LIVING VIOLET

LIVING VIOLET

The Cambion Chronicles

JAIME REED

Dafina KTeen Books
KENSINGTON PUBLISHING CORP.
www.kensingtonbooks.com/KTeen

DAFINA KTEEN BOOKS are published by

Kensington Publishing Corp.
119 West 40th Street
New York, NY 10018

All Kensington titles, imprints, and distributed lines are available at special quantity discounts for bulk purchases for sales promotion, premiums, fund-raising, educational, or institutional use.

Special book excerpts or customized printings can also be created to fit specific needs. For details, write or phone the office of the Kensington Special Sales Manager: Attn.: Special Sales Department. Kensington Publishing Corp., 119 West 40th Street, New York, NY 10018. Phone: 1-800-221-2647.

KTeen Reg. US Pat. & TM Off.
Sunburst logo Reg. US Pat. & TM Off.

ISBN-13: 978-0-7582-6924-9
ISBN-10: 0-7582-6924-2

First Printing: January 2012
10 9 8 7 6 5 4 3 2 1

Printed in the United States of America

To Donna and the fam
Keeping it real,
keeping it loud,
and keeping me sane

ACKNOWLEDGMENTS

I would like to give special thanks to those who have not only helped improve my story, but have affected my life.

To my wacky and fabulous mother, who was the inspiration for a few of my characters. You're the one who told me to shrug it off, pray about it, and keep trying. We dreamers must stick together.

To my sister, Jade, who still keeps screaming that I need a *real* job: Thank you for reminding me why I don't want one.

To Michelle: Thanks for telling me to finish something. You told me that years ago and it's been with me ever since.

To Angela: Thank you for your friendship and letting me see biracial culture through your eyes and the eyes of your family. You taught me a lot without even trying. I love you and for god's sake, eat something!

To Bruce: You are my Dougie. Thanks for all the walks in Merchants Square and listening to me dissect my story. I would marry you, but that would be weird, not to mention gross.

To Camille, my first reader and my harshest critic: Your red pen is brutal, made from the blood of a thousand virgins. Thank you for lending me your ear for hours on end. I hope to return the favor.

To my awesome agent, the great and mighty Kathleen Ortiz: Thank you for sticking your neck out for me, for talking me off the ledge on more than one occasion, and for going above and beyond the call of duty. You are utterly and truly divine.

To my sister clients, Jennifer, Dawn, and Sarah: Words can't express how much I love you guys . . . so I won't try.

To my editor, Selena: Thanks for having my back in all the major decisions. You're a real trouper. Seriously.

To J.J. and Stacy: Your advice and feedback were priceless and I'll never forget it. Much love to White Harp.

To all my online followers: U know who U R & U know what U do. Thank U, thank U, thank U!<3::huggles::

To all my readers and fellow writers: Without you there would be no point in any of this, aside from my own selfish amusement. Writing is way cheaper than therapy, so thank you for letting me vent on your couch.

Finally, to my quirky little town of Williamsburg: Whether good, bad, or downright weird, you are my home. That will never change, no matter where I go.

1

Love indulged the masochist.

Truer words have never been spoken, if I do say so myself. It's a philosophy that has kept me sane for as long as
I can remember and helped me survive the weirdest summer of my life. On the flip side, it's very entertaining
what love will make people do. It's a great way to spend
your lunch break.

Sitting on my car hood, sucking down a Big Gulp, I
watched the pinnacle of love unfold before my eyes. My
best friend, Mia, and her on-again off-again boyfriend,
Dougie, squared-off like prize fighters in the middle of
the outlet center parking lot.

This week's drama included props. Dougie pivoted
along the concrete, ducking and avoiding death by the
finest designer handbag money could buy. Through the
litany of screams, cusses, and purse swinging, I figured
Mia had caught Dougie hanging out with another girl.
Mia could be a little high-strung sometimes, but when it
came to her man, she advanced to straight head case.

That jealous insanity went both ways, depending on the day, and much amusement awaited all who watched.

"God, you're such a liar! How could you do this to me?" she raved.

"Chill, baby! She was my cousin!" Dougie escaped the oncoming blow from Mia's handbag by an inch.

"You lying piece of crap! I've met all of your relatives, Douglas. She never came to your house before."

Dougie ran in circles around her, the blood rush turning his face beet red. "She just came into town! I swear, baby."

"Why didn't you introduce me, huh?" Mia wiped her sweaty brown hair from her forehead. "What, are you ashamed of me?"

He paused, clearly hurt at the suggestion. "No! Why would you say that?"

"Liar!" Her purse swung at his head, but missed.

Dougie grabbed one of the straps, and the two began a full tug-of-war in the middle of the parking lot. Weekend shoppers watched in horror, covering the ears of their children from the curses flying in the air. At any moment, someone would definitely call security, so I decided to leave the lovebirds to their own devices.

"Hey, guys," I yelled behind me. "I gotta get back to work, but I'll see y'all later, okay?"

"Okay, I'll call ya!" Mia yelled back before shoving Dougie in the chest.

I dumped my cup in the trash, then entered the side door of Buncha Books. The air-conditioning slapped me in the face and pushed the June heat back outside. Mellow jazz rang through the speakers in a chronic loop from the satellite radio. Tourists and townies overran the floor in a slow, indecisive dance around the bookshelves.

I strolled through the main aisles, past the kiosk of new releases and bestsellers toward the customer service desk in the center of the store. Working at Buncha Books since sophomore year taught me a few tricks of the trade, namely to never get caught on the actual book floor. I also discovered that if I didn't make eye contact with the customers, they wouldn't talk to me. That policy remained tucked in my back pocket until my shift started. Casting a wary glance over my shoulder, I singled out an empty computer and clocked back in.

Stealth infiltration and quick reflexes allowed me to reach the other end of the store without incident. When I breezed by the magazine aisle, I caught something odd in my peripheral, a scene disturbing enough to break my stride. I stopped, blinked a few times, and then backtracked to the Home & Garden section to confirm what I just saw.

Caleb Baker, the assistant manager in the music department, held some redhead in a devastating lip-lock. She didn't seem to have a problem with the public tonsillectomy, but this wasn't the type of customer service the managers urged us to practice.

Just as I turned to leave, his gaze met mine.

Caleb's looks would never stop traffic, but he was worth a second glance with his deep dimples, and the most intense violet eyes I had ever seen. Despite his claim of authenticity, eyes that color shouldn't exist in nature—eyes that now reflected every purple tone of the color wheel.

Light brown strands draped over his face as the two continued to slob each other down. If they didn't come up for air soon, Caleb would no doubt suck the life out of her. From what I hear, cheap hotel rooms existed for such an occasion, and there were plenty in the area to choose from.

Of the year and a half I worked here, that kid weirded me out in one way or another. Not to mention the number of women who chased after him on a regular basis. This fact went unnoticed and unaddressed by everyone in the store, including the managers, which disgusted me even more. Having seen enough, I walked away toward my station before my lunch came back up.

Cuppa-Joe was a coffee shop in the back of the bookstore, the place where people kicked back and talked trash about everyone; the cesspool of company gossip and customer-bashing.

I closed tonight with my weekend partner in crime, Nadine Petrovsky, a Polish exchange student at The College of William & Mary, and one of the most cynical people I ever had the pleasure of meeting. Guys came to the café just to hear her exotic accent and watch her work. One glimpse of her explained why.

Model scouts would salivate over her European beauty: her long wheat-colored hair that reached her butt, and her freaky green cat eyes. Too bad none of the attention interested her. Having no time for the BS left the girl cutthroat and caustic. She was just too focused to let a guy or anyone else slow her down.

Nadine stood in front of the barista machine, rinsing the steam wand, when she caught me in the corner of her eye.

"You're late," she noted without looking up.

"Sorry. Mia and Dougie were having it out in the parking lot again." I tied my hair into a bun and grabbed my apron from the back kitchen.

"Oh yeah?" She craned her neck, straining to see the front of the store. "Their fights are good. They need their own sitcom."

"I told them that."

Worry lines etched her forehead as she shook her head in disapproval. "Their relationship isn't healthy, Sam."

"What relationship is?" I tightened my apron, then went to the sink to wash my hands.

"The sane kind."

"Well, as soon as I see one of those, I'll let you know what I think."

While drying my hands, the second reason why I hated customers approached the counter. A kid dressed in all black with a dog collar leered at me.

Nadine kept herself conveniently busy, so I made my way to the register. "Can I help you?"

"I'd like an iced chai latté," the boy said, deadpan. It was hard to tell if the kid was high or half-asleep, or whether he was, in fact, a boy. His parachute jeans dragged the floor like a prom gown, the cuffs frayed and dirty, hiding the clown boots underneath.

I rang up his order and shot Nadine a look, which she mirrored perfectly. After he left, I leaned against the counter and laughed.

Nadine didn't smile, no matter how hilarious the joke, which I'm sure made her a real delight during the week-days when she babysat preschoolers in daycare. Instead, she wiped down the work area with aggravated swipes.

"I hate those Elmo goth kids," she griped. "What self-respecting sociopath drinks chai anyway? What do they know about real torment? Let them survive a concentra-tion camp and then they can complain."

"It's called 'emo,'" I corrected her. "And your great grandparents didn't even get to the camp before the U.S. troops came in."

Nadine moved to the back counter and checked the timers on the coffeepots. "It's still torment. And if you say 'emo,' I say 'Elmo' because they are equally childish."

Shaking my head, I watched her in amusement. "You don't know what his home life is like."

"*Everyone* knows what his home life is like. He doesn't get along with his parents. He stays in his room and whines and writes bad poems about being a vampire."

Laughing, I stepped to the espresso machine and stole a shot.

"Hey, it's your turn to wipe the tables." Nadine tossed me a rag. "And don't forget to put back those magazines."

Groaning, I dragged my feet to the sitting area and gathered the discarded cups and straw wrappers. Seeing no one else in line, I took a moment to return the magazines to the racks. When I had finished, I turned around and met Caleb, still as idle and unproductive as when I last saw him.

He sat on a reading bench by the window, holding his head in his hands. Afternoon light showered his back and crowned his dark hair in a golden halo. Normally, I would've ignored him were it not for the slight tremors that rocked his body. Was he crying? Did he and his new arm candy have a falling-out? It was just off-putting to see a guy cry, but no tears fell and none were wiped away by his hand. His body teetered back and forth, and I half expected him to start begging for spare change. How long was his break anyway?

I went over to him and tapped his shoulder. "Hey, Caleb. You okay?"

"Yeah," he mumbled from under his hands. Thankfully, I didn't smell any alcohol on him, but he definitely wore the hungover look. Then again, he always looked like that.

One hand reached for the sunglasses hooked on his collar, while the other shielded his eyes—whether from shame or the glaring lights, I wasn't sure. I also wasn't sure about the source of the purple rays leaking between his fingers.

For a split second, a cast of purple flooded his eyes, swelling in a florescent glow. Caleb quickly turned his head, leaving a streak of color dragging through the air in a residual haze. That was an interesting trick for someone who supposedly didn't wear contacts.

He rose from his seat and paused at the shocked look on my face. He shifted his feet and messed with his hair, trying to play it off as if he'd been caught with his fly open. However, the only things I caught were vision problems and a bad vibe.

I took a step back. "You sure you're okay? Are you sick?"

My question made him laugh, but it sounded dry and full of bitterness. "You have no idea," he said before marching back to his end of the store.

My mom taught me not to judge people, but damn, that kid was out there. I didn't know much about him, but that only made the fact that much more tangible. Something told me that ignorance was bliss when it came to Caleb Baker, so I went back to work, hoping for a distraction. But the damage was done. My curiosity had been piqued, and that hungry creature wouldn't let me rest until I fed it.

2

After another four hours of retail hell, the closing announcements piped through the store.

Customers ambled toward the counter to make last-minute orders. There was always one person who insisted on leaving when we did, and trust me, they were more than welcome to shut down the cook station for me.

Because Nadine did let's-get-the-hell-out-of-here better than anyone, she wrapped up the food while I stacked the chairs and mopped. Rock music blared through the intercom, letting everyone know that business hours were officially over. After forty minutes of shutdown, it was time to call it a night.

"Don't forget, we have reading group tonight," Nadine reminded me.

"Oh, crap!" All joy and enthusiasm vanished. Staying after hours without pay took more patience than I could give.

I flung my apron behind me and turned off the back kitchen lights. After gathering our things, we clocked out, then moved to the restroom hallway toward the break room.

Half the employees were already there, drinking stale coffee to stay awake. The sour expressions and defeated postures made it clear that no one wanted to be here on a Sunday night, so I was in good company.

The monthly book club strived to keep the work morale up, but it usually led to fights. The sales reps from on high thought it was a good idea to have the employees read the new releases and recommend them to customers.

One thing I loved about my coworkers was that they disliked this activity as much as I did. That mutual hatred brought us together, and it made this pointless hour bearable. We could let our hair down and talk true literary smack without censorship. At the end of the night, a book was voted as the store's choice of the month.

Nadine stood by the broken soda machine talking to Caleb. Though out of earshot, her reddened face suggested that the topic didn't involve the latest bestseller. Fingers pointed at the other person, teeth bared, features twisted in anger.

Caleb and Nadine barely talked at work, just brief exchanges and whispers in secluded corners of the store. I suspected that Nadine and Caleb shared a thing that went sour before I started working here, but I thought it was better not to rehash the past. No matter how bad the breakup, Caleb was the only guy she seemed to respect.

Trying hard not to look nosy, I slinked over to the low-budget refreshment stand and commandeered day-old snack food.

Placing a doughnut on a napkin, I almost jumped at the deep voice behind me. "Hey, I had my eyes on that powdered one."

I turned around and met those freaky purple-blue eyes again. In all honesty, that was the only thing going for him, at least in my book. Caleb was pasty, even for white-boy standards, and he was in dire need of a haircut and shave. With hands shoved in his tan khakis, he looked at me under thick lashes.

"Too bad. It's the last doughnut, and it's all mine." I allowed the treat to hover in my hand for good measure.

"No way I can change your mind?" His eyes ran the length of my body before meeting my gaze again.

"Nope. Sorry." I took a huge bite of the powdery confection and scooted to the folding chair next to Nadine. I could feel him watching me, no doubt coveting my sugary prize. Caleb was skinny with a swimmer's build, so who would believe that this guy could wipe out an entire sugar plantation in one sitting? His sweet tooth rivaled mine, and that was no small feat.

Linda, the store manager and the queen of bling, barged in and slung her bag on the floor. Her stilettos clunked against the linoleum tiles, signifying that the bedazzled badass had just arrived. Propping hands on her hips and car keys clasped in her jewel-covered hand, she addressed the group.

"All right, let's get this over with. I got an hour drive ahead of me, and I'm not trying to be here all night." She took a seat and pulled her dreadlocks into a bun on the top of her head. "Okay, let's begin with the young adult section." She turned to the short, curly-haired girl to her left. "Alicia, what book did you read?"

Alicia Holloway sat up straight, grinning, sporting wide eyes and dimples. She was a freshman at my school—well, sophomore this fall—and the youngest employee at BB. Her work permit was probably still tucked inside her Hello Kitty purse. Alicia had come a long way from the frightened deer who always brought a nightlight when she slept over my house. I used to babysit her when I was in junior high, and even then she tried too hard to act mature. I saw right through it, and it was my duty as a friend to hug her to death.

"I read *Specter*, by Nan Jacobs," Alicia chimed with excitement, holding the book up so everyone could see the worn cover.

A number of groans filled the break room. People adjusted their chairs, preparing for the diatribe that would surely follow.

This was the book series that every bookseller loved to hate, and its popularity boggled the minds of everyone in the room. But no one could deny the number of sales among teenage girls, and an entire shelf in the store was devoted to the saga. Anything that mainstream was enough to keep us from reading it. Well, most of us.

"Okay, first off, I have to say I loved this book. It's so romantic and sweet, and the characters were so believable, and I felt like I was right there with the main character and, *Omgoodness*, Nicolas Damien is so hot!" Alicia bounced in her seat and swallowed a lungful of much-needed air.

"Have you met him?" Nadine leaned back in her chair and allowed her hands to touch at the fingertips. "This Nicolas Damien—has he come to the store or something?"

Alicia frowned in confusion. "Uh, no. He's a character in the book."

"Then how do you know he is hot?"

"Because the book makes him hot, that's how," Alicia snapped, then addressed the group again. "Anyway, the story's about a young girl who goes to detention and falls in love with a gorgeous new guy. But there's something mysterious about him."

"Let me guess, he's a serial killer?" Caleb piped in. He sat at the opposite side of the circle with one leg resting on his knee and his arms folded. Every so often, I caught him watching me, probing me with an open curiosity that had no shame. I tried not to stare at him, tried not to squirm in my seat, but his stare had a physical presence.

I couldn't wait to get out of there.

"No, he's not a killer." Alicia rolled her eyes. "He's dead."

"How romantic," I mumbled. "Forget *Teen Beat*; go to your local cemetery. Corpses are the new heart-throbs."

"No, I mean he's a ghost," Alicia explained. "Anyway, the girl doesn't know that at first, and the thing is she's the only one who can see him. Nicolas thinks it's a sign that Angelica is his soul mate."

"Angelica?" Nadine and I mimicked in unison.

Alicia spun her head at the jeering. "What's wrong with that?"

"It's reaching, isn't it?" Nadine asked. "Let me guess, Nicolas calls her 'his angel'?"

Alicia snarled in our direction, then continued, "Anyway, it's about forbidden love. They can't be together because Angelica is still alive and he's a ghost, and they can't even touch. The story follows her search to figure out how Nick died, all while fighting their attraction."

"Why is she the only one that can see him?" Linda asked.

"Because Angelica is a rare and unique snowflake," I answered, picking at my doughnut.

Redness rushed to Alicia's cheeks, giving her skin a rich mahogany tint. Her fist slammed down against her knees. "Shut up! You're just jealous of Nicky and Angie."

"Wow, we're on a nickname basis with these made-up people?" Caleb asked, his chest shaking with laughter. "It's just a book, Alicia. Relax."

Applying some serious neck action, Alicia contended,

"Look, you write a bestselling novel and then you can complain about someone else's book."

"Will someone else go now, please?" Linda rubbed the bridge of her nose and squeezed her eyes shut. That vein on her forehead looked ready to pop, so I jumped in.

"Okay." I reached behind my chair and pulled the book from my shoulder bag. "*Trick of the Light*—I love that title—by Harriet Coffman-Frost. It's about this male prostitute, Ren, who runs into some bad luck and gets evicted from his house, and ends up rooming with one of his lady customers, named Janice. Janice is emotionally unavailable—some Madonna-whore complex where she can't sleep with someone she has feelings for, so she buys male company. The tables slowly turn as they get to know each other. Ren ends up having feelings for Janice and tries to woo her, but she clams up and ignores him. So he ends up using his hooker money to buy her affection. I'm almost to the end; I'll let you know what happens."

Alicia sucked her teeth in disgust. "That's sick."

I grinned. "Isn't it, though? But the characters are real to life, unlike your oh-so-perfect Nicky."

"Can't be too perfect if Nicky can't remember how he died," another employee added.

"All right, settle down people," Linda broke in. She turned toward Caleb and smiled. "Okay, how about you? What book did you read?"

Caleb unfolded his arms and presented the paperback to the group. "*Snap Shot*, by Orlando Hutchins. It's about this demonic photo booth in the middle of the Jersey boardwalk. When Mark Daniels goes inside, the camera flash gives him a subliminal message to murder people. And out of the photo slot are pictures of five people he has to kill. So Mark goes on a mindless killing spree, but he only figures it out when a friend comes to kill him. The friend also has a strip of pictures with Mark's face on the last square. It's a crazy, vicious circle."

"Wow, that's awesome." Linda jotted something down on her notepad.

"Yeah, it's got plenty of gore and violence," he agreed, glancing over at me. "Good family fun."

After another twenty minutes of show-and-tell, we all decided on Caleb's book choice. Sighing in relief, everyone got up and filed toward the doors. I grabbed my bag and walked out, ignoring the prickling feeling on the back of my neck, the warm humming over my skin, and Alicia giving me the stink eye.

Linda stayed behind to lock up, while outside an ambulance and two cop cars flanked a vehicle at the end of the lot. Aside from the employees' cars, the parking lot was empty.

Nadine leaned into me and asked, "What's that about?"

"Your guess is as good as mine." I stepped to the side as the rest of the crew moved in to watch.

Nadine's eyes widened with excitement. "You think there was shooting or something? I would kill for action in this town."

She had a point, but I wasn't sure if this was the way to go about it. Williamsburg was one of the most boring cities on the planet. It was a far cry from Mayberry, but this town still had some sleep in its eyes. It was a resort town, the hotbed for tourists for the summer, and most of its revenue banked on the hotels and restaurants in the area. So any sign of a skirmish proved enough to keep the townsfolk talking for a while.

A group of skateboarders sat on the grass, watching the fallout from the opposite side of the lot as a heavyset officer took statements from each of them.

I looked to the dark blue SUV parked near the store

when the driver's window rolled down. Mr. Holloway popped his head out the window. "Alicia, come on!"

"Coming, Daddy!"

Alicia rushed from behind me and bumped my shoulder. Obviously, she took her book rejection personally and needed someone to blame.

Reaching the van, I straightened my back and saluted Alicia's dad. "Captain Holloway, sir!"

My foolishness never failed to make him smile, no matter how hard he tried not to. The man was too serious, as was the military fade cropped close to his head. "At ease, soldier," he said. "You guys are coming out late."

Alicia climbed in the passenger side. "Yeah, we had our book club tonight. Sorry you had to wait so long."

"Hey, what's up with the police?" Nadine asked before I could.

Mr. Holloway turned his head to the flashing lights. "A woman had a heart attack in the parking lot. Some kids found her unconscious in her car; I guess they called the cops. God, for a minute there I thought it was my little girl."

"Daddy, I'm fine," Alicia chided. "You're such a drama freak."

"Hey, kid, mind your elders!" I pointed a finger at her. "My mom's got me on lock like that too. It's a parent thing."

Alicia snickered. "Whatever, thumb-sucker."

I spread my arms wide, inviting the challenge. "Anytime, training bra."

"Ladies." Dragging a hand over his face, Mr. Holloway lifted his head and sighed. "You two will never grow out of this phase, will you?"

"Well, your daughter's a bad influence," I said in defense.

He gave me a hard look. "And you're not?" Not waiting for my answer, Mr. Holloway revved the engine. "You guys be safe going home—lots of weirdos out there."

"Will do." I drifted up the lot with Nadine at my side. I dangled the keys on my finger, all the while trying to sneak a peek at the action without appearing too obvious. The emergency team eased a body out of the driver's side. I recognized the slim build and long red hair right away. That was the same woman Caleb performed the poor man's CPR on earlier today. From the look of her unconscious state, she needed a professional.

Linda moved to the scene and talked to one of the officers by his car. A few head nods and shakes followed, but relayed no solid info to go on.

"She looks awful young to have a heart attack," I told Nadine.

"You can have attack at any age. It depends on person," she returned, riveted at the sight before her.

Nadine held an affinity for all things macabre, so something like this was right up her alley. But behind her normal blank-slate expression laid a note of contained anger. "Did you recognize the girl?" she asked.

I had no idea why I said no. Maybe I wasn't up for a police interview in the middle of the night. Maybe it was just a freaky coincidence. I just knew I needed to get home.

"See you tomorrow." I chucked my bag in the passenger seat.

Nadine waved and inched to her car two lanes down, struggling to break from the draw of tragedy.

As I turned to get in, that feeling returned, that electric zing on the back of my neck. Swallowing hard, I spun around and jumped.

Caleb stood behind me, staring, as if waiting for me to hand over the doughnut I inhaled earlier. I returned the

look, slowly backing away until my body wedged between him and the car door. His hand reached for my
face. A scream was about to break from my throat before
he brushed the side of my lips with his thumb.

"You've got something there." He pulled back his
hand and examined the smudge of powdered sugar on
his finger. "See ya tomorrow." He strolled up the lot to
his Jeep, unfazed by the flashing lights and his chick getting wheeled off by paramedics.

That's no way to treat a make-out partner, no matter
how bad they kissed. If he owned any decency, he would
at least follow the ambulance to the hospital. Just watching his proud swagger made my stomach roil.

For the eighteen months I'd been on this job, at least
twelve girls had hung on his arm, and there were no signs
of stopping. Mr. Too-Cool-for-School was a man-whore
of the highest order.

I couldn't think about it anymore. I was already late,
and I didn't want to be the last one in the parking lot. Ev-
idently, this wasn't a safe place for a girl to be alone.

3

It was a good thing I lived five minutes from work. I was dead tired.

Warm air rushed through the window, carrying the whiff of yeast that drifted for miles. Commuters on I-64 labeled the smell as one of the many Williamsburg staples.

Most areas of Williamsburg were historical sites. Every child within the state was forced on a field trip here and shown how tobacco was made. It's a quiet city that reeked of beer from the local brewery and the smell of mildew from the old money that circulated through the area. It was wall-to-wall old people, the new Florida, with dozens of golf courses and country clubs. It became tradition to those who grew up here to only return when they needed somewhere quiet to die.

I lived in a pretty decent middle-class neighborhood, just off the main strip of James City County. No one could ever call us wealthy though, that's for sure. Our home was a two-story colonial-style house with a wrap-around porch, though it had seen some better days. The white paint curled and chipped, but the tall pines bordering the yard fought to hide that fact from our neighbors. An unexpected bee infestation had slaughtered our bed of gardenias, yellow button poms, and daisies.

Gravel crunched and popped under my tires as I pulled up to my house and met a silver Lexus parked by the curb.

Whimpering, I turned off the car and gathered my stuff. I avoided this situation for a reason, and some people just didn't know when to take a hint. Mom had left the porch light on for me. As always, she worried about her baby.

Entering the house, the smell of sautéed onions and garlic hit me immediately. The aroma dragged me to the kitchen, kicking and screaming. Mom stood over the kitchen island, chopping mushrooms on the cutting board, while Dad sat on the bar stool peeling potatoes.

This was an odd pairing if I ever saw one, but my folks were anything but normal. Unlike most estranged parents, mine actually got along. They rarely argued, and if they did, it was about something stupid on my end. With that said, I couldn't shake off the feeling that this was a setup.

Mom's yellow sundress cast a glow to her fair, lightly freckled skin and revealed more than a peek of cleavage. Her hair was pulled up in a loose bun with brown tendrils framing her face.

Though she had put on a little weight over the years, Julie Marshall was a nice-looking woman. True, I got my curly hair, flat butt, and ultra-sensitive skin from her, along with the Wolf-Man eyebrows that required waxing every week. But not even that could detract from her round, honest face and the best legs this side of the Mason-Dixon Line. All the same, if I had a kid at sixteen, I would probably look like a MILF at her age too.

Dad was dressed casual tonight, a far cry from the corporate takeover suits he usually wore. His white button-down shirt made a bold contrast to his dark chocolate skin. The overhead light bounced off his shaved head.

They worked in silent harmony, oblivious to my presence, even as I dropped my bag on the kitchen table. Against its original purpose, the table overflowed with coupons and unopened mail. Mom's laptop, the only thing the woman had ever splurged on, chimed away, letting her know more unread mail waited in cyberspace.

"You can't speak now?" Dad's deep baritone stopped me in my tracks.

"Hi, Daddy." I bent to kiss his cheek.

"You're home late, honey," Mom said while cutting green peppers.

"Monthly book meeting. Sorry."

Rubbing my back, Dad asked, "Is there something wrong with your cell phone, baby girl? I've tried calling you all day, and all I got was your voice mail."

"I was at work," I explained quickly. "I can't have my phone on at work."

"Uh-huh. I figured as much, so I decided to pay you a little visit." He set down a peeled potato and reached for another. "So your mother told me you agreed to our arrangement with your car."

"Yep." The thought brought a smile to my face.

My current car had served its purpose, but it was time to put it down. It was a 1998 Honda Civic with chipped white paint and a busted air-conditioning unit. My phobia of public transportation was the only thing that kept me from chucking it off a cliff.

Dad frowned in thought. "I'm glad to hear that, but she didn't say anything about you watching Kyle and Kenya."

My smile dropped. "Who watch what?"

"You heard me." He seemed amused that he had just ruined my victory party.

"Samara." Mom sighed, knowing this song and dance all too well. "You're their big sister. You need to show them some support."

Oh yeah, this was definitely a shakedown. I stole a glimpse at my traitorous mother before saying, "Well, now I gotta pick up more hours at work to save up for the car. I don't think I can take the time to watch the twins."

Dad nodded. "You know it's your stepmother's and my anniversary next weekend, and it would mean so much to us if you could take the time out of your busy schedule to help us out."

"Why can't Nana watch them?"

"Nana's in Atlanta until next Tuesday. Plus the doctor told her to take it easy after her hip surgery. She couldn't keep up with a pair of six-year-olds."

"Well, Dad, sorry about your luck. Have you broken the news to Rhonda?"

Dad dropped the peeler and locked eyes on me. For anyone else, that look would involve imminent death, but I was lucky to get away with a sound reprimand. Though the spankings had stopped years ago, the look in his dark eyes told me the legendary belt was about to make a comeback.

Instead, he spoke in the calmest voice. "Samara, it would mean a great deal to me if you did this favor. I haven't gotten a weekend off in months, and the reservations I made are nonrefundable."

I must have gotten that stubborn streak from him, because I managed to stand my ground.

"If you don't help me," he continued, "I may have to retract my end of the deal involving your car."

The statement hung in the air on a dangerous note.

My body went rigid. "What? You can't do that!"

"I'm an adult, and unlike you, I can do whatever I want with my money."

I wanted to scream. I wanted to break something. I wanted to slap him across his big bald head. I had to play it cool, but how could I when injustice was purely on my side? It was no secret that I didn't like Rhonda and her minions, and my reasons were justified. He knew I would do anything for him but that. I loved my dad, but nothing would stand between me and new wheels.

Clearing my throat, I whipped out the SAT vocabulary and my best diplomatic voice. "Father, you of all people should know how injudicious it is to renege on a verbal contract."

"Verbal contracts rarely hold up in court," he disputed.

"Not unless there was a witness to the concurrence." I shot a look to Mom. "Mom is a participant and standing witness to the pact. This new clause was not present during the concord and therefore is not germane to the original contract. In addition, your retraction will result in the infringement with the agreeing parties, signifying that a man's word means nothing, in turn, placing your personal ethics into question."

Now I stood, waiting for the backhand of justice to strike me dead. But nothing came.

Mom stopped stirring and looked over her shoulder. The sizzling vegetables in the pan replaced the quiet.

After a two-minute stare-down, Dad spoke. "Quite the litigator you are."

"I learned from the best."

Slowly, a brilliant smile melted his hard features. "All right, what do you want then?"

I paused. "What?"

"What do you want? Like I said, I can't get a refund on my reservation, so I need you to watch the twins. Since I can't extort you, I'll use old-fashioned bribery." His smile widened.

I couldn't believe this. He had granted a carte blanche to anything I wanted. I quickly grew drunk with power. Usually, my mind teemed with mischievous deeds, plots of world domination and the overthrow of Hollywood, but nothing came to mind.

Mom finally spoke. "Might I make a suggestion? Since you can't omit the prior contract, then add to it. If she watches the twins, you will ensure that she'll have enough to afford her car, no matter how short she is on her end. You will not only match what she has, you'll pay the difference."

Dad rubbed his chin in thought. "So basically, I'm paying for the car."

"No. What purpose would that serve? She'll put a nice chunk of her own money in it."

My shoulders sagged.

Her blue eyes narrowed at me. "Don't give me that look. I've watched those Sweet Sixteen shows with those brats getting Ferraris and yachts for their birthdays, and talking back to their parents who pay for the whole thing. Life doesn't work that way, and it's better that you learn that now than later. Your father and I believe in hard work, and if you want something, then you earn it. Education is more important than whose name you've got on the back of your jeans. Heaven knows I don't want you ending up like Mia."

For as long as Mia and I had been friends, Mom had always held a modicum of patience for Mia's flashy lifestyle. Though Mom had once lived in one of the wealthiest neighborhoods in Williamsburg, her early take on motherhood popped that bubble indefinitely. From then on, Mom was a straight coupon and blue-light-special woman.

"Mom," I whined.

"I'm serious. Little Miss Trust Fund is giving you the wrong idea about wealth. I see her with her designer shoes and purses that could pay our mortgage for six months. I don't want you to be like that, Samara."

"I'm not."

"Then you won't dispute the arrangement your father and I set for you. Whatever you earn at work, we'll match it, and you'll have your car by the fall."

I stood quiet for a moment, whipping out the mental calculator. Two thousand dollars already in savings, plus two months' worth of slave wage. I still didn't have enough to reach my quota.

I knew the suggestion was dead in the water, but I had to try. "What about my college fund? I could use some of that."

"Over my cold, dead body! You don't touch that account until you're eighteen. You're going to college even if you have to walk there." Dad didn't even bother to make eye contact, which rendered the subject closed.

"I'll ask Linda if I can pull a few double shifts at work."

"Don't hurt yourself, baby," Mom warned. "You still need time to be a kid. Time will pass quicker than you think."

I moved around the kitchen island, took my mother's hand, and placed it over my heart. Putting my sophomore drama club acting to work, I declared, "All things must end. 'Tis a heavy challenge you proffer me, but I accept, my lady."

Mom chuckled.

Dad cut his eyes at both of us, not amused by this

transaction at all. "There's no way to get out of this, is there?"

"Nope. Do you accept the terms?" I extended my hand, waiting for the verdict to fall from his lips.

After what felt like days, he shook my hand and almost broke all of my fingers. My heart jumped, and as soon as my stomach stopped doing cartwheels, I was going to call Mia and rub it in her face. Yes, victory would be mine!

"At least it's for a good cause. This trip means a lot to Rhonda." He stared off with a secretive smile, anticipating the alone time with his significant other. Only God could understand why.

"Where are y'all going anyway?" I asked.

"D.C. I have us booked at the Capital Hotel. We have a whole tour planned out, with dinner and dancing—the whole nine yards."

"Sounds nice," I said as an explosion of clattering dishes came from the sink.

Dad and I looked to Mom, who leaned over the counter. Every muscle in her body looked tight. After a deep breath, she excused herself from the room, her arms glued to her sides, her fingers balled into fists.

Dad watched Mom vanish around the corner before he turned to me. "What's with her?"

"She's going through a thing right now." I turned off the stove, then removed the food.

Eyeing me carefully, he leaned closer. "Talk to me."

"Well, you really expect her to be happy about you traipsing off with that woman?"

He scowled. "You mean my wife?"

"Semantics. You were practically flaunting your relationship in front of her."

Dad shook his head. "I didn't mean to."

"I know, but she's still a little sensitive about it. She's

almost thirty-four and unmarried. She only dresses up when you're here. Did you know that she's been looking up dating services online lately?"

Dad's expression was a long, dumbfounded blank. "Wait, this is the same woman who warned me about that scandal on Craigslist?"

"Desperate times call for desperate measures. I'm just saying, don't give her mixed signals, and don't flaunt your new life in front of her, 'cause I'm gonna be the one who'll have to talk her off the ledge when she finally snaps, not you."

"You know I love your mother. It's just—"

"You love her like you love me," I interrupted. "It's not the same."

Mom and Dad were high school sweethearts, and well, things got a little too hot and heavy. In the spring of their junior year, I showed up, and that's when the epic family feud began. Grandpa all but disowned Mom for having a baby with one of "those people," so Dad's parents practically adopted us. I knew very little of the white side of my family, and you can't really miss what was never there. Things soon fizzled between Mom and Dad after high school, and they went their separate ways, but Dad had more luck with moving on.

Dad got up from the stool and strolled to the door. "Maybe I should go. Tell your mom I had to run. I'll call you later on in the week."

"Okay." I followed him out.

When he opened the door, he pulled me in for one of his suffocating bear hugs. Though my dad was a big guy and stricter than a drill sergeant, his power showed the most through his hugs. No matter where I was, his oaky cologne would always remind me of home.

"For what it's worth," he whispered, "I'm sorry."

"I know. Love you, Daddy."

"Love you too, baby girl. Thank you again for bailing me out." His lips brushed the top of my head.

I pulled away and forced a smile that I didn't feel. "No problem. Drive safe."

As soon as I closed the door, the voice of Joni Mitchell rang through the house, one of Mom's old angst-ridden CDs used to jump-start her pity party. I knew she wouldn't crawl out of her cave until she was good and ready, which meant it was all on me as far as dinner was concerned.

After setting the security system, I returned to the kitchen to clean up. Two slices of last night's leftover pizza rotated in the microwave while I wrapped up the half-cooked food and took ice cream from the freezer. I balanced the load upstairs, careful to avoid that annoying creak on the eighth step. Stopping in front of Mom's door, I tapped a code against the wood, but didn't expect a reply. I set the ice cream and spoon on the floor, then went to my room.

A click of the light switch revealed the crash site known as my bedroom. The color scheme was lime green, but the clutter hid that fact from all who entered. My bed stood against the wall, giving me plenty of floor space to work on my Tae Bo moves. Half of my wardrobe was slung about the room along with countless books, DVDs, and magazines.

Still buzzing off the high of getting a new car, my first course of action was to call Mia and spread some I-told-you-so her way. Judging from the last time I saw her, she needed some cheering up. I grabbed my phone and plopped on the bed with a plate of meaty, cheesy goodness warming my lap.

After three rings, I heard a stuffy voice on the other end. "What? Just let me die in peace."

I stared at the phone, then put it back to my ear. "Mia? It's Sam. What's wrong with you?"

"My life is over, that's what's wrong." After twenty minutes of sniveling, squealing, and blubbering, I pieced together that Doug really did have a cousin from out of town, and now he won't talk to Mia because she clipped him in the shin with her BMW when she pulled out of the parking lot.

"Is he gonna press charges?" I asked while scarfing down my second slice.

"No, he wouldn't do that. He's just mad."

"Maybe this is for the best. It's good to make a clean break now."

More nose-blowing blasted through the phone. "You don't get it. I love him."

I rolled my eyes. "If that's what you wanna call it."

"What's that supposed to mean? I don't expect you to understand. You've never been in love."

I scoffed. "Look, if it's anything like what you and Doug got going on and what my mom's going through, y'all can have it."

"What's wrong with your mom?"

"She's looking at online dating sites."

The sniffing stopped on the other end of the line.

"Hello?" I asked with a mouthful of crust.

"You gotta be kidding? This is the same woman who made us sit down and watch every episode of that *Dateline* predator show."

"Yeah, well, I think she's getting lonely. You know, that empty nest thing. And the fact that she's still holding a torch for my dad," I explained.

"How is the black Mr. Clean?"

I snickered. "I'll pay you twenty bucks to call him that to his face. I dare you."

"Oh, hell no. Your dad scares me."

After I updated Mia on Dad's request to babysit his demon spawn, she said, "Wow, that sucks. I suddenly feel better now. You coming to V.A. Beach tomorrow?"

"Naw, I gotta work in the morning." The word "work" conjured up thoughts of the day's excitement. I wondered about the girl in the parking lot and the boy who pretended she didn't exist.

When I ended the call for the night, I scrounged around the floor for a T-shirt. I crashed on the bed, twiddling a strip of pizza crust between my fingers, and delved into the mind of my creepy coworker.

I didn't know a whole lot about him, except that he was nineteen, an army brat who had lived in Europe most of his life and owned an unhealthy obsession with baked goods and bad techno music.

Caleb always held a candy bar or a doughnut in his hand when he went on his break. He also kept a coin jar under the register for every time a customer asked him if he wore contact lenses. Talk about vain! The way he tossed women off like used Kleenex didn't improve my opinion of him either. But those eyes sure were strange, so I could understand the curiosity. He certainly held mine and wouldn't let go, trapping me in that luminous and haunted gaze. . . .

Oh god, I had to stop. Thinking about him made my head hurt. I had work in the morning and this guy wasn't worth another moment of thought. I just had to tell my brain that.

4

Ah, Mondays. The starting line of the rat race, and the end of all free will.

Mondays ran pretty steady at Buncha Books, with the usual business folk needing their morning rocket fuel. I didn't get the real jerks until later in the afternoon and weekends. The book floor jumbled with stragglers, looking lost and enjoying icy caffeine from Cuppa-Joe. I strolled to customer service and met Linda, who wore "don't mess with me" like a name tag.

I scooted past her and clocked in. "Tough night?"

"Yeah," she replied. "I talked to the police last night about the girl in the parking lot. They wanted to know if anyone saw anything before the incident."

"Why? I thought she had a heart attack."

"That's what the paramedics say, but police are coming in today to ask the staff a few questions. The victim had a store bag in her car, and the 911 call came from inside the store," she said, trying not to fall asleep at the computer.

I nodded while my brain worked overtime. Linda's explanation raised a red flag and an accusatory finger in one direction.

After haggling extra hours from Linda's greedy clutches, I marched toward the back of the store, where Nadine was pulling fresh cookies out of the oven. The aroma performed a siren song for all the sugar-holics within a two-block radius. However, for the sake of bathing-suit season, I had to fight the temptation.

"What up?" I called, reaching for an apron.

"Same old crap. People buying their own means of demise." She shrugged.

"You're bubbly today."

"Yeah, well, I opened today, so I leave early, and I have time to finish my term paper."

How Nadine managed to work three jobs and attend classes during the summer stretched past my span of logic. Not only was she runway gorgeous, she was smart and worked like a dog, upstaging us lazy Americans in every way possible.

But somehow Nadine and I gravitated to each other like kindred spirits, and we manipulated the schedules at the store just so we could hang out. Oh, and work.

"We need to make more decaf." Nadine examined the timer in her hand.

Aside from the usual summer tourist and mallrat prosti-tots, business was kind of slow for the next three hours. There was always one guy who abused the purpose of name tags, and slaughtered the pronunciation of my name, all for the sake of friendliness.

Oddly enough, this didn't tick me off. I just smiled and pronounced slowly, "Sir, it's Samara. Suh-MAIR-uh. But if you want, you can call me Sam. In fact, I insist."

After the lunch rush died down, my favorite customers approached the counter: the historical actors who work at the heart of Williamsburg in Merchants Square.

These people tripped me out with their white tights, buckled shoes, and powdered wigs. This town was a living, breathing American history class. Tourists came far and wide to walk the cobblestone streets of Colonial Williamsburg and see the tavern wenches, the silversmiths, and the freed slaves reenact olden times.

The only strange thing was when they were off the clock and the town crier text messaged his girlfriend. Or when Thomas Jefferson showed up at Costco and stocked a thirty-day supply of toilet paper and frozen dinners in his cart. On the way to work today, I saw a sharecropper zoom past me on a motor scooter with spinning rims. Seriously, I couldn't make this up if I tried. Not a day goes by where I don't see that sort of thing at least twice, and it's the best tourist attraction in town.

After Martha Washington left with her cappuccino, I needed a pick-me-up. Sneaking my second espresso shot of the day, I heard a guy behind me say, "Yo, SNM, got a minute?"

I knew who it was before I could turn around. Only one person had the perverse humor to turn my initials into a dirty joke. I swallowed my shot and slowly faced the counter. "What you want, Dougie?"

He stood with hands in his baggy jean pockets. His upside-down visor pushed back spiky black hair. Though it shamed me to admit, Dougie was cute in that wigger sort of way, and his green polo shirt brought out his hazel eyes and olive skin. But that popped collar had to go.

"Have you seen Mia?" he asked. "She's not picking up her phone."

"I thought you weren't talking to her."

He looked down at his unlaced sneakers. "I'm not. I just—I just wanna see if she's all right. She was really upset. I'm not trying to have her stalk me, that's all."

"So instead, you're gonna beat her to the punch."

"It's not like that."

I crossed my arms over my chest. "Then please, tell me what it's like. 'Cause from this side of the counter, you're trying to out-stalk a stalker."

Turning away, he mumbled, "Forget it, man. I knew you couldn't help me."

"If help's what you need, Eastern State Hospital is right up the road." I pointed to the exit.

He stopped, then walked back to the counter. With his head down, he looked up at me with the saddest puppy eyes I ever saw. "Look, Samara, I know you don't like me, but you can't go around judging something you don't know about. Mia and I got something not many people have, and I just wanna know if she's all right."

Oh, B-boy was laying it on thick. "You know good and well I love you to death, so put your violins away. If you must know, Lady Moralez is at Virginia Beach, trying her best to look like me." I extended my arm to him.

He observed the brown limb, then asked, "Who is she at the beach with?"

"Some of the gang. Why?"

His eyes narrowed. His lips tightened. "Is Garrett with her?"

"He would be part of the gang," I hedged, watching the green-eyed monster wake from its sleep. Garrett Davenport was the walking stereotype of the football playboy with all the beer-guzzling shenanigans the label entailed. Not saying another word, Dougie shot to the exit with car keys in hand and murder in his eyes.

With that bit of conflict over, I looked at the clock and realized it was time for my break. I yelled to the back kitchen to let Nadine know I was taking off and unhooked my apron.

Soda in hand, I meandered through the aisles, perusing the new releases. Nothing looked appealing enough to waste a week of reading, so I moved to the bestsellers. It was hard to ignore the shrine dedicated to the *Specter Saga* and the squealing tweens bowing down at its altar, but I tried anyway.

By doing so, I caught the silhouette of law enforcement leaving the music section. The voyeur in me itched to know what was going on. At first, I assumed the cop had come to catch a punk shoplifting, but then I remembered what Linda had told me earlier. They were still investigating the incident in the parking lot. It would only make sense to interview the last person seen with the victim.

Curiosity had me by the throat as I reached the metal detector of the music department. Not seeing anyone at the counter, I strolled around, picking up random CDs and reading the covers.

"You break it, you buy it," someone said right behind me.

I jumped and saw Caleb holding a half-eaten chocolate-chunk cookie the size of my hand.

I put the CD back and faced him. "Are you following me?"

"You're in my department, so I would have to say . . . no. You see something you like?"

"Not really. It's all the same."

He took a bite of his cookie and nodded. "Most of it, but there're a few diamonds in the rough. Here, come listen to this."

Caleb led me to the endcap and stopped in front of the music sampler. He placed the headphones over my ears before I could object. Long fingers punched away at the display, and in seconds, a deep, soulful voice caressed my eardrums. I closed my eyes as the drum and bass picked up tempo, bringing my heartbeat along for the ride.

Once the thirty seconds of heaven ended, my eyes

opened and found Caleb behind the counter with a customer. He met my gaze for a moment and flashed a smile before steering his focus to the young woman in front of him.

I removed the headphones and took my time approaching the register, overhearing the woman stammering and giggling. What this guy did to get these girls to act stupid around him was beyond me. The woman looked well put together, and she didn't appear to have a problem getting a man, if the wedding band was any indication. But she gawked at Caleb like a man hadn't crossed her path in decades.

And Caleb, the cocky SOB, rang up her order as if drooling women were part of standard procedure. He went along with the company spiel about membership cards and clearance items, and the woman scrambled for her credit card.

Not wanting to waste any more of my lunch break, I inched toward the exit. "That was a good song. Thanks."

He threw me a look that told me to stay and handed the woman her merchandise.

"I knew you'd like it." He turned to face me. "It's a group from Brazil. I have all of their albums, back when they did underground house music. This one's a bit more mainstream."

"Oh. Well, I'll be sure to check them out."

"I'll let you borrow the CD, if you want," he offered.

"Okay. Thanks."

Caleb watched me, studying me, possibly trying to learn the mechanics of my existence, when the woman spoke up.

"Um, I'm sure you're asked this a lot, but, um . . ." She licked her lips and fingered the chain on her neck. "Do you wear contacts?"

Caleb's eyes dragged from mine as he regarded the customer. "Do you have a quarter?" Seeing her obvious confusion, he threw in, "It's for a charity fundraiser."

"Sure, let me see." She dove into her purse, no questions asked. Unsatisfied with the delay, she deposited all of its contents on the counter. When she found a quarter, she presented it to him, her chest heaving from her rigorous search. Charlie wasn't even that happy when he found the golden ticket in his Wonka Bar.

Smiling, Caleb plucked it from her manicured fingers and reached to the shelf under the register. The clatter of coins soon followed, announcing the latest donation into the Caleb vanity bank.

Having kept his audience in suspense long enough, he put the woman out of her misery. "Thank you, and the answer is no. This is all natural."

"Wow," she gushed.

I rolled my eyes and went to the music sampler again. There had to be a reason for that woman to throw herself at Caleb. It was distracting the way he kept looking at me, and I completely forgot the name of the band I just heard. He said that he would bring me the CD. Or maybe he just said that to be nice, like when people say they'll call you back when they really mean, "I'm done talking to you." Why *was* he being nice all of a sudden? He had barely talked to me before. I still had no idea what the police said to him, so I really needed to think up a game plan before going for round two with that fool.

These thoughts plagued me while I scrolled through the display, trying to find the song that echoed in the back of my head. So it didn't come as a big surprise when Caleb snuck me from behind again.

"It's called 'La Boya,'" he whispered in my ear.

I spun around to him sporting that smug grin that I

wanted to slap away. Before I lost my nerve, I went down the list of questions I had memorized.

"Is your girlfriend okay? What did the cops say to you? Why are there so many chicks on your jock? Do you have a sugar deficiency, or what? Are you really gonna let me borrow that CD, or are you just as flakey as I suspect?" This was not the smoothest way to get into someone's business, but I had to pour it all out before he distracted me again.

His eyebrows shot to his hairline. "Yes, I promise to bring you the CD. I'll even bring you a playlist that you might like."

My jaw dropped. *He's gonna make me a playlist? That's kinda sweet.*

"And I just like junk food. I have a fast metabolism, and sugar is the only vice I have, so cut me some slack."

I was still on the playlist part.

"I did go by the hospital, and the girl is fine. She's getting released day after tomorrow."

That got my attention. "The girl? You don't even know her name?"

His eyes lifted to the ceiling for the answer. "Megan, Meegan, Morgan, or something."

The warm and fuzzy feeling was officially gone. "You don't even know the name of your girlfriend?"

He looked at me like I was crazy. "She's not my girlfriend. I just met her that day."

"And you just start molesting her on the book floor?"

"She jumped on me. I was on my break." He shrugged, unapologetic.

"You—what?"

"The police asked if I knew her, and I told them I saw her in the store, and it's true."

I just shook my head, my mouth open in shock.

"Chicks dig me." He shrugged again as if that answered everything. To prove his point, he winked at three more awestruck women circling the counter.

Not one to be ignored, I stepped into his line of vision. "Do you have any self-restraint?"

He met my gaze for a long beat before saying, "Plenty."

"You might want to apply some of it to the workplace." With my chin hiked in the air, I left the music section.

I couldn't believe this guy. His arrogance was breathtaking. A woman almost died, and he was completely nonchalant about it. Those women remained camped out by his register, waiting for him to grace them with his presence. If they started slinging underwear at him, I was going to have a talk with Linda. In fact, I should talk to her either way out of general principle.

I wove through the maze of bookshelves toward the break room when Caleb leapt out of nowhere and blocked my path. "If I didn't know any better, I would think you're jealous."

I tried to walk around him, but he blocked me with a side step.

"Jealous of what?" I asked.

When I moved to the right, he did the same. "Of my popularity."

I stopped moving. "Oh please. I know practically everyone in this town."

"I mean with the opposite sex."

My hands pinned to my sides, my fists clinched. He may stand over six feet, but my killer right hook could bring him down to size. "Are you implying that I don't have game?"

The side of his lips curled. "No. I'm implying that you have a tendency to scare people off. You don't have the same reaction with me that most women do. For a while, I thought you hated men."

At his words, my muscles relaxed. I gave up worrying what people thought of me long ago, but that didn't lessen the sting. "I don't hate men."

"Then prove it. Go out with me."

My mind went blank for a second, so I wasn't sure if I had heard him right. "Go-who-what?"

"Go out with me. Nadine gave me two tickets to Europia Park since she works there, and I want you to come with me."

"Get Nadine to take you."

He gave me a weary look as if I should know better than to ask. "Catching Nadine on a day off is as common as Halley's Comet."

He had a point. Vacations and sick leave must be against her religion or something. "Then why don't you call one of your disciples to go with you?"

"Because I want *you* to come with me. Besides, they would be all over me, and I actually want to see the park. I've been in Virginia for two years, and I've never been there."

Indignation came back with a vengeance. "You are so arrogant!"

"Yet you won't say no."

"Oh yeah? Check this out. No!" I tried to skirt around him. When that didn't work, I raced to the other end of the aisle and ran into his chest.

He tapped his chin in contemplation. "Tomorrow would be a good time. We're both off tomorrow. Why don't we meet here and we can take my car?"

"How about I stay home, and you go get your little groupies to show you around?"

"I already told you why, and this would be a great way to get to know me."

"I don't wanna get to know you," I argued, sounding every bit the five-year-old.

"It's not a date. I just want to hang out."

Jabbing a finger in his chest, I met his gaze dead on. "First off, how do you know when I work? Second, you're assuming I have nothing else to do but show you around a theme park all day, and why isn't it a date?"

"Because you don't want it to be. And our work schedules are posted in the break room."

"Oh." I dropped my hand. "Well, I'm still not going."

His advance made me retreat until my back pressed against the shelf.

"I'll tell you what, meet me here at noon, and if you're not here by twelve-fifteen, I'll go alone. No pressure, though I'm sure you wanna know why what's-her-name had her heart attack."

He slowly backed away, his eyes watching my reaction. And boy, he had quite a show. All kinds of horror scenes flashed before my eyes in every subgenre, from psycho killer to swamp monster.

"What do you mean?" I called after him.

"Tomorrow. Noon."

"What? What the hell kind of cliffhanger is that? If there was foul play, there's no way I'm going anywhere with you."

He turned and walked on. Now it was my turn to chase. He only made it to the end of the row before I caught his arm. "Did you have something to do with it? Did you poison her, or something?"

Dude had the nerve to laugh. "No."

I pulled his arm again. "Then what?"

Instead of answering, he scooped my face in his hands and kissed me, if one could call it a kiss. His mouth barely touched mine, which made it that much more powerful. The soft pillows of his lips traced the seam of my mouth, seeking access as he gently nudged mine apart.

At the feather-light contact, a sudden heaviness pulled at my chest. My arms began to tingle as if they had fallen asleep. The sensation soon reached my feet, and I couldn't feel the floor under me.

My eyes flew open and met an eerie purple abyss. His eyes were odd from afar, but seeing them up close scared the bejesus out of me. They possessed a soul of their own, a life that shouldn't exist, an entity that shocked the eyes and confused the senses. It stared back at me, sending an electrical charge through my nervous system, a feeling that made my lower region ignite. Just as I thought I would pass out, Caleb pulled his lips away.

Firm hands gripped my shoulders as he pressed his forehead against mine. Taking a deep breath, he whispered, "Tomorrow. Noon."

And with that, he walked away, leaving me to question the state of my sanity all on my own.

5

Mia stretched across my bed, staring up at the ceiling. "Let me see if I got this right," she began. "That creepy guy at your job asked you out on a date?"

"It's not a date!" I yelled from the hidden vortex in my closet.

"Okay. If it's not a date, then why am I here, and why do you wanna borrow my top?"

"Because I can't fit into your jeans," I replied.

"You can wear my sweatpants; the ones with 'Juicy' on the back."

"Mia, there ain't nothing juicy about what I got back there." I looked over my shoulder toward my butt. "That would just be false advertisement."

Though I needed Mia's keen fashion sense, I also needed her as a solid alibi. I had told Mom where I was going, but left out who was coming with me. Mom wouldn't let me out the door without a thorough FBI background check on Caleb Baker. Then she would probably call Dad, and I wanted Caleb to live long enough to give me the music he had promised me. My parents' nondating rule derived from their error in judgment as teenagers, and they didn't want to relive the sequel through their daughter.

"Why does it smell like feet in here?" Mia asked with a wrinkled nose.

"I was working out earlier."

She glanced at the DVDs on top of my television. "What's the big deal about Tae Bo? It's so old school. Why don't you do the stripper workout? Dougie seems to appreciate my workout regimen very much."

"I bet." I shuddered. "Unless I plan on working the pole after high school, that particular skill is not gonna benefit me. Besides, Tae Bo is way cheaper than a kickboxing class."

"You're so strange, Sam." Mia sprang up and dove into the suitcase she brought over that was armed for any fashion emergency. "Let's see, something to wear . . . oh, what about the capris?"

I tossed a shirt over my shoulder. "Muffin top."

"The cutoffs?"

"Wedgies."

"Well, damn. I don't know what to do. You didn't give me much notice here."

"It's cool. I got a backup plan." I went to the door. Mia was right on my heels on the short trip to Mom's room.

Clicking on the closet light, I surveyed the lay of the land. My eyes stopped at a pile of summer clothes in the back of the closet. On the top sat the infamous "skinny clothes" that Mom didn't have the heart to toss out in case she stuck with her diet. Unfolding a pair of black jean shorts, I realized it was a lot of wishful thinking on her part. Mom still owned a great figure, but that dime piece had some rust on it.

Turning to Mia, I presented two pairs of shorts. "Which ones—the red, or the white ones?"

Leaning against the doorjamb, she scrutinized each item, assessing the style, the cut, and the age of the textile worker who wove the fabric. "The white ones. They make you look more . . . *virginal.*"

I moved to the dresser drawers. "Keep on with the jokes."

"I'm just saying. I think it's cute that you have a crush. You know, it's the summer of love."

"Blasphemy! You dare speak such guile under thy kinsmen's roof."

"I love it when you get all medieval on me. That means I've hit a nerve." Mia plopped on my mom's bed. "So, what are you gonna do with your hair?"

"You're looking at it."

She grimaced. "How does it naturally stand up like that?"

"Physics," I answered, knowing exactly what she meant. As the sworn enemy of the humid Virginian summer, my funky riot of curls would not be denied. Today, my hair was pulled back in a huge Sistah Soldier afro puff on the top of my head. A red and white streak on the right side stood out against jet-black curls, resembling the Bride of Frankenstein with a candy stripe.

I slid on the white shorts, moved to the full-length mirror, and took inventory of the one known as Samara Nicole Marshall.

Dad called me "baby girl" for a legitimate reason. I had a baby-doll face. A great deal of cheeks and forehead catered to small features bunched in the center with barely a chin to anchor it. My wide eyes were so dark they looked like two big pupils. There's something to be said about biracial kids: they all have great skin, a rich caramel complexion that defies the gods of dermatology. I had to smile at that, my one crowning glory.

Mia stepped beside me and struck a pose, her brown ponytail slapping me in the face. Right on cue, she cataloged her microscopic flaws: claiming to be the only Filipino in history who couldn't tan, plotting to remove the light bump on the bridge of her nose, and debating whether to inject fat into her thin upper lip.

She stood two inches taller than my five and a half feet, sporting a sleek, fat-free physique that I secretly envied. I looked down at my boyish figure, which carried all its weight in the midriff, leaving scrawny limbs swinging in the breeze. It could be just baby fat or the inability to put the fork down, but my Treasure Troll beer gut would not go away. These were not the enduring qualities of a hottie, but rather a starved orphan in need of a child sponsor.

"So if you don't like this guy, then why are you going to Europia Park with him?" Mia asked, combing her hair with her fingers.

"He said he knew what happened to that girl in the parking lot, and it's a free ticket."

"You think he was involved? Maybe he's a drug dealer and he gave her some bad stuff."

"I don't think it's that. There's something odd about him."

Mia's look was incredulous. "And you wanna go off with him? Good thinking, Sam."

"That's why you're here. I need you to come with me."

She leapt back in surprise. "What?"

"I need a buffer and witness to any possible homicide. My cell phone has a GPS, so in case we split up, at least someone can find my body."

"What if he takes the phone?"

I rushed to Mom's nightstand, opened the drawer, and pulled out the razor she kept under her Bible. "Then I'll have to cut him."

"You can't take that into the park."

"I can put it in my shoe."

Mia sighed. "In that case, Dougie's got some brass knuckles."

I scoffed. "Too bad he can't hit worth a damn."

During my scavenger hunt for the perfect ensemble, Mia caught me up on the fallout at Virginia Beach. Dougie had gotten there and seen Mia hugging Garrett Davenport. Though Mia insisted that the hug was friendly, and expressed no romantic interest in the strapping linebacker, that hadn't stopped Dougie from going completely bat shit. The odds would have been in Dougie's favor were it not for half the football team voicing their concern for their injured comrade. For some reason, Mia found jealous rage and a head contusion sexy, and she and Dougie were back together.

"Leave my man alone. He was just defending my virtue." Mia propped her hands on her hips.

"You might need to upgrade your security," I shot back. "So are you coming with me, or not?"

"Yeah. I gotta stop by the house first and grab my season pass. I'll meet up with you later."

"Where?" I asked.

"In front of the Hall of Feasts. If I leave now, I should get there at two. Can you hold out for an hour?"

"I think I'll be fine. I just need some backup, just in case. I don't think he's stupid enough to do anything in public. Plus, Mom taught me how to jump out of a moving car."

"Tuck and roll." Mia smiled.

"That's what's up." I nodded and walked with her to the door.

Cruising into the Buncha Books parking lot, I found Caleb standing by his Jeep, eating an éclair.

I pulled into a vacant spot three lanes down then climbed out. Taking my time, I gave him a detailed perusal. He looked pretty good in civilian gear: a plain white shirt, tan cargo shorts, and sneakers. The heat was a likely motive for his much-needed man-scaping. He almost looked like a kid without that Unabomber facial hair, which provided an unobstructed view to his angular jaw and full, bow-shaped mouth.

Once he spotted me, he pulled the dark shades to the top of his head. His eyes locked on mine for a moment before examining his watch. "Twelve-eighteen."

"You didn't expect me to come right on the dot, did you?"

Caleb smiled and looked to his feet. "Would you be mad if I said yes?"

I nodded.

"Then yes. I don't know, I'm just—"

"Used to women dropping everything and running to lick your boots," I interrupted.

"No. Not my boots." He sucked the icing off his fingers.

Tossing him a murderous glare, I asked, "Are you gonna tell me about the girl?"

"You're quite curious about her. Are you sure you two don't have a thing?"

"No, I just don't like suspense. Spill it, Cake Boy."

He leaned against the back of his Jeep, engaged in a quiet moment of reflection. I didn't know what was worse: watching him inhale his high-calorie stimulant or that he hadn't offered me any.

Taking his sweet time, he said, "I kissed her."

I waited for the punch line.

"That's it." He tossed the wrapper in the backseat.

"That's it? I waited a whole day for that?"

With a sly curl to his lips, he placed the shades back

over his eyes. "Didn't know I had you on pins and needles like that. Besides, you wouldn't have joined me otherwise."

I threw my hands in the air. "You're such—"

"A great kisser?"

"A freak!" I yelled.

Dangling keys in his hand, Caleb circled his Jeep to open the passenger door for me. "Yet, you're still here. Come on, I wanna get on Poseidon's Wave first. I heard it was cool."

There had to be more to it than that. Infuriating as he was, I wasn't immune to his excitement, like a little kid at recess. The boy was plain goofy—probably not a physical threat. I was more concerned with internal injury, the kind that could penetrate through Kevlar and hurt worse than any bullet. In light of all this, he made the thrill of escape contagious, and I wanted the adventure.

After climbing in, I waited for him to start the ignition before I asked, "Are you a drug dealer?"

He paused. "Why? Are you wearing a wire?"

"No. Did you give her something laced? Or did she have an allergic reaction?"

"Sam, I didn't give her drugs. I was at the magazine aisle, she saw me, and we started talking—"

"About?" I cut in.

He stole a quick glimpse before he pulled out of the lot. "Grown-up stuff—not suitable for your young ears."

"You're only two years older than me. Now spill it."

He didn't answer right away; in fact, he didn't speak at all. Perhaps he was thinking of a good lie. If so, my BS meter had a hair trigger, and I would catch the first crack in his story. When we reached the interstate, he spoke up.

"She was flirting and touching me. One thing led to another, and well . . ."

I sucked my teeth in disgust. "I hate when people say

that. It's such a cop-out. People are fully aware of their actions."

He shook his head. "Not with me."

I cut my eyes at him. "Dude, really, how can you *and* your ego fit in this car?"

"I'm just being honest. Females are drawn to me. It's beyond my control."

I pointed to my chest. "Not this female."

"You're different."

"Different how?" I asked.

"You're not open."

Leaning away from him, I stared him up and down. "What's that supposed to mean?"

"Just what I said. You're too guarded and cynical to let anything into your world."

"What's that got to do with a woman suffering cardiac arrest in her car?"

He combed his fingers through his hair, which the wind pushed back in his face. "Look, would you just relax and enjoy the day? It's my day off, and I want to absorb the oncoming adrenaline rush. Don't you ever have fun?"

"Not with potential killers," I mumbled.

"I haven't killed anyone."

"Yet. And I intend to keep it that way."

He leered at me through the shades. "You really think I would hurt you?"

"I wanna believe you won't, which is why I agreed to come. As much as it pains me to admit, you've sparked my interest."

He chortled. "The kiss that good?"

I crossed my arms over my chest and stared out the window. "That's it. I'm done talking."

6

A side from the outlet stores, Europia Park was every kid's first job in Williamsburg.

However, no one else in their right mind would want to deal with that amount of people, not for minimum wage. Europia Park's theme mimicked all the major countries in Europe: France, England, Italy, Scotland, Germany, Ireland, you name it. That fact left tourists asking the question, "Why are so many Mexicans and Asians working here?"

Corporate America wanted to market Europe with family-friendly clichés with all the comforts of home. They didn't anticipate the language barrier with the imported employees. Good luck asking directions in this place. If visitors couldn't read the map, they'd be so screwed! So it made sense that Caleb brought me along as a tour guide. I could navigate through the park blindfolded. Regardless of how many times I came here, I still found the scenery breathtaking.

Surviving twenty minutes of parking-spot hunting and

a perilous trolley ride, Caleb and I strolled down the flowered path through the entrance. The first stop in our continental tour was ye olde England. Though he mentioned seeing the real thing before, he stood in awe at the medieval model of Big Ben near the entrance.

I've had my paranoid moments, that eerie suspicion of being watched, but the feeling intensified while in Caleb's company. Dozens of female eyes followed him through the park, where I tried to look everywhere but in his direction. When the fourth chick "accidentally" bumped into Caleb, I tried to ditch him, but he caught me before I could escape. For a ladies' man, he went out of his way to avoid his admirers, and shield me in case a riot broke out.

We wandered through France, where singers preformed in the street with camisoles and berets. Caleb's nose led him to the ice cream parlor by the portrait stand. This was his second stop within thirty minutes, and his appetite only seemed to get stronger.

While waiting for Caleb, I smiled at the woman in a revealing peasant dress operating the tavern-style lemonade stand. Her long blond hair fell over her shoulder in two long braids. She leaned her elbow on the counter, sweaty and extremely bored by her conversation with a customer. The man carried a drink in each hand and stood in the process of ordering another to keep her interest.

Once tired of the stall tactic, he took the plunge. "So, I was wondering what are you doing—"

"No," she snapped.

He tried again. "Well, how about—"

"No."

"Can I at least get your—"

"No."

"Fine!" The man skulked away with his head low and his dignity crumbling in his hands.

Laughing, I went to the booth. "What's up, Poland?"

Nadine's emerald eyes lit up, and that was as close to a smile that she would ever reach. "Sam! Hello! What brings you to ninth ring of hell?"

I summed up my crisis in one word. "Caleb."

Nadine leaned back, blown away by this news. "Oh! He's finally using those tickets I gave him?"

"The tickets were collecting dust while he waited for you to take a day off. How can you work so much? Honestly, when do you sleep?" I asked.

"I'll sleep when I'm dead. For now, I have rent and student loans. I'm still young with energy to burn."

Trust Nadine to make me look like a slacker on my day off.

"So, you're here with Caleb, hmm?" She leveled me with her eyes and twirled her braid. A bad idea since that one gesture brought three old dudes to her booth. Before they could speak, she yelled, "If you don't buy anything, piss off!" which succeeded in scaring the men away. Leaning over the counter, she drew closer. "So, are you two on a date?"

"No."

Her eyes narrowed. "You answer awfully quick."

"It was a quick question. I'm not interested in Caleb like that. I just wanna know what he's about. You know he's weird. Doesn't it bother you that he has women falling all over him?"

Nadine simply stared. "You're talking to *me* here."

I gave Nadine a good look from head to toe. "Well, yeah, you got guys all over you, but at least you're hot. Have you looked at Caleb? I mean, really looked? Dude has *no* swag and his hygiene is suspect."

Nadine shifted her lips from side to side in debate. "He's cute in scruffy, indie kid way. He has good taste in books. I just finished first chapter of book he recommended, and I had to tear myself away."

"You're missing the point. He's weird."

"You just want him to be weird so you cannot like him. He has bad moments and can be stubborn, but he's a good guy, Sam. I should know."

"Oh yeah? Aren't you two like 'frenemies' or something?" I asked coolly, but secretly anticipated her answer. Nadine and I talked about everything, but the subject of Caleb Baker came with a warning label and a combination lock.

If the question shocked her, she hid that fact from me. "In a way," she replied. "We are just friends who look out for one another, whenever he lets me."

"I think it's the women who need the looking out," I said dubiously.

Disappointed, she fell back behind the booth. "Thou doth protesteth too much."

Getting into character, I replied, "I fear not enough, lest haste awaken calamity from its rest."

She stared at me and shook her head in awe. "You are so strange, Sam, yet you pick fun at my poetry."

"So does that mean you won't hang with us after work? It'll be fun."

Before she could answer, the man of the hour approached the booth, holding a small mountain of frozen custard. On sight of Nadine, he tipped his head. "Nadine."

A chilly, impersonal welcome if I ever heard one, a mere acknowledgement of one's existence.

Returning the greeting with equal apathy, Nadine assessed his new grooming habits with heavy scrutiny.

Oh yeah, they were so doing each other. Probably one of those New Age European "arrangements." But if she wanted to keep it on the DL, then why did I care?

No really, why did I care?

I stared at the ice cream dripping down Caleb's fingers and cringed. "You're an insulin shot waiting to happen— you know that, right?"

"Does my sweet tooth make you uncomfortable?" He asked the question with such earnest curiosity, it caught me off guard.

"No. I—I just worry about your blood sugar. I'm surprised your teeth haven't fallen out of your head yet."

He rolled his eyes. "Thanks, mom, but this dessert will tide me over until supper's ready."

I heard Nadine snort behind me.

"Fine, but when you pass out from sugar shock, don't expect me to help you."

"Good to know who to rely on in a jam." Caleb strolled away, but stopped when I didn't follow. "You ready to go?"

I moved to join him as Nadine's taunt buzzed around my ears. "You *like* him. Admission is first step to recovery."

By the time Caleb and I finally made it to Germany, I was an hour late for my rendezvous point with Mia. I could tell Caleb was annoyed with the delay and wondered why I was stalling. He was eager to get on the rides, but I needed to sit down. I took a seat on a bench near the Hall of Feasts. Laughter, polka music, and profuse whiffs of beer bumbled in the air. I scanned the immediate area and found no sign of her. I decided on waiting another five minutes before calling her cell.

Caleb stared down at me, rocking on the balls of his feet. The afternoon sun hit his back, shooting gold light through his brown hair.

Wiping the sweat from my temple, I broke the ice. "We should talk about that kiss."

"I thought it was self-explanatory."

Shielding my eyes, I looked up at him. "No. Why did you kiss me?"

"Because I wanted to. I wanted to see what would happen." Though the reply was simple, something in his expression told me otherwise.

"What exactly did happen?" I asked.

"You saw me." The rocking stopped as he met my gaze. Flecks of purple light peeked from under his lashes. "The real me."

Before I could say anything else, he searched around, sniffing the air. "You smell funnel cake?"

Not knowing what else to say, I pointed to the food stand to my right.

Following my hand, he sprung into action. "Ah, I'll be right back. You want anything?"

"Water."

His head volleyed between me and the food stand. "You sure you'll be okay here? I don't think I can see you from there."

I waved him on. "Yeah, I'm fine. I'll wait here."

Put to ease, he disappeared into the crowd, leaving me to reflect on his peculiar statement.

What was his deal? True, he was vain to the tenth power, but he also seemed sad and lonely. I mean, if I had that much attention, I'd be milking it for all it's worth.

And why was that shrub talking to me?

I turned in the direction of the bush next to my bench. "Psst!" it said. "Hey, are you okay?"

I just stared at the rustling leaves. "That depends. Am I hallucinating?"

"No. It's me," I heard Mia say through the foliage.

"Why are you in the bushes?"

"You said you needed backup, and I'm doing surveillance."

"Wow, I've never seen your stalking firsthand. It's quite disturbing. How does Dougie sleep at night?"

The leaves rustled viciously. "I don't stalk him!"

"Whatever. I'm not gonna talk to a bush. Come out."

In seconds, Mia appeared with a tan trench coat and shades. Someone forgot to tell her that the Cold War was over, and that getup made her look even more conspicuous.

I lifted my head to the sky. "Why can't I have normal friends? Why is everyone around me mental?"

She took a seat next to me. "You attract them. So, did you really kiss Caleb?"

My eyes snapped back to her face. "What? How long have you been listening?"

"Five minutes. Why didn't you tell me?"

Oh man, I underestimated her undercover work. "Because it wasn't important. You kiss boys all the time."

"Yeah, but it's the same boy. And we're talking about *you* here."

"I don't want you to make a big deal about it."

"It must be a big deal if you wanna talk to Caleb about it. What happened? Did he try something? Did he touch your private parts?" she teased.

I kicked the side of her leg. "Stop it. I can't explain it to you. I can't understand it myself. And he's acting all cool about it, like that kiss didn't spook him out too."

"Well, from what you told me, he's got some mileage on him."

"Yeah, and another thing, why is he in my face all of a sudden? Ever since I caught him bustin' slob with that girl at the bookstore, he's been all over me."

Mia stood and removed her spy gear. "Guys do that

sometimes. We need a guy's opinion on the matter. Let's ask Dougie."

"Sure, as soon as he comes out of surgery," I mumbled.

Mia sighed, perturbed. "It wasn't that bad of a fight. And he's right over there."

I turned to where she pointed, and saw a laid-back and thoroughly beat-down Dougie exiting the men's room. After spotting us, he limped to our side and sat next to Mia.

"Damn, Dougie, you got your clock cleaned!" I exclaimed, taking in what was left of his face.

"Shut up," he grumbled.

Mia reached her arms out to him. "My brave man! My hero!"

While stomaching five minutes of lip-smacking and moaning, I wondered what was keeping Caleb. I craned my neck to see the food stand, but I didn't see him in the line.

Finally coming up for air, Dougie prompted, "So, SNM, I hear you got man trouble."

"I don't," I replied.

"Then why are we here?"

Mia bumped his arm. "I told you, Sam needs backup."

Dougie's body went stiff and on high alert. "Did he try something?"

I turned to him. "Relax. He hasn't done anything. Don't strain yourself; I'd hate to have you bust some of those stitches."

Dougie rubbed his bruised jaw. "Joke all you want, but Garrett's a douche. I don't like how he looks at Mia, and I've heard some things about him that ain't cool." He held Mia closer.

She looked up at him. "I told you it was a hug, nothing more."

"His hand was on your ass."

"And I pushed him away," Mia countered.

Knowing this argument could go on for days, I broke in. "Hey guys, we'll get back to your drama after the commercial break. Right now, I wanna ask you about boys."

Dougie's eyes widened. "Wow, this must be serious. What's up?"

I gave him the ninety-second abridgment of the weekend's events.

Giving a studious nod, he decided. "He likes you."

And that was it: the profound pearls of wisdom from the lips of Douglas Emerson III.

"How do you know?" I asked.

"You said he's got girls all over him. If he's taking the time to talk to you, then he wants you. And the fact that you don't drool over him is a turn-on. You're a challenge, and guys like to chase."

I looked sideways at him. "What is he trying to catch?"

"That's something you gotta ask him." He shrugged.

"All I'm saying is that he better not try anything. I'm not some conquest to mount on his wall, and if he tries something, I'll shove my foot so far up his—hey, Caleb! You've met my friend Mia, right?" I asked, taking the bottled water from the man in question.

Balancing a plate of fried dough, Caleb extended his hand to Mia. "I've seen her in the store a few times."

Mia's eyes dragged up and down Caleb's body before shaking his hand.

"And this is her *boyfriend*, Doug," I announced with an elbow to Mia's rib.

"What's up, man?" Dougie reached over and knocked fists with Caleb.

"So you guys tagging along?" Caleb asked.

"If that's okay?" I gave him my best puppy face.

"Sure, as long as I finally get on some rides. For some reason, Sam was bent on coming to Germany. Trust me, I lived in Germany for four years. I don't want to see any more of it."

A commotion made us all turn around. Tourists made room for the park's first-aid crew steering through the crowd. Two medics yelled for onlookers to move as they carried a woman on a stretcher. When the parade passed our way, the woman stared at me under her oxygen mask, her watery eyes wide and twitchy.

My stomach lurched at the scene. She was a pretty woman, not even middle aged, yet she looked as though every breath was her last. For some reason, she decided to use that precious air supply to speak. Her runny eyes grew wide on sight of something just over my shoulder. A shaky hand clutched at her chest while the other pointed in our direction. Her mouth flapped, like a fish, and hot air fogged the plastic mask, but whatever she tried to say went unheard as the convoy drifted from view.

"Whoa, what was that about?" I turned to Caleb, whose face now bore a ghostly cast under his shades. I gave him a wide berth in case his funnel cake resurfaced.

"She probably suffered a stroke. It's hot as hell out here." Mia wiped the sweat behind her neck to underline her point. Springing to her feet, she guided Caleb by the arm. "You ready? The Dragon Horn is just this way. You need to start off right."

We spent the next six hours riding, laughing, and riding some more. The lines were ridiculous, but it was to be expected and well worth the wait. I must have lost fifteen pounds from the walking alone, and the ninety-degree heat index did me no favors.

We reached Italy and stopped to eat and cool off on the water rides. Caleb insisted that I stay hydrated and bought me a gallon jug of lemonade. When another woman was wheeled away by medics, I didn't argue with him.

Though Nadine flaked out on me *again*, she kept paging me every twenty minutes, demanding a play-by-play and checking if Caleb was behaving himself.

By nightfall, we were exhausted, but I wanted to walk the bridge in Italy. The lights were spectacular, and I got lost in the romance. I wasn't the only one, with Mia and Dougie making out by a lamppost.

"You look happy," Caleb mused. "Where's my camera?"

"You got jokes. How can I not be happy? I mean, look at all these lights."

Caleb swept his eyes across the expanse. "You sound like my mom. She was a sucker for a good view."

"Oh yeah? Where is she now?"

"She died five years ago."

That wasn't the answer I had expected, and Caleb seemed to have difficulty giving it.

"I'm so sorry. I didn't know." When I touched his arm, he finally looked at me.

"Yeah, it was part of the reason I came back to the States. My dad took her death hard, and I couldn't watch him get dragged down with her." He took a sharp intake of air and held it.

"He loved her a lot?"

He exhaled slowly. "That is the mother of all understatements." For a moment, Caleb was no longer with me, but someplace beyond time and distance.

"How's your dad holding up?"

"Don't know. Haven't spoken to him in over a year. I've kinda distanced myself from my entire family. I don't want to get sucked back into all that strife for nothing to get solved. I love my family, but I'd rather express that love from afar."

I searched his eyes for what he didn't say. "It's that bad?"

"Yup."

I leaned away from him. "You don't have mob ties or a warrant for your arrest, do you?"

That made him smile, something I knew he needed right now, but it didn't make the question any less relevant. "No, Sam. I'm squeaky clean, probably the dullest guy you'll ever know."

"I seriously doubt that." I looked out to the water, enjoying the lights tickling its surface. "Where have you traveled around the world?"

"Everywhere. The only bad thing is I can't pick up a language to save my life. My brothers and sisters lost their American accents, but I lived in the States longer, so mine sticks no matter where I go. I can speak more German 'cause I spent more time there, but French, Spanish, and Japanese fly right over my head. Nadine's trying to teach me Polish, but I'm a lost cause."

At the mention of Nadine, a new question arose. The issue bothered me more than it should and I hoped Caleb was more forthcoming with answers. "Did you and Nadine used to date?"

To my surprise, the thought made him shudder. "Oh God, no! Why would you ask that?"

"I see you two looking at each other and how you guys talk, but not really. It's always tense," I began. "Did you break her heart? You didn't cheat on her, did you?"

His upper lip curled as if tasting something rancid. "No. We never dated. Our families have known each other for years, what with traveling and all that. Since I'm the baby of my family, Nadine likes to play big sis and designated cockblocker." When he saw my puzzled look, he continued. "She thinks I'm a womanizer or something, and we all know her attitude toward men. She won't let me forget it."

He had a point. Nadine had a way of cutting a man at the knees and even higher, should the chance arise. I shook my head, knowing that if she couldn't end Caleb's wicked ways, nothing would.

I could tell he wanted to change topics, so I asked, "Where's your favorite place to visit?"

Caleb stepped behind me and wrapped his arms around my waist. Without hesitation, he said, "India. The music there is insane. Love it."

Normally, I would have clocked a guy for invading my personal space, but the action felt appropriate for this personal moment. I may be guarded, as Caleb had proclaimed, but I wasn't dead. Feeling the heat of his body coaxed me into a peace I'd never known I lacked. The way his chin tucked within the pocket between my neck and shoulder, the light whisper of hair touching my skin, and the gentle thud of his heartbeat made my own speed up to match his pace. I nestled my head against his chest and listened to his tales of international exploits.

As the youngest of six children, Caleb received abundant coddling and hand-me-downs, something that I could tell he despised. He attended seven private schools and was expelled from three for causing unrest with the female student body. One of his teachers was suspended due to an unseemly event with him in the boys' locker room. He swore he didn't embellish these accounts and was willing to provide photographic evidence.

He excelled in track and field, soccer, and anything involving a bull's-eye. All the men in his family learned to shoot before they could ride a bike, but Caleb mastered archery and offered to show me his crossbow. Displaying a collection of medieval weapons to an already suspicious girl did not incite the best confidence, so he decided to hold off until our third date. And here I didn't even know we agreed to a *first* date.

Mr. Caleb Baker was a walking contradiction. He could shoot a target from a hundred yards, but he got squeamish around knives and avoided hand-to-hand combat at all costs. He came from a wealthy family, but he kept the lifestyle of a gypsy. He had friends all over the world, likely females in countries I never even heard of, but a heavy blanket of loneliness cloaked his body. Dude was a hard book to read, but he was definitely a page-turner.

By the time we parted, I felt a little better about being alone with Caleb, but I still held suspicions of his motives. He seemed interested in more than friendship, but how far was he trying to go? We said nothing on the ride back to my car. My feet were killing me, my clothes were still wet from the water rides, and I smelled like hard, sweaty fun.

When he parked his car next to mine back at Buncha Books, he reached in the glove box and pulled out a memory stick with my name written in silver marker. "You thought I forgot, didn't you?"

I couldn't argue because I had surely forgotten about it.

"Thanks, I'll let you know what I think." I slipped his music in my bag.

He leaned over me, his eyes fixed to mine. His sudden movement scared me. The scent of powdered sugar on his breath tickled my nose. His lips parted, hovering mere centimeters over mine when a dull pop came from my door. I spun my head in time to see his hand on the latch, prying the door open.

"Drive safe," he whispered.

I wasn't sure what to make of the entire day, or why he hadn't kissed me, or why I cared that he hadn't. But I felt him watching me as I climbed in my car, pulled out of the lot, then left the shopping center. Even throughout the short drive home, I still felt it—the deep purple of curious eyes and unknown intent. It was a hard thing to get used to, and I wasn't sure if I wanted to.

7

The next few days went by in a blur. Nothing exciting happened anyway.

I was so swamped at work from summer tourists that I practically had to smuggle a lunch break. But the music Caleb had given me kept me entertained to the point of distraction.

I got through the entire file in one day, and I transferred a number of tracks to my playlists. There were some weird Euro-trash techno songs that had me raising an eyebrow, but the rest was unexpectedly . . . *awesome*! He owned an eclectic taste, from rock, to blues, to old-school hip-hop. I found myself humming a folk melody as I whipped through my work.

I needed to adjust my hours so I could free the weekend to watch the twins. Swallowing two mouthfuls of pride, I sought out Alicia, who alternated between the café and book floor. After a great deal of groveling on my part, she agreed to take my shifts. Today she whisked by me on her way to the magazine aisle, giving me the you-owe-me-big-time glare.

Restocking the cream and sugar bar, I went through the agenda in my head, estimating how much time was required to go home, shower, pack a bag, and head to Dad's house so I could chaperone his brood.

Just before my shift ended, a voice rang out, "What's up, Sam?"

I turned around and saw Garrett sporting a nasty shiner on his right eye. I took a step back and admired Dougie's handiwork.

The guy was about six-foot-four with wide shoulders, built solely to intimidate weaker beings. With spiky blond hair and a square jaw, Garrett Davenport was the text-book definition of a *Chad*.

> *Chad [chad]—noun.*
>
> *A young Anglo-American male with athletic build, typically named Chad, who is very popular with the opposite sex, and usually the alpha male of a social group. Chads are often found in fraternities, tailgate parties, sporting events, and anywhere within the vicinity of a light-beer kegger. Staple attire consists of the following: baseball cap, wife-beater undershirt or T-shirt with ironic slogan, cargo shorts, and leather sandals. Prone to utter inappropriate phrases like, "What's up, bro?" or "Yo, dog."*

"Hey, Cha—I mean Garrett," I corrected. "What up?"

Hiking his chin in greeting, he browsed around the store. "You've seen that little bitch Doug around?"

"No. I heard you two had a misunderstanding." I tucked my lips to stave off the laugh.

He dragged his tongue over his top row of teeth and nodded. "Something like that. You tell him to stay out of my way, if he knows what's good for him."

I gave him a firm salute. "Will do."

"You coming to Robbie's party next Saturday?"

"Wouldn't miss it."

Garrett looked over to the bookshelves and spotted Alicia. "Doesn't she go to our school?"

Seeing the predatory lust in his eyes, I dropped my box of straws and rounded on him with both barrels loaded. "Yeah, but the thing is, *you* don't anymore. Back off, Garrett. She's only fifteen."

He lifted a blond eyebrow. "Your point?"

"I can sum it up in two words: *jail bait!*"

The words hit him like a bucket of cold water. "See ya on Saturday, Sam," he mumbled and left my sight, but not without stealing another glimpse at the forbidden fruit on the book floor.

Once I finished my cleanup, I tossed off my apron and went to clock out. At customer service, I felt a tap on my shoulder. I spun and saw nothing but violet.

"Hey, you." Caleb's voice carried more enthusiasm than any normal person should have while at work.

"Hey, yourself." A smile crept through despite my efforts to keep cool.

"I listened to the music you gave me. It's good. Thanks." He went to the opposite computer to clock in.

"Glad you like it. I like your stuff, too."

He looked over his shoulder. "Oh yeah? You're not just saying that, are you?"

I was about to reply when an unmistakable tune rang from my bag. The man must have ESP or something, because he seemed to know when a guy was in the general area of my person. Dad sure knew how to kill a mood. He had blown up my phone all day, ensuring that I didn't back out of our agreement.

Groaning, I reached in my bag for my cell. Caleb

watched with an amused look on his face. "Is that *The People's Court* theme song?"

"Yeah."

He snorted. "As your ring tone?"

"My Dad's anyway. He's a lawyer. It's our little joke." I groaned, digging into the dark recesses of my bag.

"Well, I gotta get back to work. I'll see you on Monday." He gave me a quick peck on the cheek, then left the desk, both actions so random and awkward that I wasn't sure they had actually happened. I just stood there, probably wearing "shell shock" on my face for all to see. Shaking out of my trance, I went back to my hunt. By the time I found my phone, the music had stopped.

Passing through the main aisle toward the entrance, I saw a tall, muscular man talking to Caleb. Seeing them together made it painfully obvious they were related, but the heated subtext of the exchange reached far from loving. I wasn't prone to listening in on others' conversations, but what little I did hear sounded ominous and shady as hell.

Caleb glared up at the man, his jaw tight and fists clenched. "Don't come here again, Haden. I told you I don't want anything to do with it, and now you bring this bullshit here?"

When Caleb tried to leave, the man known as Haden spun him around. With a faint hint of an Irish brogue, he said, "You can't turn your back on this. Deny and starve yourself in this hick town all you want, but it's as much a part of you as it is me."

Caleb swatted the hand away. "I have a new life now. It isn't much, but it's mine. If you were smart you'd stop chasing ghosts and do the same."

"Not everyone is as cold as you are. Don't you feel the loss? *He* certainly does, and he's asking for you."

"Good for him. I'm not going to see him, so this little

trip of yours is wasted. And you better not tell him where
I am—"

"He already knows," Haden interrupted. "You can't
hide from the patriarch, and no matter what, we all must
return to our source."

"You may be quick to forgive, but I'm not, and I have
long-term memory. I told you what I would do if I saw
him again, and I keep my word. Leave me alone. Forget
you ever saw me."

Caleb stormed away, leaving the man slumping against
the bookshelf, straining for control with his eyes closed.
As if he sensed being watched, his head popped up, but I
scurried off before he looked in my direction.

This was none of my business. Everyone had their family problems, and Caleb was no exception. Then why did
it feel different, freakishly different? I couldn't blame him
for ducking out on a guy who resembled a bounty hunter,
but what did Caleb do to have the angel of death track
him down?

I reached the main entrance when a hand shot out to
open the door for me. When I looked up to thank him, I
nearly jumped out of my skin. How did he cross the store
so fast?

The man's big body towered over me, leering in cyni-
cism. His rugged features spoke of hard knocks and way
too much sun. He exhibited the world-traveler appeal,
and telling by the dirt on his clothes, he spent his time
raiding ancient tombs for buried treasure.

His violet eyes came alive with amusement as if he
reached some great revelation. "So *you're* Caleb's missing rib. Wouldn't have pictured it."

His gruff tone made me recoil. "Excuse me? How do
you know me?"

"I saw him kiss you a few moments ago. Caleb never
makes the first move. He never had to, until now." He

placed a thick hand over his chest and gave a slight bow. "I'm Haden, his older brother."

Seeing him up close, the similarity was uncanny; however, the man's wide, husky build and slick, coal-black hair threw me off. They even had the same eyes, the weird amethyst shade, but his held a mystical glow as if he wore florescent lenses.

"So are you in love with him?" he asked, but it sounded like a demand.

The question snapped me back to the present. "Whoa! That's *so* none of your business." I passed through the open door.

"I'll take that as a yes." Haden followed me out and teetered back from the hot gust of summer air. "I can understand if you are. The men in our family are irresistible. It's kind of a curse, actually. But I warn you, the women who love us don't have happy endings. So guard your heart. One kiss will seal your fate."

Was he for real? How this "don't hate me because I'm beautiful" routine worked on women stood as the mystery of the ages. Waiting for cars to pass before crossing the lane, I called back, "Apparently, conceit is a hereditary trait as well." I halted midstep and turned to him. Not sure of his reaction, I averted my gaze while confessing, "I couldn't help but overhear you talking about a patriarch. Is your father royalty or something?"

He paused to consider his answer, his expression gentle and composed. "We have a legacy, a birthright of sorts. But Caleb in his pigheadedness refuses to claim it. He's ignoring his obligations and that may cost him in the end."

I nodded, though more questions emerged with each obscure answer, questions that I didn't have the right to ask. "I hear the family ties are strained. I'm sorry."

He stood next to me, so close his arm brushed against

my back. "So am I. Perhaps you can talk some sense into him, help him bridge the gap."

I bristled. "Me? That's personal, and I'm not that tight with him to offer family counseling. Besides, he doesn't seem like the type to disown his family without good reason."

"True." He gave a lazy smile. "You're not easy to impress and you have boundaries. No wonder he wants you."

Hefting my bag on my shoulder, I spun around to face him. "Why are you telling me this?"

"Because Caleb won't. I told you, he's stubborn, something I reckon you two have in common. You have a wild ride ahead of you." He flicked my name tag with his fingers. "Who knows, *Samara*, you might live to tell about it." He shoved his hands in his pockets and strolled away, with no apparent destination in mind.

I stood still for a full minute, watching his big body dissolve into the throng of window-shoppers on the sidewalk. That graceful stride exuded carnality, danger, and all the things mothers warned their daughters about. I noticed that was one of many attributes that ran in the family.

Both brothers had those strange, luminous eyes that tricked the mind, a power that crooked its finger to invite me in. I'd come across enough players in school to know when to cut and run, but Caleb Baker operated on a whole other level of seduction. Against my better judgment, I had to know what waited on the other side. I just hoped I didn't go insane in the process.

8

___

Once dressed, I dragged my rolling suitcase down the stairs.

Though it was only a two-day sentence, I went down the checklist of needed items and artillery. Grabbing my keys, I headed for the door, but cringed at the sound of approaching footsteps.

"You heading out now?" Mom asked from the dining room.

I winced. "Yeah."

"Okay, honey. Call me as soon as you get there. And make sure you lock all your doors, and watch your speed. If a cop flashes you, make sure you stop at a public place, with plenty of people. There was a story on the news about this man impersonating police by using one of those party lights in his car. Anyway, you don't wanna know what happened to the poor woman he stopped. They like to get you in a wooded area, somewhere where there're no houses or buildings you can run to for help."

There it was. This wouldn't be a proper sendoff without the parting gift of terror. I knew Mom worried, but she needed to work on her timing. This woman struck fear in the hearts of everyone in my neighborhood and friends brave enough to cross our threshold. So was it really a wonder where I got my suspicious nature? I've lived under this woman's roof for seventeen years; something was bound to rub off on me.

"Come on. Give me a hug." She spread her arms and pulled me in.

Trying not to wonder what happened to that victim's body, I said, "I promise, I'll call you as soon as I get there."

"Okay, honey. You got a sweater?"

"It's June."

"Just in case. And you know the number to Triple A?"

"Uh-huh."

"Phone charged?"

"Yep." I nodded and pulled the door open.

Wheeling my suitcase to the car, Mom rushed after me with a bottle of water. "And make sure you have plenty to drink. I don't want you having heat stroke like those women at Europia Park."

I popped the trunk then stopped. "What?"

"Two women collapsed in Europia Park a few days ago."

After dumping the load inside, I turned to look at her. "Where did you hear this?"

"Where have you been, Samara? It was all over the news."

"You know I don't watch that show. Plus, I got you here to fill in all of the good parts. So, when did all this happen?"

"Tuesday. I thought you knew about it. You didn't see anything while you were there?"

My mind rolled back to the day in question. "I saw two women fall out, but I thought it was from heat exhaustion."

"Maybe. But it resulted in a full-blown heart attack and stroke. Luckily, they survived, but they're in bad shape. It can happen at any age, Samara. So be careful."

Mom handed me the water, then moved in for another hug. Though Dad lived only an hour away, Mom still acted like I was going off to war. I didn't look forward to the devastating farewell when I left for college next year.

I climbed in the car while she stood on the porch and waved. She smiled, as if pleased that her baby had received her daily helping of bewilderment and paranoia. But in this instance, the suspicion came with a good reason. A girl can never be too careful, especially alone.

I pulled up to Dad's place around five. Mr. Watkins and company lived in a gated community on the outskirts of Richmond. Dad would never be featured in *Fortune* magazine, but his house told everyone that he carried a little change in his pocket. I cruised up the path, admiring the geometrically groomed shrubs and the endless stretch of lawn.

Dad was in the process of loading the trunk of his car when he turned and waved.

After I climbed out or my car, a warm hug greeted me.

"Hey, baby girl. Thanks so much for doing this. I know it's short notice."

"It's cool. Nothing personal; it's just business," I murmured against his chest.

When we pulled away, I saw Rhonda coming out of the house with more bags. Though a tall waif, Rhonda wouldn't be strutting down a runway anytime soon. She was afflicted with extreme butterface (everything looked good but her face), and she seemed deathly allergic to tact.

Two hyper children flanked her sides like pups begging for scraps. Those playful cherubs deceived all unaware, most of all their mother. Kenya stood to the left, giving me the neck-and-eye-roll combo, and Kyle was straight "mean muggin'." Staring at those *darling* faces, I could see a little bit of Dad flashing behind their eyes.

Deep, deep down I loved my siblings, but they played too much and owned an endless supply of pointless questions like, "Why does your hair look like that? Why do you talk like a white girl? When are you gonna untie us from this chair?" And so on and so forth.

Bottom line: I didn't look like them, and they saw me as an outsider—an outsider who had no qualms with whipping out a belt in public. With any luck, they would outgrow this animosity. But today wasn't that day.

Doling out a smile she'd likely practiced all day, Rhonda chimed, "Hello, Samara. Good of you to come."

I returned the gesture. "Is it?"

"Yes, of course it is. You know you're welcome here anytime. I've invited you to come to church with us every Sunday, and you never come."

I unloaded the suitcase from my trunk. "We have several churches in Williamsburg, Rhonda."

She must have taken that as a challenge. With quirked eyebrow and raised chin, she asked, "Oh? What church do you and your mother attend?"

"The ones on TV."

Lifting her eyes skyward, she let out a loud, exasperated sigh. "Samara, it's not the same. There's nothing better than fellowship person-to-person. There's a support system to help you through those troubled times."

"You mean people getting all in your business and gossiping about you in the name of goodwill? No thanks. I like to keep my spiritual life private." Translation: I don't answer to you, so keep it movin'.

"Still the little spitfire. You get that from your mother, you know. It's a shame how certain habits pass down to children." She glowered at me with pity in her eyes. "I'll pray for you. You need it."

And you need a hot-oil treatment, *stat*, I wanted to say, but Dad stood next to me, holding his breath.

I'm the last one to talk about ethnic hair, but home girl was positively nap-tastic! My dad was a good-looking dude; he could have done better than this. Plus she's mean! But Dad loved this woman enough to marry her, so she must be doing something right. I saw the love in his eyes, a look that he could never give Mom. I didn't have the heart to cuss Rhonda out. Dad looked so excited about this trip, and I needed to conserve my energy in order to survive the weekend.

Rhonda shooed the children back into the house with a flimsy warning about disobedience. Their innocent smiles slid away the moment her back turned. Kenya served me a look of malice, and Kyle dragged a finger across his throat to illustrate his point.

I shook my head, wondering which was worse—that a six-year-old boy could issue a threat with the best of them or that he meant it.

Once the preliminaries were over, Dad and Rhonda went down the emergency numbers and security precautions and then set out. I waved good-bye, squared my shoulders, and prepared for battle.

The inside of the house was spacious and surgically sterile, like those model apartments inside rental offices. Everything was white, with no sign of organic life, but rather a mock-up of a human family dwelling. How they managed to keep the furniture clean with two worrisome kids running around expanded the boundary of belief.

The rumble of footsteps on the second floor declared that the battle of Armageddon was upon me. To say that the twins were a handful was an understatement of epic proportions, not suitable for the faint of heart or those with back problems. As expected, the next four hours consisted of random flashes of traumatic events the brain fought to suppress: Running up and down stairs twenty-six times (yes, I counted), chasing Kyle a half mile when he ran out of the house, hurdling over toys and bikes, getting peanut butter stuck in my hair from Kenya's "beauty shop treatment," wringing a steak knife and Dad's power drill out of Kyle's clutches before he hurt himself, or me, and hiding my cell phone from Kenya, who had developed an obsession with buttons. During all this, I clung to the image of my new car like a talisman, the only thing that kept me going.

Thank goodness for technology. I put on a movie they both agreed on, and urban street fighting kept them distracted long enough for me to prepare dinner and draw their baths.

Once the kids were asleep, I crashed on the couch, listening to Caleb's music. My body relaxed as the melody dissolved into my sore muscles and joints. With the house quiet, I thought of Caleb Baker and all the mystery he encompassed.

The boy was interesting; I'd give him that. He gave me butterflies, though I would never reveal that to the rest of the world. I couldn't explain it, but the more we talked, the better he looked. My mind drifted to the night at Europia Park and how he held me on the bridge in Italy. He smelled of sweat and vanilla ice cream. His arms around me felt like home. All I wanted to do was stand there all night.

Slicing through the cotton-candy cloud, logic intervened. Its opening argument featured two women who had collapsed in a theme park on Tuesday. Both had encountered heart attacks, not even thirty yards from where I'd stood. That was the third time that a woman had had a bum ticker within a span of a week.

I never believed in coincidences, so there was no point in starting now. The common variable stood out in bold neon, daring me to overlook it. I thought of Haden's warning about guarding my heart around his brother. It was a rhetorical statement, of course, but it haunted me nonetheless. So much power and magic invested into a tiny organ.

Caleb certainly held an air of enchantment, a shadowy aura that prickled my arms, but never broke the skin. There had to be a logical explanation for all of it somewhere. But there just wasn't enough hard evidence to convict him of anything aside from liking me. Above all else, that notion was the hardest one to believe.

No matter how loud that little voice kept screaming in my head to keep away, an even louder voice demanded to know more, to see more, to feel more. Maybe Nadine was right, I was just making excuses not to like him. This new experience quickened my pulse with excitement, and damn if I didn't want to know where all of it would lead.

9

The first few days of the new month were a bit stagnant. People prepared for the Fourth of July, wearing patriotic colors and waving banners in the air. The smell of barbecue complemented the flute songs of marching soldiers in Colonial Williamsburg.

Mia and Dougie were tighter than ever. I kept an eye on my watch, anticipating the next altercation waiting around the corner. Mia scrambled around town, hunting for the perfect outfit to wear at Robbie Ford's party on Saturday. His Fourth of July bashes were legendary, and everyone who was anyone at my school would be there. Robbie's recent graduation marked the event as the last hurrah before he and his class scattered across creation. Mia wouldn't stop talking about it, and couldn't wait to exploit our new position as the upper echelon of James City High School.

Meanwhile, Mom was still looking for love in all the wrong places online. While setting up a user profile, she tore the house apart trying to find pictures of her, sans love handles. She even signed up for a speed-dating session next week.

Dusting off that gym membership, Mom initiated an emergency makeover. She wiped the house clean of anything above ten calories, leaving nothing but ice cubes and a cool breeze in the fridge. She ate nothing but chicken broth and green tea all week. I would lose my baby fat in God's sweet time, so I had to rely on my survival skills for sustenance. But I had to draw the line when my Tae Bo DVD suddenly went missing.

The store was busier than usual, but I almost looked forward to going to work. And there was only one reason why. Caleb and I continued our customary trash talk with a side dish of public affection. These subtle spars went on throughout the week. We began swapping more music, then progressed to books and movies. He also had a thing for the old black-and-white flicks, and he wasn't afraid of subtitles. Yep, this guy was slowly growing on me.

By Saturday, I had to stop myself from bouncing when he approached the counter with hunger in his eyes. Unfortunately the look wasn't for me, but for the apple tart in the bake case.

After I rung up his order, he asked me what I was doing later that night.

I paused behind the register. "Um . . ."

"You're still afraid I'm gonna put something in your drink, aren't you?" He smirked.

Looking down, I handed him his food. "No. I just got plans."

"Oh yeah? What kind?"

"The kind that conflict with us going out."

He leaned closer, forcing me to meet his gaze. "What are you doing?"

I gave a dismissive wave. "There's this party my friend's giving tonight, that's all."

"Cool." He took a bite of his tart and walked away.

Before I could check myself, I blurted out, "You wanna come with me?"

His brows knit together as he mulled over the idea. "Would this party consist of high school kids?"

I shrugged. "Some."

"With no parental supervision?" he asked.

"Likely."

"And beer?"

"Copious."

"No thanks." He kept walking.

"*I'll* be there," I emphasized, hoping that would sweeten the deal.

He stopped, then turned around. He swallowed, then asked, "What time?"

"Nine. I'll meet you here."

Flashing a smile, he drifted from sight, leaving me to collect myself and withstand the scandalized look from Nadine.

She stood with her mouth open and coffee overflowing from the cup she poured. Catching herself, she grabbed a rag and tended to the mess.

"That's what you get for being nosy." I pranced to the back kitchen.

She looked like she wanted to say something, perhaps talk me out of it, but no reply came.

After a shower, quick wardrobe change, and another cautionary tale from Mom, I was back at the Buncha Books parking lot just before nine. Caleb stood by his Jeep, looking quite snazzy in frayed jeans and a V-neck T-shirt. When he spotted me, he almost choked on his candy bar.

I couldn't blame him. I looked good in a black one-piece halter set, an outfit I had to peel on in my car because Mom would wild out if she saw it. But my covert operation was well rewarded by the look in Caleb's eyes; a look that, for once, had nothing to do with food.

Swallowing hard, he stepped closer. "Damn, Samara, you've got great legs."

"Yeah, Mom let me borrow them for the next thirty years."

"I take it you hear that a lot?"

Feeling heat rush to my cheeks, I studied my feet. "A few times. Maybe I should keep a coin jar under the register at work like you do."

"You'd make a fortune." He dug in his pocket and handed me a quarter. "This should start you off."

"Thanks." I plucked the coin from his fingers.

"You ready?"

"Sure." I dropped the quarter in my bag as he escorted me to his Jeep.

Robbie Ford's house was huge with a pool in the back. His parents were always out traipsing around the world, doing God knows what. Why no one called Social Services or who actually signed his permission slips and report cards remained a mystery to this day. Everyone at school had believed he was an orphan until Mr. and Mrs. Ford made a cameo appearance at his graduation.

His folks were a peculiar lot, and one glimpse into their bedroom drove that fact home. There were mirrors on the ceiling and some sort of harness bolted to the wall, complete with an odd assortment of costumes in the closet. Needless to say, that room was off limits to visitors.

Robbie was an interesting one. He was going to MIT in the fall, and I still believed he blackmailed the dean to get in. He was a closet brain—the go-to guy who could hack into any database and procure just about anything. If one needed to get out of the country ASAP, he could provide a fake passport for a reasonable fee.

He greeted us at the door with a silk bathrobe, boxers, and a pipe in his mouth. "Sammy, my sweet, buttery goodness, you look ravishing," he declared in the best Sean Connery impersonation I ever heard.

"Thanks, Rob." I stepped inside to peck cheeks.

Pulling away, he took stock of the tall man in front of him. "Who's this?"

"This is my friend, Caleb."

"Friend, huh? Is there a benefit package involved?"

I punched Robbie's arm. "Shut up."

"I'm Robert Ford, host of the Shangri-La. *Mi casa es su casa*, but not the master suite upstairs." He shuddered at the thought of his parents' bedroom.

"Thanks. Nice to meet you." After shaking hands, Caleb scooted his way through the crowd.

People underestimated the power of word of mouth. The house was packed. Half of the guests went to rivaling schools and William & Mary.

Robbie had hired a deejay, who stood between four monster speakers in the corner. The house shook with hard dance music, vibrating the pulse between my clavicle bones. The air was alive and breathing within this world of dry-humping and drinking games.

Nearing the center of the madness, Caleb pulled me in for a dance. He wasn't too bad, but the music didn't require many moves, just high-energy bouncing and head bobbing. When a popular song came on, the entire continental shelf rushed the dance floor. Bodies jumped in the air, drinks splashed, voices howled and sung along. It was the end of the world, and we were going out with a bang.

Needing some fresh air, I maneuvered to the patio with

Caleb on my tail. Though it was almost eighty degrees outside, it felt like supermarket air-conditioning compared to the dance floor.

Guys plunged into the pool and floated on inner tubes. Girls squealed and raced around barefoot, trying not to get pushed in. Sparklers twirled in hands and fireworks exploded overhead. Guests walked by holding paper plates and red plastic cups. Hotdogs and burgers hissed in the grill to my left, and the line for a sample wrapped around the pool.

All of this set away into a moving backdrop of disengagement. Perhaps the detachment was purely on my end, like a phantom that haunted the last place visited while alive. It no longer felt like home, but I couldn't quite move on.

Caleb stood behind me and stroked my bare arms. "You okay?"

The contact made me shiver. His fingers did a job on a girl's nerves, but I didn't ask him to stop. "I'm fine. I needed air. You having fun?"

"Surprisingly enough. But if you wanna leave, we can."

"No. I'm just thinking about school. It's funny seeing people in the hall every day, not even friends, just the same old people you bump into. I'll never see these guys again, not like I used to, not all together like this."

His chest rose and fell against my back. "Will you miss them?"

"Some. I mean, Mia and I are thugs for life. We get to graduate together next year, but Robbie and half of the gang I hung out with already graduated. Everything's gonna change; it's a feeling I can't shake off. I'm moving up in the ranks. I'm a senior now and one step closer to the end. I'm not sure I'm ready for it."

"Just the fact that you're aware of it is enough, I guess. You've gotten used to people making decisions for you. Stay in school, go to college, get a job, and then what? There's no instruction manual on life, Sam. And not one path is for everyone."

"Is that why you didn't go to college?" I asked.

"Yeah, I know people who are about to graduate college and still don't know what to do with themselves. If I'm gonna blow fifty grand on education, I wanna know what for."

"What do you want out of life?"

He kept quiet for the longest time. Squeezing my waist tight, he said, "Consistency, independence, and something that's mine and mine alone."

I looked up at him. "Have you found it yet?"

"Not yet, but I have time. All I have is time."

I smiled. "Must be nice."

He leaned over to look at me. "What school are you going to apply to?"

"Howard. Dad went there, and he wants me to follow in his footsteps."

"Is that what *you* want?"

"God yes! It's been my dream to be a lawyer like my dad, but I wanna do criminal law."

"Well, you sure know how to argue, that's for sure." He kissed the back of my neck.

Warmth coated my belly as a tickle crawled from his lips to the base of my spine.

I shivered. "Why did you do that?"

"What? Kiss your neck?"

"Yeah."

His breath bounced against my ear. "Well, aside from your legs, that's my favorite spot on you. Does it bother you?"

"No. It's just a weird place to kiss someone."

He turned me to face him. "I can think of a better place."

I wrapped my arms around his neck. Now that I had him relaxed, I asked the question that haunted me all week, the main reason I invited him to come along.

"There's something strange about you, Caleb."

He laughed softly to himself.

"What are you hiding? Why are you hiding?"

His smile melted away, that warm sun dipping behind the horizon. "I knew it wouldn't be that easy. Do I scare you?" he asked.

It took a moment to consider it and I answered as truthfully as I could. "No. In fact, I feel comfortable. Too comfortable. I don't let guys hug me like I do with you and that's a sign right there that something's wrong. There's something you're not telling me."

The back of his hand stroked my cheek. "Tell you what; I'll answer all your questions after the party if you just give me these few moments, right now, with you."

I didn't like the sound of this at all. It held the finality of a parting gesture, a last request. Was the truth so bad that he would start avoiding me again, or skip town? Or maybe I was the one who would leave. The wait was killing me, but at least I was making progress.

"Okay? Should I be worried?" I asked.

"No. But I have to warn you, it's a long story. You might start nodding off."

"I doubt it." My lips were inches from his when something caught my eye. Much like that *Sesame Street* game, one of these things was not like the other; something just did not belong.

"What the—" I pulled away from Caleb and raced to the drink table. I made it just in time to slap the beer out of her hand.

"Hey! What are you doing?" Alicia yelled, wearing enough makeup to run her own circus.

"What the hell are you doing here?"

She folded her arms, pushing her breasts even farther up out of her top. "What's it to you?"

"This is a senior party. You're not supposed to be here. And you sure as hell shouldn't be drinking."

Her raccoon eyes narrowed. "Neither should you."

"Do you see a drink in my hand?" I looked around. "They've got soda in the cooler over there. How did you get in?"

"Not that it's any of your business, but Garrett invited me."

The answer was like a punch in the gut. Every PSA episode of *Degrassi* flashed before my eyes.

"Garrett?"

"Yes, Garrett. So, if you'll excuse me." She turned her back and began mingling.

I pulled her arm. "Come on. I'm taking you home. Your dad would have a fit."

"Let go of me!" Yanking her arm away, she tumbled back, almost snapping her three-inch heels. "You can't tell me what to do. You're the one who seemed to have outgrown your old friends, and you just hate that I'm gonna be popular now. All your little cool friends wanna talk to me. You're jealous, aren't you?"

"Oh, you're gonna be popular all right, but for all the wrong reasons. Now come on." I reached for her, but she jumped away.

"No. You owe me for covering your shift. Just let me have fun for once."

And with that, I let her go. I'd known she would call in that favor eventually. True, this party was an efficient way to climb the social ladder, but she was easy prey among a pack of wolves—a pack of oversexed, intoxicated wolves.

Caleb joined my side. "What's Alicia doing here?"

I rubbed my shoulder, working out the sudden cramp. "Making a name for herself."

The muscles in his jaw flexed as he watched her hug every man within reach. "We should take her home."

I shook my head. "It's cool. I'll just keep an eye on her."

When we got back inside, I saw Mia yelling at Dougie in the corner. From what little I could understand, some drunk girl was hanging all over Dougie and, of course, Mia walked in at the wrong moment. There was a push, a shove, and then the most violent tongue wrestle I ever had the displeasure of witnessing.

"Are they always like that?" Caleb asked.

"Yep."

"They should get their own sitcom." He shook his head and handed me a soda.

For the rest of the party, I played chastity maid for Alicia and referee for Mia and Dougie. Between shifts, I gave Caleb what he wanted: time alone with me and the freedom to get lost in the moment. For just a few hours, the world comprised of two beings dancing to the rhythmic pulse around us as well as the beat within.

One o'clock was my cue to leave before Mom took it upon herself to hunt me down. The party was dying and Mia and Dougie were already gone. Caleb waited by the car while I went to grab Alicia. I didn't care if she was having the time of her life. It was days past her curfew, and her dad was going to hit the ceiling.

I searched upstairs, then around the pool area. I asked stragglers if they'd seen her, but all I got were shrugs and incoherent nos. I was about to give up when I saw something large and blond swaying near the trees. I raced down the deck and to the wooded area behind the house.

The closer I moved, the louder the sound—a soft moaning. It wasn't a content moan, but one of protest, like a child fighting in his sleep. Whimpering soon followed, and I was on high alert. In moments, I spotted Alicia pinned to the ground underneath Garrett. He was twice her size, so she couldn't have fought him off even if she was sober.

When I saw his big hands pull at her underwear, I lost it. I couldn't explain what happened inside me, but "Oh, hell no!" was the recurring theme. In seconds, I was on the scene, and Garrett got a size-eight shoe to the face.

Dad taught me one key principle about fighting: When you get someone down, make sure they stay down. I kicked, punched, screamed, and cursed. Samara Marshall was possessed and highly pissed. All of my mother's warnings and teachings rose to the surface, all the righteous man-hate exploded in a mushroom cloud of rage.

When he was no longer moving, I climbed off and crawled to Alicia. She curled on the ground, hugging herself. Dirt and leaves tangled in her twisty braids, but I saw no visible injuries.

"Alicia." I kneeled over her, and she shied away. "Did he hurt you? Are you okay?"

"Daddy," she whimpered and curled into a ball instinctively. The strangled sound made me want to commit murder. I reached down to help her up when something large knocked me to the ground.

I looked up and saw Garrett looming over me, looking unpleased with the rearrangement I had made to his face. He clutched at his chest and pulled at his ripped undershirt.

After spitting a mouthful of blood, he wheezed, "You should have stayed out of this, bitch."

His advance was intersected by something dark and fast from the left. It came at him in a blur and with such unnatural momentum, it sent Garrett's body flying behind a row of bushes.

I blinked a few times, unable to truly process the sight. When I finally stood up, low gurgling echoed through the trees, followed by a dry wheezing sound. I inched toward the shrubs and saw Caleb leaning over Garrett, giving him mouth-to-mouth. Caleb was so quick—I never saw him roll up—but I was glad he was here to help. The force of that push must have knocked Garrett out because he had stopped moving.

I shifted my feet, debating over which to do first: collect Alicia, go for help, or call the police.

Where was my bag anyway? I dropped it around here somewhere. And what was Caleb doing?

Between all the medical shows and emergency drills at school, I never saw CPR like this. Caleb's lips locked on Garrett's, not once pausing to pump his chest. I expected Caleb's cheeks to puff out as he pushed air into Garrett's mouth, but it was just the opposite.

I thought I walked into the middle of a *Brokeback* moment, until I saw Garrett was no longer moving. Still, unblinking eyes stared up at the sky, immersed, yet focused on nothing. His skin, a filmy, translucent sheet, looked more like gelatin than flesh.

"Omigod!" I gasped. "Caleb, something's wrong. We need to call—" was all I could say before Caleb lifted his head in my direction. Every last bit of sanity left my body in one scream.

10

That Sunday, I took my ass to church.

I was virtually a stranger around these parts, and it came as a relief to step inside the building and not burst into flames. I sat in the first row, probably taking someone's seat, and shaking like a junkie. But I needed some spiritual counsel among godly folk. Rhonda had said that they were good for those troubled times. Well, times couldn't get any worse than this. The sermon drifted in and out of my mental range, for I hadn't truly seen or heard anything since last night.

I had seen Garrett's lifeless body and that string of white vapor being pulled from his mouth; the raised veins collecting around his cheeks and hands; his skin sinking in as though it was drying out from the sun. His body twitched in a final effort to stay alive, his face locked behind the grotesque mask of horror once the inevitable took root.

I bore witness to the greedy swipe of Caleb's tongue as the last of the strange mist passed his lips. I could almost feel the violent spasms contorting his body. I heard his growl fill the night, a battle cry inspired by the ecstasy and rage haunting his eyes.

Those glowing, purple eyes.

Caleb crawled along the grass, trembling with tears streaking his cheeks. "Get Alicia home. Now!" he ordered between breaths and tossed me his keys.

He didn't have to tell me twice. I found my bag, got Alicia to her feet, and dragged her back to Robbie's house.

It took all my combined faculties to get Alicia home in the vehicle of a man who had just sucked the life out of a potential rapist, but it was accomplished. Driving straight proved a true test of strength. Alicia was pretty out of it, so she hadn't seen how Garrett died—one less thing I would have to explain.

I wanted to blame Alicia for being the typical horror-flick damsel. I would always yell at the screen at stupid girls who went off in the woods in high heels, but it's a whole other story when it's someone you know, and when you know her parents.

When I reached Alicia's house, I parked up the block. Knowing her dad was an ex-marine, I wasn't about to get accidentally shot. Alicia teetered in and out of consciousness, her head rolling along the seat. Her dark cheeks glistened with tears and sweat.

I took a tissue and wiped some of that glam-rock makeup off her face, and sat her up straight. "Come on, wake up. You're home."

Moaning, she looked around, then jumped. Clinging to me, she began crying. I wasn't sure what scared her more, what could've happened, or what *would* happen when she entered her house. Stroking her hair, I whispered words of encouragement, then opened the door for her. She didn't thank me, but her eyes spoke for her.

I waited for Alicia to reach the stoop before I started the engine. Once the porch light clicked on and the door swung open, I took off, leaving skid marks in my wake.

My brain went on automatic shutdown, taking one task at a time; trying not to think, or else I would bug the hell out. That could wait until I got home. I parked Caleb's car back at Buncha Books, tucked the keys under the visor, and bounced.

When I got to the house, everything was as it should be—no sign of predators with glowing eyes, though that did nothing for my accelerated heart rate. Thank goodness Mom was already asleep. I couldn't talk tonight. What could I tell her anyway?

My mind tried to provide a logical explanation, but logic didn't drive through my neighborhood anymore. I wasn't half asleep, I wasn't seeing things, and I wasn't high on anything but caffeine and fear. Just as sure as I knew the night's events were real, I knew I would have to confront it. The question was who would make the first move, me or him.

Once church ended, I received a barrage of sympathy hugs and pats. The congregation saw my haggard state and assumed the worst. The deacon offered me a few dollars until I got back on my feet. Once his back was turned, I snuck some vials of anointing oil and went home. I circled my house, my car, even made the sign of the cross over my door with the oil.

When I called in sick to work, it didn't surprise me when Linda revealed that Caleb had done the same. With that accomplished, I called Alicia to see if she was all right. Mr. Holloway kindly informed me that Alicia was on restriction and could not receive phone calls. I was just glad that she was safe, so I didn't argue the point.

I shut off my cell and took another shower. Pain and

guilt washed over me with the spray. I grieved for Garrett and for his parents when they heard the news.

I'd known Garrett since seventh grade, back when he was still a beanpole who hadn't grown into his body, the shy kid who helped me burn my Barbies in the backyard. He didn't get into his asshole years until he joined the junior varsity team. His behavior was inexcusable last night, but that didn't stop the tears from stinging my eyes. He was a shining star in our school with a bright future, and now he was gone.

I began thinking about *my* future. What would the police think of all the bruises on Garrett's face? Would they come after me? Would I be sharing a prison cell with a large hairy woman named Jerome? The disappointed look I imagined on my dad's face made the tears flow in a torrential downpour.

By six o'clock, I curled into a fetal position on the couch. To Caleb's credit, he forced me to partake in an activity I never thought possible: watching the news with Mom. My eyes stayed glued to the screen, waiting for any word about a murder.

"Honey, are you all right? You've been acting strange all day."

"Fine, Mom," I mumbled from under the blanket.

When she stroked the top of my head, I flinched. "Baby, what's going on? Are you sick?"

"I'm good. I'm just tired."

"Well, go upstairs and lie down," she ordered as the doorbell rang.

From under the covers, I expected Mom to go through her customary greeting to *anyone* who came to our door. "Who are you? What do you want? Are you a registered sex offender?" And so on.

Instead, soft voices and giggling accompanied her line of questioning.

I pulled my head from its hiding spot as footsteps approached. I had no idea how I made it to the other side of the living room, but there I was, with an iron poker in my hand.

"Samara, that is no way to treat company. This young man was kind enough to return your wallet. You're scaring him." Mom reached over and stroked Caleb's head.

I held the poker like the Excalibur sword. "Mom, go to the kitchen and call the police."

"Samara, what is wrong with you?"

"I mean it, Mom. Back away slowly."

Mom rolled her eyes and turned to Caleb. "I'm going to the kitchen to make some green tea. Would you like some, honey?"

"I'd love some, thanks." Caleb's eyes slid in my direction, heated with intensity. "Is it all right if I speak to Sam alone?"

"Of course you can. You're more than welcome to stay." Mom continued playing with his hair, dragging her fingers along his nape and twirling the ends.

"Mom, could you stop petting him and call the police?"

"What for, baby? Caleb hasn't done anything. Now you two just have a seat, and I'll be right back with your tea." With visible reluctance, she wandered into the kitchen.

Caleb simply stared, his expression blank. For every step he took, I took one back.

Before he could open his mouth, I said, "Don't even give me the 'we need to talk' spiel. Just give me my wallet and get out."

"I can't do that."

"Why not? You had no problem walking in here." So much for the anointed oil. Next time, I'll try holy water.

"We need to resolve this," he said.

"I swear, if you hurt my mom, I'll—"

"I'm not here for your mother."

That chilled me even more. His tone, his intent stance— it all screamed "predator."

After a hard swallow, I asked, "Would I be asking too much for us to just forget about last night, and go our separate ways?"

"Yes."

"Why?"

"You know why. And we *are* going to talk about it, so you might as well get comfortable." He took a seat on the couch and placed my wallet on the table. "I'm not here to hurt you. That was never my intention. If that were the case, I would've done it the first day you started working at the bookstore."

That fact didn't ease my anxiety in the slightest. I stood my ground.

"I know you have questions. What do you wanna know about me?" he asked.

"Only what I need to do to get you to leave."

"You have to listen to me. That's all." He patted the cushion next to him.

I scooted to the armchair in the corner. "I'm good here."

"Fine. I'm sorry you had to find out this way. I wanted to find the right time to tell you, but—"

"Here you go, sweetie." Mom floated in, all buoyant and domesticated. The only things missing were the vacuum cleaner and pearls.

Caleb set the cup on the coffee table and smiled. "Thank you. Could you leave the sugar bowl?"

Watching the exchange, my mouth gaped open. When Mom left, I asked, "What did you do to my mom?"

"The same thing I do to all women. Nothing."

"Oh, you did something. That woman is queen of the

feminists. How you managed to get through the front door without an X-ray is a miracle."

"You've seen how women act around me. Are you really surprised that your mother would have the same reaction?"

"Why? What makes women do that?"

"It's what I am; what's in me."

"What's in you?"

He didn't answer right away. He just piled five spoonfuls of sugar in his tea. After blowing the steam from the cup, he snuck a glance at the entryway. Satisfied with our privacy, he asked, "What do you know about spirits?"

"That I'm too young to drink any," I threw back.

"I mean sentient beings, or souls."

"I'm sorry; I've already had my dose of church today."

"I doubt they'll tell you what I have to say in church. But spirits are all around us, and I'm not talking about ghosts." He set down his cup and balanced his shoulders. "Let me explain."

"Please do."

His elbows rested on his knees, his hands clasped together. "I suffer from a type of possession."

"Like *The Exorcist*?"

"Not that bad. Let's just say that there's more than one conscious life inhabiting my body."

"Ah, you have a roommate," I chided. "What's his name?"

"He doesn't have one." Caleb leveled me with a stare that swept all humor from the room. "Sam, I need you to listen to me. This isn't a joke. There are different types of spirits around us. Some are good, some are bad, and some are downright evil."

I crossed my arms with the poker held tight in my hand. "What category does yours fall under?"

"The bad," he replied in a noncommittal tone. "The

spirit in my body is just a piece of a much larger entity, a creature older than time. Even after centuries of human experiences, my being still carries a few of the traits from its origin. A creature that's still among us today, one that is known throughout folklore as an incubus."

"Which-bus?"

"Inc-u-bus," he pronounced slowly.

My eyebrows rose. "Like the band?"

"Like the demon that seduces women and sucks the life out of them."

I was speechless, motionless, and officially struck stupid. Meanwhile, Caleb just sat there like we were swapping chemistry notes instead of tales from the underworld.

He extended his hand in appeal. "I know this sounds farfetched, but—"

"You think?" I snapped. He might be all blasé about ghouls hijacking his body, but it would take a minute for me to drink this in.

"If you have a better explanation for last night, I'd love to hear it." Eyes locked to mine, he reclined on the sofa and waited.

As if to reinforce the creepy atmosphere, his eyes ignited in a purplish glow. They possessed their own power source, which detained and refreshed with each blink, a feature that no optometrist or contact lens could achieve. Watching the light fade, or simply return to its violet origin would easily take hours out of one's day. No trick of the eyes, no second-guessing, no room for error or denial, but a formal introduction to an unknown presence. Then just like that, it disappeared, and Caleb sought his tea.

I knew there were forces among us that I couldn't understand. However, I had never held a fear of the supernatural. Mom kept me busy with a healthy fright of creatures in the tangible realm. Man did far worse things than any demon could contrive. But all the things I'd seen left no doubt that what sat across from me, sipping liquid sugar, was not normal.

He paused halfway through his drink and said, "I don't mean to scare you. I'm just giving you the backstory, where my spirit originally came from, what it used to be. See, everything in existence has three components: a vessel, a spirit, and life energy. Trees, birds, humans, even demons—believe it or not—encompass all three in some form. What lies inside me has no viable life and no body, just a spirit. To compensate, it uses me as a vessel, and feeds off the energy I supply.

"It's like electrodes. Little sparks and neurons and wavelengths, an entire switchboard of life going all over your body. That's what you saw coming out of Garrett's mouth."

"You ate his life?" When he affirmed, I asked, "How?"

"It pulled from the mouth. The kiss of life . . . and death," he intoned.

"Like a dementor."

He looked confused. "A what?"

"Dude, you've worked in a bookstore for two years, and you've never read *Harry Potter*?"

"No," he returned; although his expression seemed to shout, *Why would I?*

I sighed. "I'll lend you the series. But why does it only attract women?"

"Because it's male. That's his weapon. The spirit gives off a signal that draws females in, kinda like pheromones. It pulls them in with an allure so powerful they lose all sense of control. When they kiss me, the spirit pulls at their energy. The magnetism works best on vulnerable females. Most unhappy or lovelorn women are especially drawn to me. The more desperate they are for love, the stronger the attraction."

"And my mom?"

"If you weren't in the house, she would probably be all over me."

"Ugh. I think I'm gonna be sick," I replied, more to myself than to my strange company. The thought of Mom going cougar on Caleb left a bad taste in my mouth. "So, what does this mean? What do you do about it?"

"I try to ignore most of them. But things happen, as I also told you before. As a result, the girl in the bookstore parking lot. She jumped me and—"

"And your little roommate heard the dinner bell," I cut in.

"Yeah."

"Has this happened before? Is there any way to resist?"

"Yes and no. It's like having a pet tiger. It's wild and carnal, but it has recognition. After a period of time, it recognizes people. I have sisters and female cousins and the spirit never reacted. It won't draw from anything it recognizes."

"Well, you know what happened to Siegfried and Roy."

Wearing a mask of boredom, Caleb darted his finger at me. "All right, look, that tiger didn't attack his owner. An excited fan approached the stage and spooked him. The cat acted in defense and pulled Roy away from potential danger and forgot his own strength. That's pretty much what happened with the women at Buncha Books and Europia Park—"

"So it was you! You were the cause of their heart attacks." I accused.

He at least owned the decency to look shamefaced. "The spirit only attacks when confronted. Those women jumped on me, and it responded. It really has no conscience when it comes to the unfamiliar. It just knows what sustains it. If it can't feed on others, it will feed from its host."

That got my attention. "What?"

"Over the years, I discovered that the spirit can be appeased by large amounts of endorphins, the ones that come with excitement or when I eat sweets. It's a passable substitute if a life source isn't available, but I have to be replenished constantly."

At his words, his weird baked-goods fetish began to make sense.

Wait, no, it didn't. "So it feeds off euphoria?" I asked.

"Euphoria, fear, anger, adrenaline, excitement. It all produces dopamine, a different quality or grade of energy. Do you know what life is? It's not flesh, blood, and bones. It's the spark. It's that universal core that makes us what we are, the beginning of all things. It's not the body, not the soul, but the bridge where the two meet; what keeps the soul in the body. That is what it eats."

I tried to follow, I really did. "Okay, then why didn't the women die? They just had heart failure."

"Because I fought against it. If they held on any longer, the spirit would have taken more, and . . ." He raked a hand through his hair. "I don't wanna hurt people."

"Then how do you explain Garrett?"

He brooded over the question while sipping his tea. "That was my fault, not the spirit's. That can never happen again."

I leaned away from him. "Your fault?"

"Like I said, the spirit's primary prey is women. I'm a slave to its cravings, but I can curb the appetite. When I saw Garrett hurt you, I reacted, and things got out of control. I couldn't stop."

"Why?"

"Garrett had an unusual amount of energy. He'd been using an artificial stimulant."

"Like steroids," I supplied.

Caleb nodded. "It was killing him before I even touched him. I started giving him CPR when I felt his energy in my mouth. The spirit got one taste of that and went completely haywire. I couldn't stop if I wanted to. Then there's the fact that I *didn't* want to stop. I wanted Garrett to pay for hurting you and Alicia. And the pull was so damn good, so painfully exquisite, it brought me to tears."

I reared back. "And here I thought you were crying out of grief."

"I just know what I felt, and remorse wasn't it. But it scared me, Samara. I've never let it go that far before. I've never . . . killed anyone before."

His features twisted with anguish. I noticed his skin appeared paler than usual, and he likely hadn't slept all night.

"What did you do with Garrett's body?" I asked.

"I went to Robert's house and called the police." Scowling, he leaned forward in his seat. "What? You thought I buried him in the backyard?"

I lifted my hands in resignation. "Hey, I don't know how these things work."

He just stared at me, disappointed and greatly offended. "I'm not a monster, Sam."

"Then what are you?" I demanded.

"How's everyone doing in here?" Mom chimed from the hall. She made a beeline for Caleb and continued with the touchy-feely.

He handed her his empty cup. "We're fine. Could I have some more tea, please?"

"Of course. You can have anything you want," she assured in a breathy voice that made me cringe. I tried to ignore how her fingers caressed his when she took the cup.

When Mom left, Caleb turned to me. "I'm not a monster. We call ourselves 'Cambions,' because of the spirit's origin. I am one-hundred-percent, flesh-and-blood mortal with a few stipulations, that's all. I've had this thing all my life and I can control it."

"What if you run out of doughnuts and your little pet is starving for energy?"

His face set in a hard block of determination. "I see to it that it doesn't happen."

Mom's head popped from around the corner. "Did you want milk or lemon with your tea? I forgot to ask."

"Nothing. Plain is fine," Caleb called back.

Flashing a wink, Mom disappeared.

He looked back at me. "I can control it, Sam."

I shook my head. "I can't rely on that."

Mom's head reappeared. "Do you want some cookies to go with—"

"Mom!" I yelled. This fixation was getting on my nerves. And where did she get cookies? I scoured the four corners of the house and found not a crumb of junk food. "Could you give us a minute to talk, please?"

"Huh? Oh, I'm sorry, sweetie. I'll be in the kitchen if you need me," she announced, almost running into the wall to leave.

"Let's take this outside." I went to the front door with Caleb fast behind me.

The heat felt like an octopus latched onto my head—clammy, suffocating, and highly intrusive. The smell of charcoal and barbecue drifted up the block, escorting the sun on its journey west.

Leaning against the railing, I folded my arms. "All right, let's take this from the top. Act one, scene one. How did you get a demon in your body?"

His eyes narrowed at me. "I don't like the word 'demon.'"

"And I don't like the word, 'conversate,' but people say it," I shot back.

He stared down at me with open impatience. "It. Is. Not. A. Demon. Not completely. If you wanna be technical about it, it's a sentient, a being capable of conscious thought and emotion. A soul." Caleb ruffled his hair and dragged a hand over his face before continuing.

"True demons still have their physical bodies, have unspeakable power, and they're evil as fuck. They have no morals, humanity, or conscience. 'Demon' is a very sensitive word among my kind. We try not to use it."

"Duly noted." I shook off the chill creeping up my neck. "But if this 'sentient' once had a body, then how did it get inside you?"

"I don't know. My dad says that I was born with it, but I never felt it until I was about twelve."

"Whoa, back up. How does your dad know?"

"He's a Cambion too. There's another thing about this entity. It can multiply and spread, kinda like a gene or a curse." He chuckled bitterly.

I reared back. "Can I catch it?"

"It's not a germ. You can't get it from touching. It's passed down at birth and it's been in my family for centuries. My children will have it."

"Let me guess, your brother Haden is just like you, too?"

"Yes," he confessed, though he seemed reluctant to do so.

"So that's what he meant by *legacy*." I nodded, not having the brainpower to do anything else. I suddenly felt tired and drained, and I hadn't even touched Caleb. "Does Nadine know what you are?"

His cold stare locked me in place. "It's not something that should ever come up in conversation, Sam. Can I trust you to keep this to yourself? Tell no one, not Nadine, or even Mia."

Was he kidding? People would think I was just as crazy as he was. "Yeah, sure. I won't tell."

He sighed as if my silence offered some great relief. "Samara, I like you, I really do. You're about the only woman in this town who doesn't have this reaction. I would never hurt you or your family. I can control this; I've done it for years. I'm able to live a normal life. I told you, this spirit has recognition. The more time you spend with me, the less likely it is that it will draw from you. My parents were married for twenty-eight years without any problems."

Just as I was about to respond, Mom opened the door and yelled, "Honey, Mia's on the phone for you. She sounds upset."

My shoulders sagged as I let out a breath. Mia had probably heard the news about Garrett. All the events from the past twenty hours slammed into me like a crosstown bus. When Mom saw me nod, she went back inside, but not before undressing Caleb with her eyes.

"Listen, I gotta go. Thanks for bringing my wallet back." I started for the door but stopped when Caleb touched my arm.

With a look that echoed torment, he asked, "So, are we cool?"

I pulled back. "No, Caleb, we are not cool. A friend just died last night, and that's something one doesn't shake off right away."

His features hardened, his nostrils flared. "How can you call him that after what happened?"

"With ease. I know it's a lame excuse, but Garrett was drunk and probably high. He deserved a serious beatdown, some jail time, and a taste of his own medicine by the fellow inmates, but not death. Death is a little permanent for me, and I prefer that it be applied sparingly. You just threw a lot of information my way and I need to process all of it. I don't hate you, especially after you helped me last night. But no, we're not cool, Caleb. So if you'll excuse me, I need to comfort my friend and find a black dress." I went inside and slammed the door in Caleb's face.

11

Garrett's funeral took place the following Wednesday. The student body, extended relatives, and half the commonwealth were in attendance. Those who couldn't find a seat stood in the back. Within the ocean of black were the tear-stained faces of children, friends, and teammates who awaited the answer to the universal question: *Why?*

The autopsy report verified Caleb's claim of steroid use. Though the cause of Garrett's bruises remained unknown, police speculated the injuries came from a brawl during the party, a pastime he was known for. Medical examiners concluded that his sudden heart attack was caused by the FDA-banned horse pills that polluted his bloodstream. The fact that Garrett hadn't dropped dead in the middle of the practice field was a true act of God.

Seated in the third row were the dreaded Courtneys. Yes, our school had a clique of girls who shared the same name. Rumor had it, they had also shared Garrett. They were nicknamed the Brides of Dracula, because every other week, one hung on his arm, wearing his class ring.

They traded off like the Changing of the Guards. They now huddled together, dabbing their eyes with tissue and checking their makeup.

I sat near the back in the second to last pew. I didn't own a black dress, so Mom had let me borrow her old turtleneck dress with the football shoulder pads. Mia looked no better, dressed like the opening scene of *Breakfast at Tiffany's*. She leaned against Dougie, who still looked like the closing scene of *Fight Club*. Dougie and Garrett were far from blood brothers, but Dougie wanted to pay his respects. He held Mia tight, as if afraid that Garrett would make a pass at her from beyond the grave.

After a quick sermon and group prayer, the service moved right into open-mic night. People approached the podium, sharing delightful anecdotes and fond memories of the departed.

I wondered why people only praised others after they died. Was death the ultimate street credit? Dad told me that you could tell how one lived by how many people attend their funeral. Seeing these solemn faces left no doubt that Garrett would be missed.

The service was brief, dignified, and uneventful as all get out. I'd only attended one other funeral in my life, and it was nothing like this. When Grandpa Watkins died, Nana went all to pieces. She fell out in the church, screaming, and pulling the body out of the casket. Cousin Tameka's water broke, announcing the arrival of her fifth child. And Uncle Rudy had some warrants out on him, resulting in his arrest at the gravesite.

Now that was entertainment.

This, on the other hand, was Melancholy and the Infinite Sadness. Not a cough, crying child, or whisper as the silence carried its own noise throughout the building.

I couldn't even look at the Davenports. Garrett was

their only son who hauled their dreams on his back. They sat in the first row, showing a brave front, and all I could think of was my own parents.

There was something cosmically perverse about burying one's child. It left several questions in the air. What were those past eighteen years for if he was going to leave? What was the point of expectations and hope? And how would they, could they, move on with life?

Once Garrett was laid to rest, I hugged my friends and left. I wasn't in the mood to talk, and I preferred to grieve in private. Halfway home, I pulled over on the side of the road and cried. It came from out of nowhere, one of those nasty, snot-bubble, I-hope-no-one-is-watching-me cries. It was a delayed reaction that was long overdue.

After collecting myself, I stopped for a slushy, because turtlenecks in July were never a good idea. I couldn't even smile as Captain John Smith held up the line by blowing his paycheck on scratch lotto tickets. A cloud of depression hovered over my head and wouldn't go away.

Then there was Caleb. What on earth was I supposed to do about him? I had to think fast because he was parked in front of my house, and I didn't know what to do.

I spent the past three days avoiding him, which he made easy for me. He didn't look at me at work, and that bothered me more than I liked to admit. I still needed to take everything in, process and analyze it to death— which only produced a new batch of questions. Aside from Hebrew scriptures and some very entertaining fanfic, the Internet was not a stable reference for this particular issue, so I thought it better to consult the source directly. Today he decided to take matters into his own hands and pay me a visit. He leaned against his Jeep as if I was running late.

Despite it all, I liked Caleb.

There, I said it. I liked Caleb.

I often wondered why girls were attracted to dangerous, mysterious men. The answer was simple. It's exciting and provocative. They're constantly on edge, nothing's ever boring, and danger is a turn-on. Wearing faded jeans, a tight-fitting black T-shirt, and aviator shades, Caleb epitomized the bad boy.

I got out of my car and strolled down the driveway. "What are you doing here?"

"Waiting for you." He pulled the shades to the bridge of his nose and dragged eyes down my outfit. "Holy 1985, Batman!"

I almost cracked a smile. Almost. "You're just jealous that you can't pull off this look."

"You got me there." He nodded. "How was the service?"

My eyes lowered to the grass. "Sad."

"Sam, I'm really sorry." The words sounded urgent, almost desperate.

"I know. It shouldn't have happened that way. I don't expect you to understand, but Garrett was a friend. I've known him since—"

"Junior high, I know, but he's not the same boy you knew. The drugs he took changed him and not in a good way."

"Well then, leave me alone to grieve for the boy he used to be." I treaded across the lawn, then stopped. "Wait, how did you know how long I've known him?"

"I know a lot about him now." His tone carried a hint of suggestion.

"Like what?"

"He wasn't a good person. Alicia wasn't the first girl he attacked. There were others."

If that didn't get someone's attention, nothing would. "Who?"

Caleb shifted his feet and shoved his hands in his pockets. "Someone named Courtney."

"Which one?"

"I'm not sure."

I stepped closer. "How do you know all of this?"

"The energy consumed comes with a type of fingerprint of its past, memories. I know all about Garrett. Everything."

"Like?"

"He was allergic to cashews. He loved kung fu movies. He was very insecure about his body for a while, which is why he took drugs. He had a crush on you when he was fourteen, but he wasn't sure how his parents would react to you."

"What do you mean *react*?"

"Let's just say that there are some members of his family who aren't as open-minded as most." Caleb's gaze lowered toward my chest. "Did he really pay you ten dollars to touch your breasts freshman year?"

I dragged my hand over my face. "I completely forgot about that."

"Garrett didn't. You want me to go on?"

A rush of dizziness rocked my body. "No. Yes. I mean, no. What were you saying about the Courtneys?"

"I wouldn't be surprised if they're not sad to see him go." The look on his face told me that he didn't want to elaborate.

I shook my head. "I need to go inside. I'm roasting in this dress, and I'm tired." I moved toward the house.

"When can I see you?" he called after me.

"When you always do. At work."

"I mean outside work."

I spun around. "What do you want from me, Caleb?"

He pushed off his car and met me halfway. "For you to be close to me. I need you near me so—"

"So what? So your roommate and I can bond? I don't think that's a good idea."

"Why?"

"Because it's weird, because it's dangerous, and I've got better things to do on my day off." I walked away.

"Please?" Though the word was barely audible, its meaning rang loud and clear.

That one word was enough to stop me in my tracks and put a crack in my dam. "What do you get out of this?"

"Company."

I watched him draw closer. "Is it really that lonely?"

He pulled the shades from his eyes, removing all barriers from getting his point across. Capturing my full attention, he said, "Sam, women want me, crave me, but none of them *like* me. My family lives all over the world, and the guys in this town are nuts. You're the only person I truly have fun with. I'm at peace with you. You like me, don't you?"

I glanced sideways at him. "You a'ight."

"Sam."

"What do you want me to say? We've just started talking"—I checked my invisible watch—"a few weeks ago. We're still in the introductory stage. This is all new to me. I'm not a big fan of dating, not counting dealing with whatever it is you are, and that you accidentally helped kill my classmate. Top it all off with the fact that I'm wearing polyester in eighty-degree heat. What do you want?"

He took a deep, controlled breath, as if trying to conjure patience. "Fine, go change and let's go."

I stared him up and down. "Go where?"

"To eat. I want waffles."

I jumped back, appalled. "Waf—are you insane?"

"No. I'm hungry, and we can talk. I'm sure you have a new list of questions for me. Now go change. You've got fifteen minutes."

"I've got as long as it takes for me to shower and get dressed. Don't rush me." When I got to the porch, I turned back to him. "Mom doesn't come home until seven. Come inside. You can wait downstairs."

He stepped closer. "Are you sure? You don't think I'll come after you, or something?"

"You could try. The Marshall women don't die easily, and we always go out shooting. Besides, you should worry about yourself. You have no idea what's inside the rest of my house."

12

I've never considered myself a finicky eater. No pie ever crossed my path and survived.

However, watching Caleb get his grub on removed any trace of my appetite. I sat on the other side of the booth, watching him ingest his second stack of waffles. Blueberry syrup, berries, whipped cream, sprinkles, nuts, Skittles, and one of those little drink umbrellas formed a Tower of Pisa at the top.

My upper lip curled. "Dude, you're gonna die."

"Naw. I'm a professional. Don't try this at home."

"Or anywhere else," I mumbled. "How can you stomach all that?"

He drizzled more syrup on his already soggy plate. "I have a fast metabolism. It goes right through me, and it takes a lot of fuel to feed a spirit."

"Oh yeah, I forgot you were eating for two." I reached into my bag. "And you're right. I do have a few questions."

Cheeks crammed to capacity, Caleb waited for the interrogation to begin. After a noisy swallow, he griped, "Tell me you did not whip out flash cards."

"I like to be organized and thorough during the interview process, Mr. Baker." I shuffled the cards in my hands.

Throwing his head up, he exhaled. "Fine, go on."

"Okay." I cleared my throat. "Why heart attacks? Why don't they just drop dead?"

His shifty eyes darted to the surrounding patrons; then he leaned closer. "It has very little to do with the actual heart, but stress *to* the heart. In most cases, women just faint or pass out for a few hours until their energy's restored. The body is constantly producing energy, so a simple kiss isn't as potent. If the kiss goes any deeper, the body tries to fight back, straining to build enough energy. If unsuccessful, the blood pressure will drop, causing shock and possible cardiac arrest."

"Within what span of time?" I asked.

"The delay depends on the amount of energy pulled and the individual. It could be immediate if too much is taken, or drag out to about forty minutes of suffering."

"The girl at the bookstore had her attack hours after you kissed her."

"No, about an hour. She kissed me twice. The first time when you walked in, and another when we were closing. The second kiss was longer than the first. She hid in the storeroom, waiting for me. When I was closing up she snuck up on me from behind and . . ."

"Order up," I finished.

"Yeah. I finally got her off me and showed her out. She must have had a fit in her car while we had our book meeting."

"If you knew what could happen, why didn't you help her?"

"Who do you think called the ambulance? It can only go so far until they need medical attention." His body tensed at the horror of his own explanation. Anger lines marked his face, then slowly disappeared.

I controlled my breathing and shook off the chill of what could've happened. "What is it that draws these women in?"

"My eyes, for one thing. They think purple is pretty." He batted his lashes.

I snickered. "Speaking of which, the night at Robbie's party, I saw your eyes glow. It happened before when in the magazine aisle at the bookstore. I thought I imagined it, but you did it again when you came over to my house. Why do they do that?"

"When the spirit is anxious or excited, it shows itself. It happens right after I feed. But outside of that, it usually occurs when I'm mad or really horny. It only lasts a moment. And they change colors, from indigo to lavender."

"So, you've got mood-ring eyes. That—I—that's just creepy." Albeit peculiar as hell, this little fact made Caleb a lot easier to read. I consulted the list again to keep occupied. "You said that your, um, spirit didn't have a name. Does that mean he talks to you?"

"Not really—not with words, anyway," he said. "You can tell if a dog is happy, scared, or when he needs to go outside. Yet he can't talk—just signals and indications. I can feel his mood, and that's how we communicate. He feels my emotions and responds."

"That recognition thing works with emotions?"

"Every person triggers a different response. When you see your parents, you feel one way; when you see someone you don't like, you feel another. My spirit tries to memorize each one."

"So it's like 'oh, I feel uncomfortable and I don't know you so it must be lunchtime'?" I summarized.

He shrugged. "Basically."

My eyes traveled to every item in our booth, all except the boy across from me. "So how do you feel about me?"

He considered his answer for a moment. "At ease. Happy."

"And that doesn't fill you up?"

"Yes, it does. I'm full of excitement and energy. My pet is quite pleased. You are his Scooby Snack." Another cocky grin shot my way.

I tossed back my hair. "I bet you say that to all the girls. But does it have a name? I mean at all?"

Caleb shrugged and shoveled a week's worth of carbs in his mouth.

"We should name him. I have suggestions." I sifted through my stack of cards.

Caleb stopped mid-chew. "What?"

"Hey, if this is gonna work, you need to personalize your demon."

"It's not a—"

"Whatever. I have some suggestions that I wanna run by you, and see if he likes it." I cleared my throat again. "Pookie, Balthazar, Damien, Zulu, Obi-Wan—"

"Remind me to never have children with you. Those names are hideous. Why can't he have a normal name?"

I rubbed my chin. "Something mysterious and exotic like . . . *Fernando.*"

"Hell, no."

"Or Diego, or Bruce."

He grimaced. "Bruce?"

"Yeah, it's a good tough-guy name." When Caleb shook his head, I moved on. "Loki, the god of mischief."

He paused. "Maybe."

"I know, how about Leroy?"

Jabbing his food, he shook his head. "You are so—"

"Yes, I have ghetto tendencies, but it's a good family name."

Caleb's expression was pensive as he stared off into space. "You know what? I think he likes it."

I perked up. "What, Leroy? Really?"

"No!" he snapped, then continued eating.

"Fine, let's see, what's a nice tough-guy name? Ooh, Capone. That's straight gangsta."

Caleb leaned back in his seat and watched me. Slowly, a curl formed in the corner of his mouth. "Capone. I like that. I think he likes it too."

"So it's official. Your sentient being will hereby be regarded to as Capone," I declared as we shook hands.

Wiping the syrup from my fingers, I noticed the waitress approaching us again. This should've annoyed me, but I wanted to observe the exchange from a scientific perspective, to watch the predator operate within his natural habitat.

The waitress asked if Caleb wanted more waffles. She barely looked at me, not even when I jangled my empty cup at her for a refill. She bent over to take Caleb's first plate, showing him the benefits of having a good plastic surgeon. But Caleb seemed more impressed with the stack on the table slathered in butter. Cake Boy was on a mission and nothing could distract a guy from his food.

When she left, he looked at me. "Hope that doesn't make you uncomfortable."

I stared at my hands. Needing something to do with them, I rummaged through the condiment rack at the end of the table. "Occupational hazard, I guess."

"I'm not interested, Sam."

"Hey, who am I to get jealous?"

He looked at me under heavy lids. "It's okay if you are. It shows that you care."

"It just shows that your ego is bigger than your stomach."

Resting his elbow on the table, he leaned forward. "If a man could have any woman in the world, except the woman he wanted, how happy would you think he'd be?"

I shrugged. "He'd be preoccupied."

"And empty. I feel sorry for those women, really. Women's attraction for me only translates that they're unhappy."

I shifted in my seat. "Elaborate."

"Take the woman in the bookstore. What little energy I took from her, I could tell she was unloved. She was abandoned at a young age and never found her real parents. That one at Europia Park, her husband left her after twelve years of marriage for his personal trainer. And the other was a widow. All those women were hurting and wanted to be loved. The need was so desperate, they left themselves open to anyone. That's not a good way to be, especially in my case."

"What about my mom?" I asked.

"She doesn't act as bad as most, but she needs to get out more. I like your mom a lot. She reminds me so much of my mom, it's scary."

"Oh yeah?"

As if to confirm his remark, Caleb dug in his back pocket and retrieved his wallet. I waited while he sifted through each compartment. A moment later, his hands reached out to me with a small photo clamped between two trembling fingers.

I recognized the woman before he spoke her name. Caleb's mother was not only a beautiful woman, but Adriane Baker and my mom could've passed as cousins. Though their similarities were notable, so were their differences. The main difference being that one of them died half a decade ago.

I returned the picture and awaited Caleb's response. He took his time, gently tucking the photo into its secret compartment, careful not to rip or bend the edges. His entire body centered on that simple action, and he wouldn't utter a single word until the task was complete.

Tension spread over the table like a vicious rumor. Breaking the ice, Caleb spoke up. "You're mom is a very intriguing woman. It's hard to believe she has problems finding a man."

"She's going on a speed date on Saturday."

Caleb's eyebrows rose. "Oh yeah? Do those things work? They kinda remind me of some sort of love musical chairs."

"Well, we'll find out on Saturday." I looked down and played with the index cards. "Mmm, Caleb, is there something wrong with me?"

"Of course there is," he affirmed.

"No, I mean emotionally. Why doesn't the draw work on me? Am I an ice queen, or emotionally handicapped, or something?"

Caleb dropped his fork and he reached for my hand. "Samara, look at me. There's nothing wrong with you. Like I said, not all women are affected by it. The fact that you've never been in love and don't want to be makes your resistance very high. Among other things," he mumbled the last part, then lifted his fork.

"Like what?"

Dodging my curious stare, he murmured, "I don't wanna embarrass you."

"You won't."

"Well, the same reason why my allure doesn't affect Alicia or children. The draw doesn't normally work on . . . the chaste." His eyes slowly met mine.

I was now thankful for the disclaimer. It was beyond disconcerting to have someone, especially a guy, put my virginity on blast.

The red flush to his cheeks revealed that I wasn't the only one uncomfortable. "I told you you'd be embarrassed."

"Is that why you're after me all of a sudden?"

He snickered. "And you talk about *my* ego."

"Well, you barely looked at me in the year and a half I've worked at Buncha Books, and now I can't get rid of you. What's up with that?"

"I looked at you a lot. You just never looked back. As far as how this started, you approached *me*; you came to my side of the store and sparked a conversation with *me*, and I took the opportunity for what it was. Like I said before, you're pretty standoffish when you want to be, and you have every right in my case, but man, would it kill you to say hello once in a while?" His reply came out a little tart and tangy, showing more hurt from my avoidance than he would ever confess.

Heat spread to my cheeks, but I kept my posture of indifference. Pouting my lips, I whined, "Aw, poor baby. I figured all the attention you had, you wouldn't notice me anyway."

"I did notice, and you left an impression on me. For what it's worth, I like you this way, snide, cautious, and just plain weird. You're not blinded by the draw. You can see me for who I really am and you're still sitting here with me."

"Well, we came here in your car. I'm not walking home."

"Sam." He laughed softly. "What else is on your list?"

"Oh, yeah." I skimmed down my notes. "What powers do you have?"

"I already told you."

"No, I mean like super powers. Are you strong?"

"I work out." He winked.

"Can you lift a bus?" I asked, ignoring his cheesiness.

"No. What extra strength I do have comes from my spirit, similar to an adrenaline rush. It doesn't last long."

"Do you have super speed?"

"Not really. I'm pretty quick, but I won't be dodging any bullets in my future."

"You might wanna rethink that when you meet my dad," I said. "So can you fly, or read minds, or teleport, or disappear through walls?"

"No. I'm human, Sam. I can bleed; I catch colds, and can die just like everyone else. All I've got is my looks," he said, offering more cheese and grinning the entire time.

I tossed the index cards on the table. "Well, damn, you're like the worst superhero ever! How are you gonna fight crime?"

"The same way everyone else does. Call the cops."

"You can use it to your advantage, you know."

His eyes narrowed in suspicion. "You want me to become a gigolo like the one in your book, don't you?"

Avoiding his gaze, I continued the construction of my sugar-packet fort. "Okay, the thought did cross my mind, but you know how much money you would make if customers didn't die?"

He returned his focus to his plate. "Next question."

"All right. You said you had sisters. Do they have a 'Capone' also?"

"No. Like I said, my sentient is male, so it only affects the men in our family. Female Cambions exist, they come from the line of the succubi—the female counterpart of the incubi. If my mom carried the trait, then only my sisters would have the affliction."

I fought to hold back my alarm. "How many siblings do you have again?"

"Three brothers and two sisters. And they have healthy relationships. My oldest brother has two children."

"Oh." I directed my attention to the window.

I couldn't fathom dating this guy, let alone marriage and kids. Though he was human, there were just some things I couldn't overlook. If Caleb had the soul of a demon in his body, I would hate to see the real deal. And if such creatures existed, then logic suggested other beings loomed in the shadows, a territory I never wanted to explore.

I could feel his eyes on my every move; its silent demand forced me to look his way. He sat up straight; his laid-back demeanor fell away, presenting an image of unabashed humility. "I can have a normal life. I *want* a normal life. All I need is time with you. Can you do that?"

I never answered the question. It dangled in the air between us all the way home. I had only gotten through half the flash cards when we left the diner, and Caleb saw it as incentive to go on another date. He would've walked me to the door but decided against it when he saw Mom's car parked in the driveway.

When I went inside, Mom met me in the foyer with the phone. "Honey, it's your dad for you."

I took the phone and made my way upstairs. "Hey, Daddy, what's up?"

"Hey, baby girl. I tried calling your cell, but I got your voice mail again. I'm sorry about your friend. How are you holding up?"

"As good as expected."

"If you need to talk about anything, you know where to reach me."

"I know." I entered my room, then plopped on the bed.

"Well, the reason I'm calling is because I need the information to the dealership that's holding your car. I wanna see if they're willing to go down on the price."

That brought a smile to my face. If anyone knew how to haggle, it was my dad. I scrambled for the dealer's information hiding on my desk. I rattled off the contact number and thanked him. A true knight in shining armor. His talent for slaying monsters might come in handy. I just hope I never had to make that call.

13

Linda stood behind the folding chair, not even bothering to sit down.

"All right, I want to make this cut and dry. I've got plans, and none of you are going to make me late. So who finished their book? Raise your hand."

Half the employees lifted their hands with me. I looked across the break room and saw that Caleb's hand remained on his lap. He snuck a fleeting look at me, then shrugged before Linda asked, "Okay, how many of you actually liked the book?"

When three hands remained in the air, Linda prompted, "Great. Who wants to start off?"

Nadine presented her paperback. "*The Pale Hue*, by Collette Devoirs. It's about frustrated artist who hasn't finished a painting since his wife's death. One day, he finds a woman in alleyway who looks exactly like his dead wife. He nurses her back to health as she tries to regain her memory. Meanwhile, he gets his inspiration back and paints again. When the woman remembers she has husband and two children, she wants to go home.

But the guy freaks out and holds her hostage. Eventually, she escapes, and the guy gets depressed, drinks paint thinner, and dies."

"Wow, Nadine, you're one, big bundle of sunshine." Linda turned to Alicia. "What about you? What did you read?"

Alicia twitched, then sat straight. She wore loose-fitting clothes, along with that well-scrubbed modesty one would see in a trauma victim after a shower. All traces of femininity had been scraped off with a scouring pad, leaving nothing but a chaste and sanitized child. She didn't even wear lip gloss.

"The second book to *Specter*." Alicia waited for the groans to die down before continuing. "Angie still tries to find out how Nicky died. Her parents are worried about her because she's closing herself off from friends, and she's apparently talking to herself. Angie soon discovers that Nicky isn't really dead, but in a coma. She sets out to find the hospital where he's held. When she tells Nicky's parents what's going on, she's escorted from the property and her parents decide to commit her. But there's something wrong with Nicky's mother. She seems way too eager to pull the plug on Nicky's respirator."

"So what happens to Nicky?" I asked.

"His ghost still visits Angie in the mental ward, urging her to fight, and they plot to escape in time to save him. I'll have to read the last book to find out what happens."

Linda nodded, then looked to me. "Sam, what did you read?"

"*Image*, by Jodie Holcomb. It's an urban fairy tale about a young girl named Holly who doesn't think she's beautiful. Her reflection disagrees and offers to trade places. The reflection goes out to see the world, and lives life to the fullest, not caring what people think, and her confidence makes her the object of everyone's desire. Holly sees what she could have had through the mirror and wants to switch back. The reflection refuses to trade back and removes all the mirrors in her house. When she goes to a department store, Holly tries to break free through the mirrors in the dressing room. There's a big fight and the mirrors break. Holly returns to the real world, but her face is all cracked and disfigured from the battle."

"She's no better off than when she started," Alicia disputed.

I held her gaze, conveying my message directly to her. "But she now sees herself as beautiful, and she has more to live for."

When Alicia looked away, I addressed the group. "It's a lesson on body image, but told in a creepy, Brothers Grimm sort of way."

"Interesting," Linda muttered, glancing at her watch for the tenth time. "Well, let's wrap this up. Pick a book and let's get out of here."

The group agreed on Nadine's book for some ungodly reason. After the meeting, I caught up with Alicia by the main entrance. She jumped when I touched her arm.

"Sorry. I didn't mean to scare you. Are you okay?" I asked.

She nodded, though it looked more like a tremor.

"Alicia, I know it's been kinda weird between us, but you have my number and you know where to find me, okay?"

She nodded again, this time with a smile that seemed painful, and was even more so for me to watch. Her brows bunched together as if she was searching for reason, yet terrified of what she would find.

Nadine met us by the doors. "Hey, Alicia, you okay?"

She stared up at Nadine, her head tilted in thought as if recalling something from memory. Before she could respond, Alicia's dad pulled up in front of the store, and she raced outside as soon as Linda unlocked the door.

Nadine turned to me. "Is she all right?"

"Yeah, she's got a lot to think about: lost innocence, inner growth, life and death, back-to-school shopping. You know, the usual depressing issues."

"Childhood's over the moment you know you're going to die." Nadine's voice carried a low, uncommitted tone, the words of a jaded old woman.

My head lifted to her face. "Another one of your poems?"

"No. It's from *The Crow*. Great movie." She led the way to the parking lot. "You want to grab something to eat?"

The question made me laugh out loud. "The *one* time you decide to hang out, I need to get home. Mom should be coming back from her speed date. I wanna know what happened."

She shook the sudden fog from her brain. "Your mother dates now? This is same woman who warned me about mail-order bride scams here in the U.S.?"

"One in the same. I'll let you know what happens." I turned in the direction of my car.

"Please do. Oh, hey!" she called after me. Closing the distance between us, she asked, "How are you and Caleb getting along?" She leaned in, waiting for me to dish out the dirt.

As much as I wanted to lay it all on her, I had to honor Caleb's request to keep quiet. My eyes wandered to him as he strolled two lanes down to his Jeep. He graced me with a smile that in closer proximity would have been lethal, but was now merely infectious.

Choosing my words wisely, I said, "No one can ever call him boring, that's for sure."

"I can't believe it! I've never been so disgusted in all my life!" Mom raved, pacing back and forth in her bedroom.

I sat on her bed, eating the carton of chocolate ice

cream she had picked up on her way back from her debacle. The odds of her finding Mr. Right within a five-minute meeting were slim to none, but the night exceeded all disappointment when Mom bought junk food and popped *Thelma and Louise* in the DVD player. Mia sat next to me with a carton of butter pecan and a bag of popcorn. When I told her about Mom's date, Mia had to get a front-row seat to the commentary.

"Okay, the first guy was fine, until he told me that I look like his third ex-wife," Mom began.

I sucked in a sharp breath. "Ouch."

Mom kicked off her shoes and unzipped the back of her dress. "Then during our talk, he kept calling me Sheila."

The spoon dropped from Mia's mouth. "Whoa."

Mom continued. "Then the second guy kept looking down my dress."

"Well, Mom, you had the girls on display tonight. What do you expect?"

She stopped pacing. "I expect respect. Plus, he gave me that nasty handshake—you know, the one where the guy strokes your palm with his finger."

Mia shuddered. "Eww! People still do that?"

"And the others were either fat or had a comb-over."

"Well, Mom, beggars can't be choosers," I tried to reason.

Planting her hands on her hips, Mom rounded on me. "I'm not begging. I don't have to lower my standards for the sake of companionship."

Mia saluted Mom with the spoon. "You tell her, Ms. M. You're still a tasty dish."

Mom bowed her head. "Thank you, Mia. Then the last guy had horrible breath and gold teeth. I could have overlooked that, but he decided to whip out the wallet photos of his eight kids."

I stopped mid-chew. "Wow, can you say 'child support'?"

With slumped shoulders, Mom moved to the closet to change. "So the entire night was a bust. Maybe I was meant to stay single."

"Everyone is meant to be single for a spell," Mia called out. "A time of self-discovery and achievement. If you think now is the time to branch out, then go for it, Ms. M. Don't let one lousy speed date bring you down."

I grabbed a handful of popcorn. "Wow, you're just a fountain of wisdom today."

Mia lifted her chin with pride. "Well, being in a long-term relationship, I've learned a few things."

"You mean a long span of short-term relationships with Dougie," I corrected.

"Whatever." Mia shoved my arm. "Ms. M., you could always go to social clubs or banquets."

"Mom," I called. "Don't be that lady at the supermarket who wears cutoff shorts and no bra just to attract men."

Mom's head popped from the closet. "Does that work?"

"*Mom!*"

"I know. You're right. I just don't wanna be that old woman with the cats," Mom whimpered.

"You won't," I assured. "I'm the last person to give tips on dating, but from what I've experienced, things just happen on their own. If you want love, don't try to look for it. It's like when you were looking for the remote, and you found those earrings you lost three weeks ago. When you don't think about it, it kinda pops up."

Mia leaned in, giving me the detective stare-down. "So are you and Caleb an item?"

I fell back against the pillows and balanced the ice cream carton on my stomach. "No. We're just talking."

Mia's eyes narrowed. "Uh-huh."

"I'm not a relationship person. And neither is he. We just hang out," I explained.

Mom returned in silk pajamas. Before I could take another bite, Mom snatched the carton and spoon from me. "As long as Caleb doesn't try anything, it's fine with me, baby. He seems like a nice, young man—and very charming." Her gaze drifted at the thought of Caleb.

I stared at the ceiling. "And with a bad case of tapeworm."

A smile blossomed on Mom's face. "Oh, I love a man with a healthy appetite."

Giving her room to sit, I asked, "Mom, how do you know if a guy likes you—I mean, in a good way?"

Mom stroked my head. "Well, baby, he looks you in the eyes and not down your blouse."

"He'll make any excuse to touch you, hold your hand, pick lint off your shirt, brush an eyelash off your face," Mia added.

Mom agreed. "The main thing is that he wants to spend time with you. That should be a no-brainer."

"What if he's busy?" I asked.

"When a guy wants you, you are the center of his attention. If he says he has a lot on his mind, that just means that *you're* not on his mind," Mom answered with a mouthful of ice cream.

Mia bumped me in the shoulder. "I don't think you have that problem with Caleb, if that's what you're referring to."

"I wasn't talking about him," I snapped.

"Uh-huh," Mom and Mia said in unison and proceeded to polish off their ice cream without me.

14

"**O**kay, so, I was talking to Courtney G., right? And she was like 'I never knew Garrett took drugs.'

"And I was like 'Really?' and she was like 'Yeah,' but she was like all weird and shifty-eyed, so I asked Courtney B. And she was like, 'Yeah, I knew he was like all drunk and stuff, but I never saw him do drugs, but that would explain why he had such a bad temper.' So, I was like 'Hold up, he had a temper?' and she got all quiet and was like, 'I don't wanna talk about it,' and I was like, whoa, there's something rotten in Denmark, 'cause if they knew Garrett was all strung out, then why didn't they say something, you know? I mean, that's like, so wrong, you know?"

Mary-Beth Hessling paused to take a sip of her Frappuccino.

I just stood behind the counter in a blank daze, my left eye twitching. Mary-Beth was Garrett's blabbermouth cousin who talked like an auctioneer. If there was a drinking game based on her favorite word, people would pass out within ninety seconds.

I held up my hands in surrender. "I don't know, Mary. There are all walks of life."

"Well, my dad's gonna look into it. I'll let you know what's up. See ya." With a wave, and to my great relief, she scampered away.

"Is the coast clear?" Nadine called from the back kitchen.

"Yeah. You can come out now."

Peeking around, she crept out with a notepad in her hand. "God, those girls scare me. They are so high-strung."

"It's the caffeine." I nudged my head to her notepad. "What you got there?"

"It is poem I work on for tonight. I want to try it at Commons poetry reading."

I tried not to laugh, but failed miserably. "I still can't believe you write poetry. About what? The starving kids in Kuwait or the sweatshops in Taiwan?"

"No, not this one. This one is different grievance."

My back rested against the counter. "Well, let's hear it."

"You will hear it tonight at the poetry meeting. I want you to come for moral support."

"Really? You're serious?"

"Yes, why not?" When I looked away, she threw in, "You can invite Caleb, if you like."

My head whipped around to face her. "What's he gotta do with it?"

"You have thing for him, I can tell. I've never seen you so distracted over a boy."

"I'm not distracted."

Her eyes lowered to the cup in my hand. "Then why do you pour espresso in your soda?"

Following where she pointed, I jumped. "Oh, damn!"

Watching me clean the mess, she said, "Just admit it, you're smitten."

I slung a rag at her. "Witch, mind thy wicked tongue!"

"Why do you talk all Elizabethan when you're annoyed?" A painfully familiar voice reached my ears.

Caleb stood with hands in his pockets and humor in his eyes.

My stomach flipped. "I—I don't know."

His sweet, boyish smile crept forth. "I think it's cute, in a schizoid sort of way."

And like that, the thrill was gone. With lips tight and fists even tighter, I glared at him. "What do you want?"

"What are you doing after work?" he asked.

Nadine jumped in. "Sam is going to my poetry reading tonight."

His face twisted in confusion. "Really? I didn't know you were into poetry."

"I'm not," I was quick to explain.

"You are free to come along, Caleb. It's at the Commons Theater. It starts at eight. Tonight's theme is bohemian jazz. Dress accordingly." Nadine tossed her apron on the counter and moved through the swinging doors. "I go on my fifteen. You two have fun."

When Nadine was out of earshot, Caleb said, "Poetry, huh? This should be interesting. She's a little . . ."

"Morose," I finished.

"Yeah. You want me to pick you up?"

The question took me aback. "Uh, no, I'll take my car. You really wanna go?"

He set his elbows on the counter and locked eyes on me. "I wanna be where you are. Now, give me a cookie, woman."

Poetry Night transpired in a smoky auditorium filled with every art-house cliché ever conceived: the afrocentrics with their political agenda and head wraps, the white-guy Rastafarians with dreadlocks and "peace pipes," a ton of emo vampires, and the feminists who didn't believe in bras or hair removal. A percussion band was situated in the corner, providing a soundtrack to the gut-wrenching prose that corrupted the stage. When each poet finished, the audience countered with the *Addam's Family* snap. Seated in the center of this pretentious fog were the three of us.

According to Nadine, each meeting had a different theme from a Def Jam session to Edgar Allan Poe's greatest hits. Tonight's theme was the beatnik era. It reminded me of a Parisian jazz club back when visionaries discussed true philosophy and experimented with life. In honor of their memory, I wore a tight blue striped shirt, black beret, and scarf. Caleb wore all black with shades, and Nadine looked like a reject from *Cabaret*, including the bowler hat.

A tall man with a dashiki approached the stage. "The wind flows . . . through me . . . your lips call . . . to me. I feel the liberation, the summation, and the antici . . . pation." Then the bongo beat filled the cramped hall.

"Omigod." I banged my head against the table. "Why, Nadine? Why?"

Nadine patted my head. "Relax. I'm almost up; then we can go."

Caleb massaged his temples. "I don't get it. Why do all poets talk like William Shatner?"

"It is . . . flow." Nadine made a snake motion with her hand.

I mimicked the gesture. "It is . . . retarded."

A large woman with a buzz cut grabbed the mic. "He . . . the scourge of the sea . . . and the land. He, known as Man . . . holds the world in his hand. His power is poison to all who drink from his cup. Liar! Men will burn in the lake . . . of fire. Death to the oppressor . . . and the transgressor to the Mother Earth. Thank you." She bowed, followed by snaps from the audience.

"And she wonders why she can't get a date." I shook my head in sympathy.

Just as the woman stepped down from the stage, the host announced Nadine's turn.

Through the onslaught of snaps and whistles, Nadine shuffled through the crowd. Caleb and I gave her a thumbs-up and urged her on, mainly so we could hurry and leave.

Reaching the stage, she unfolded her poem and cleared her throat. "Time . . . the man-made device that keeps everything from happening at once. Man strives to outdo the contentious engineer who divided the day and night. Time . . . the symbolic appliance that we pick apart, then discard once its mysteries are solved, because . . . because we can. Because . . . because there is no such thing as 'well enough.' It can always be improved, because . . . man wants to edit God's rough draft. The obsession with time is an earthly quality; the autocratic government of moments. But, if everything did happen at once, there would never be a dull moment, would there? Thank you." Nadine bowed and left the stage.

Tossing three snaps in the air, I turned to Caleb. "Well, at least it doesn't rhyme."

"She really needs a puppy or something," he added.

When Nadine approached our table, she asked, "So, did you like it?"

"Uh, well, no." I stood and grabbed my bag.

"Sam!" Caleb scolded.

"I'm sorry, Nadine. I'm not deep like that. It went right over my head. Plus, it doesn't matter what I think. Look around. They loved it."

Nadine's head panned around the room to the patrons

praising her with a standing ovation. After a bow, she looked to me. "Sam, I actually care what *you* think."

"You really shouldn't. I'm not creative or emotionally sound." I nudged my head to Caleb to show my point. "Anyway, are you ready to go?"

Nadine's bottom lip poked out. "Yeah, sure."

Caleb rose from his seat. "Cool, I'll meet you guys out front. I'm going to the bathroom."

Nadine and I stood by the entrance in silence. Set a good two yards apart, we faced away from each other with arms folded. Nadine was still sore about her poem, but I tried not to lie if I didn't have to.

"Nadine, I'm sorry," I said finally.

"No, is cool. Don't worry about it," she replied, though her posture told a different story.

"I know it meant a lot to you, and I didn't want to ruin your night. For what it's worth, I think you're brave to put yourself out there like that in front of all those people."

She turned to me. "Really? You're not shy."

I smiled. "So my disguise works. I've been insecure for years. I never thought I would fit in."

"Why?"

"Look at me, Nadine. I'm a mutt. Every day I've got people looking at me funny. They ask that patronizing question, 'What are you?' like I'm a new species or something. And it doesn't help when I have to fill in 'other' on an application when asked my ethnicity. Black girls talk about me because I quote-end-quote 'act white,' and white people chuck me off as the token of the group, like affirmative action also applies to pool parties. If I don't get that, I get the people who wanna touch my hair."

"I touch your hair." Nadine pouted.

"I know, sweetie, but I actually know *you*," I countered. "And there are the ones that look at my mom like she's trash. And most of those looks come from family members. My grandpa won't speak to my mom and he won't even look at me. So yeah, I have insecurities, and I've never made a point to stand out any more than I did. But thankfully, I found a small circle of people who dig me for me. And I'm proud to say that you're one of them."

"You are trapped between two worlds. You are neither, but both." Nadine closed the distance between us, pondering the concept with a heavy brow. "I'm sorry, Sam. I never knew."

"Well, you're Polish; you can't help it."

"Shut up!" Nadine shoved my arm. "But the way you are is what draws me to you. You don't act like everyone else. You are rare, unique snowflake."

"Whatever." I chortled.

"I mean it. This is why Caleb likes you. There's something about you that keeps him coming back for more. Maybe he likes verbal abuse."

I walked to the door and peered inside. "Speaking of which, where is he?"

Nadine shrugged. "Maybe he fell in."

Not putting that possibility past Caleb, I opened the door. "I'll go find him."

I paced in front of the restrooms and saw no sign of him. After asking the third man if he had seen Caleb, I started to worry. Before I could get Nadine, low grunts down a vacant hall stopped me. I moved toward the racket of gurgling and crying. Opening the door of a storage room, I clicked on the light, and nearly screamed.

A plump woman lay half dressed in the middle of the floor, engaged in some sort of fit. I yelled for help and rushed to her side. I managed a grip on her shoulders, then cupped her head in my hands. She balled the front of my shirt in her fist, bearing down against a fruitless labor. Her heavy chest heaved in a hoarse breath, like she forgot to bring her inhaler.

Tears gathered around her bright blue eyes, her hips and torso bucked on impulse.

I recognized the nervous tick, that final attempt at survival delaying the ultimate power cut to the body. The same thing had happened to Garrett, right when he . . .

"Can you hear me? What happened?" I asked, rocking her back and forth.

Her eyes stared blankly at the opposite wall. A lonely tear streaked her temple, disappearing under the pillow of brown curls. "Lavender . . . eyes," she wheezed through her cracked lips. Without another word, her eyes closed and her body fell limp in my arms.

"No, no, come on! Please, lady, don't do this. Wake up!" I yelled, slapping her sallow cheek.

I checked her pulse and found nothing. Only a faint echo answered my cries for help, and even that abandoned me in the end.

A murky deafness surrounded me, a clamor within the silence. I searched the room, as though some solution would appear miraculously. Shadows danced around this depository of sporting gear and moldy theater costumes, a place where an overactive imagination ran amuck, a place where no one should die. This was the second time in a week that someone had met an untimely end before my eyes. All the fear and profound ramifications of life came to a head, and lay unmoving in my arms.

"Sam?" The voice came from the door.

This time I did scream.

Caleb stood in the doorway with a puzzled look on his face. When he saw the woman on the floor, the gravity of the situation deflated his posture. Drawing deep into the room, his eyes shimmered under the florescent light. Only then did the woman's words hit home: lavender eyes.

An eruption of fear and anger charged through my body with equal potency. "Did you do this?"

He halted midstep. "What?"

"Did you feed from her?" I demanded.

"No, I—"

"She saw your eyes, Caleb." I gently laid the woman's head back on the floor.

"What are you talking about?" He took another step forward.

"You stay back! Stay away from me!" I scrambled toward the stack of boxes by the wall. Maintaining eye contact, my fingers tapped around for a sufficient weapon, but only the weight of my bag showed possibilities. Panic, betrayal, and indignation spiked my system with a volatile cocktail. Most of all, I felt foolish. Though fully aware of his knack for duplicity, I didn't see this coming; or rather, I didn't want to see it.

Just when I was about to make a run for it, Nadine joined our murderous party. Her mouth formed a perfect circle as her eyes shot between the two of us.

"How did this happen?" She stepped in and closed the door behind her.

"I just found her in here on the floor having some sort of fit. She was clutching her chest. And then she died," I explained, shooting dagger stares at Caleb.

As if it was the most natural thing to do, Nadine knelt down and held the victim's head in her hands. She lovingly brushed the loose strands from the woman's face. "Caleb, how could you let this happen?" Nadine's voice broke with anger.

He slowly recoiled like an animal backed into a corner. "This isn't my fault. I was coming out of the bathroom and I heard someone yell for help. And that's when I found Sam in here."

Nadine zeroed in on Caleb as if trying to stare a confession out of him. Taking a deep breath, she declared, "We need to call police. Caleb, go take Sam home. I'll stay behind."

"I'm not going anywhere near him!" I hissed, finally reaching my feet.

Caleb stiffened. "No, I can't let you—"

In a blink, Nadine was on her feet and in Caleb's face, pushing him back a step. Her balled fist hovered at her side, waiting for confirmation to "disable target." "You *cannot* be here. This is third time you are near someone who had sudden heart attack. The police will suspect and I can't afford to have you caught. Now go!"

The command, though not directed at me, tracked whip marks across my back. I almost tripped over my feet to leave. I raced past the restroom hallway, not sparing a backward glance or a second thought. The corridor leading to the lobby was empty and judging by the drums and bongo beat, the poetry meeting was still in session. My feet didn't seem to move fast enough, but I wouldn't stop until I reached the murder-free sanctuary of my house.

A few stragglers huddled together in the parking lot, laughing and carrying on, blissfully unaware of the mayhem inside. That didn't shake the creepy feeling that I was being watched, and watched hard, for the sheer intensity left me sensitive to the slightest brush of danger.

With every step, it drew closer, its presence closing in on me from all sides. My heart battered my ribs, my lungs scrambled for air as my feet ate up the distance to my car.

Not even ten feet from refuge, a strong force yanked me around. A scream caught in my throat when Caleb crowded my personal space, a presence that relieved and terrified me in tandem.

Caleb held me captive, demanding my full attention. "Sam. Why are you running?"

He had the audacity to look mad, like corpses were par for the course, and I was just being uptight.

In light of my growing hysteria, I met his irate stare dead on. "Did you kill her?"

"No," he answered firmly.

I judged and convicted him in silence, my expression cold and unfeeling as stone.

"Not every woman who has heart problems is my fault. It wasn't me. I would never hurt anyone." His sincerity made me want to believe him, but the evidence against him piled sky high.

"Then how come she knows your eye color?" I asked.

He balked. "What?"

"The last thing she said was something about lavender eyes. Who else around here has lavender eyes, *Caleb*?" I accused.

"I don't know, but it wasn't me. Sam, I—"

"Let go of me." I tried to wiggle out of his hold, but the iron clasp trapping my arms wouldn't budge. As a backup plan, I focused on my knee making contact with his crotch, but he blocked every attempt. My claws were out, and he had a hard time keeping them from his eyes.

"Not until you listen to me. I don't need to feed off women. All this time I've spent with you, have I once fed on you?"

"What about the one in the bookstore, or the others? What about Garrett? You're out of control, Caleb, and I can't be anywhere near you."

"That was an accident," he insisted, still holding me hostage. He held an opportune position to inflict harm, but simply kept me in place.

Realizing it was no use, I stopped struggling. "A lot of those keep happening around here. And how does Nadine know about the attacks? What did she mean she can't afford if you're caught?"

He stumbled with the answer, searching the parking lot for an excuse, or an escape. He calmed his breathing and wrestled for composure before saying, "Sam, knowing what I am and what I've told you, is it really a shock that I wouldn't be alone?"

15

It took me a minute to drink in the reply, and I almost choked.

Once the dust cleared, I found my voice again. "You're telling me Nadine is a sentient thing?"

"No, but the spirit inside her is," he amended. "She's a Cambion, too—the female kind I told you about."

I just stared at him. "Are you sure you two aren't related?"

He shook his head and finally released me. "Our families go way back, but she's from an older bloodline. I hadn't seen her since I was fifteen, so I looked her up and found out she was in school on the East Coast. I figured it would be good to at least know one person in town, so that's why I moved here. Turns out, we both wanted a place that was under the radar."

"In Williamsburg?" I asked incredulously.

"Why not? It's a beautiful town. It's quiet and peaceful," he disputed.

"Well, it was before y'all showed up." I swiped a hand

over my face, hoping the action would provide me with a clean slate of thought. Caleb told me he and Nadine were close, but it never even occurred to me that she was also a Cambion. She seemed so normal. Sort of.

Not willing to take on the full blame of this oversight, I rounded on Caleb. "Why didn't you tell me this before?"

"It's not my secret to tell."

I stepped back, aghast. "What? Did she threaten to kill you, or something?"

"She doesn't have to threaten anyone," he mocked, though it sounded weak and unconvincing.

I caught his averted glance. He did that a lot when Nadine was around. Just the mention of her name made him bristle. I saw the fear in his eyes when she confronted him, how he backed down like a cub to an alpha lion. All these things added up to one hair-raising conclusion. "You're afraid of Nadine? Why?"

He didn't bother to deny it. "Well, because she's a female Cambion, and she's Nadine. That alone is enough to scare anyone. But I respect her more than anything else."

"What's so bad about Cambion females? I mean, more than normal."

He seemed to find my ignorance adorable. "Like the rest of the animal kingdom, the female of the species is more deadly than the male. Even full-blown demons don't mess with Cambion females. They're like praying mantises. You piss her off, she'll eat you alive. Literally." His tone carried a note of urgency, as if a mob hit awaited anyone who leaked this information. Though intriguing to a degree, the seedy underbelly of this mystical world only pissed me off more.

Holding my keys tight in my grasp, I inched toward

my car. "I would've appreciated a heads-up about another Cambion in town. What about your brother? Have you seen him lately?"

"No. He left a week ago."

"You sure about that? Does he have the same dietary issues as you do?"

Caleb's gaze iced over. "No. He would never hurt anyone."

"I wish I could say the same for you," I shot back, then hit him with another speed round of twenty questions. "What about the rest of your family? How come you never mention them? What did your father do to you? It had to be bad for you to close yourself off, but I can't let you keep secrets from me, not anymore. Because honestly, what's to stop you from hurting me?"

The words hit their mark, sending Caleb rocking back from the impact. His head bowed, his shoulders drooped and arched inward. No one with depraved ambitions could look so wounded and defeated.

For reasons that had evaded me since the beginning, this guy valued my opinion. A supernatural being that could drain me dry and dump my body in the woods actually cared what I thought about him. My gut tightened, my heart pulled in three different directions, but I just couldn't deal. More to the point, he hadn't answered my question and wasn't going to.

"Caleb, this is too much for me. Every time we hang out, someone's at death's door. I'm sorry, but I can't get involved in this."

The lines and angles of his face twisted in pain. "You're right. I can't tell you how sorry I am. I just want you to know that I would never hurt you."

Somewhere behind the armored tanker of my soul, I felt the truth of his words. But that insurance didn't cover everyone else. "If you know the risks, then why do you keep luring women in? Why can't you shut it off?"

"I can't just shut it off. My spirit has a will of his own."

"Then fight it, fight off the women. Don't let them come near you!"

He winced. "I don't fight. And I'm not gonna hit a woman."

"You don't need to," I argued. "Just get them off you. I don't really like to fight either. I just let instinct take over."

"I can't rely on my instincts, Sam. My instincts tell me to feed and sate my hunger. If I allow Capone to take control, even for a moment, I might not get it back. He's way too eager; his draw is getting stronger, more unstable because he wants more energy than I'm willing to give. Women are coming after me left and right, complete strangers that Capone will suck dry if they get too close. It's like he wants them to, just so he can attack. I've never had to deal with this type of aggression before."

"It's only going to get worse, Caleb. People are dying."

Clearly offended, and not in the least bit amused, he held my gaze and wouldn't let go. "For the last time, I didn't kill anyone. I swear on my mother's grave, I had nothing to do with that woman's death."

"Maybe so, but it will only be a matter of time before you do. And I don't want to be around when it happens." I walked away and climbed into my car, leaving Caleb and his willful roommate to their own devices.

16

It came as a surprise when Nadine texted me the following morning.

She wanted me to meet her at her office, which was code for the sunken garden in the middle of the William & Mary campus.

I jogged down the steps toward the vast lawn where the locals played Frisbee and lounged in the sun. I trotted across the path, watching Nadine approach from the opposite side. Her flowing blond hair and long-legged stride caught the attention of every man within a block radius. Under closer observation, the concept of her harboring a man-enticing spirit didn't seem that far-fetched. I noticed how men reacted around her, but I never would've stitched those pieces together.

Meeting me halfway, she presented a cup of frozen dessert. "A peace offering."

"What is it?" I eyed the cup suspiciously.

"Strawberry shortcake slushy with vanilla ice-cream filling." She waved the cup under my nose, fully aware that slushies were my Kryptonite.

I licked my lips, then asked, "Is this a bribe?"

"Maybe. We should talk, yes?"

"Indeed." I snatched the cup from her hand. "Caleb told me what you are. Why didn't you tell me about your affliction?"

If the revelation surprised her, she covered it well. "We don't talk about it; just something we live with."

I nodded, not knowing what else to do. If I had a life-sucking spirit in my body, I wouldn't broadcast it all over town either.

She found a vacant spot on the grass and took a seat. I watched her for a moment, trying to add this new information to the sum total of Nadine. I wasn't afraid of her, but this latest development was something that would take some getting used to.

I sat next to her and crossed my legs. "What happened to the woman?"

"Paramedics took her away," she said. "They say her weight caused heart attack."

"You believe that?"

"No. There was sign of struggle. Something scared her."

"Why did you stay behind?"

"Someone had to talk to the police. Perhaps now Caleb will allow me to help him. I kept quiet for too long, and this is out of hand." Nadine took a sip of her blueberry slushy. As if reading my thoughts, she stated, "Caleb did not attack the woman. Deep down, you know this."

"Then who did it? Are there more like you here?"

"Not sure. But I will find out." Nadine's brows puckered in contemplation.

"Could another Cambion be involved?" I asked.

"It's possible, but this is not in our nature. It's not healthy to consume *entire* life. We take a little. A whole human life gives us great power, but corrupts the insides.

You crave more and become more like demon with each life."

"What kind of power?"

"Caleb told you the origin of these spirits, its descent?" Seeing me nod, she continued, "The spirit reverts back to that, becoming true demon: immortal, indestructible, able to manipulate thoughts and physically transform their bodies into anything you desire. But your humanity is gone and your soul is trapped within for eternity."

Riveted, I leaned closer. "How many lives would a Cambion have to take to get to that stage? Just give a ballpark figure."

"Human life is great, and holds much energy. From what I hear, it takes weeks to digest; it's very large. Six should begin the change, twelve may complete it. Is estimate, of course. The spirit wants to become whole again through us, but our humanity keeps it tame."

Swallowing hard, I thought of Caleb. If he suddenly decided to go buck wild and eat enough people, he could upgrade to full-blown demon. The only thing holding him together was a threadbare shroud of humanity. It wouldn't be long before the fibers would tear, and I shuddered to think of what would break free. But the topic intrigued me. "Have you ever met one of the originals, a real incubus?"

"Yes. Most terrifying moment of my life, and I begged for more. I pray you never meet one."

Remembering what Caleb said about Cambion females, I had to ask. "Did you eat him?"

She didn't answer, but for the briefest, infinitesimal portion of a second, a look of pleasure stretched her lips. That one look rendered the subject closed.

Taking the hint, I ran down my list of possible suspects. "You think Haden killed that woman?"

Nadine's nose and lips bunched together as if she smelled something foul. "No. Haden is a lot of things— and I mean *a lot*—but he is no killer. He's peacemaker of the family."

"What about his father? What happened to cause so much tension in their family?"

She pondered the concept for a moment. "Love is strange thing with our kind, Sam. It's what we fear, what we crave, what we live for, and what we die from. If you know nothing else, know that." She held a distant, almost glassy sheen in her eyes. "There's much pain in that family from the death of the mother. Caleb turns his back on them and everything with it, including the being within. His reclusion is the root of all his problems. This is not healthy. He must feel, connect, or he will starve. I tell Caleb this many times, but he refuses. He's a good guy, Sam, but he needs to deal with his demon properly."

"It's not a—"

"I call it as is," she snapped. "My family hates that word, but I have no time for political correctness. It must be dealt with. I handled mine, and Caleb needs to, uh, man up and do the same."

"What do you mean?"

"He must collar his demon."

"Capone."

Nadine stopped mid-slurp. "What?"

"His sentient being is named Capone," I said. The *D* word suddenly made me uncomfortable. It sounded derogatory, too similar to a racial slur for my taste. The label seemed to define Caleb, condemn him, and his situation wasn't that cut and dry. There was still hope for him.

A smile pulled at Nadine's blue lips for a second before vanishing. "He finally named his?"

"Well, I thought of the name," I bragged.

She nodded in approval. "It's good start to interact with spirit. Caleb denies that it is part of him. He tries to separate himself from it. That doesn't work. He has to work with it, not against it."

"How?"

She lay back, resting her weight on her elbows. "For one thing, they need to connect. He needs to get in tune with his own feelings. Caleb told you it feeds off energy, yes?"

I tossed the concept in my head. "Kinda."

"Since we don't want to feed on others often, the spirit feeds from us, consumes our excitement, our joy, our energy, our anxiety. Caleb is in dangerous role reversal where demon dominates, and he feels powerless to stop it."

"Can you break that down a little more for me?"

Nadine flung her head back, reveling in the sunshine. "Demon souls cannot exist in physical realm without a body and energy. They try to possess weaker humans for control, but the human body dies eventually. To have immortality, it saves pieces of itself through human offspring."

"Like a living horcrux," I surmised.

Nadine glowered at me. "A what?"

"Has anyone in the Cambion community read *Harry Potter*?" When Nadine shook her head, I threw my hands up. "Never mind. Go on."

"Uh, okay. As spirit passes down generations, one body after another, it loses influence. Caleb and I come from old bloodlines that developed tolerance that Caleb must now put into action.

"I have a body, energy, and a soul. I have what my demon lacks, so I wield all power. Since the spirit lives in my house, I call the shots. If I wish to feed from person, I do. I know how much to take and when to stop. I know what will sustain it between feedings. A good source of energy is joy."

"You make it sound like potty training a dog."

"There is no real difference. Caleb needs to apply proper training. He must know himself to put leash on his demon. And he needs to feed regularly."

"What do you mean 'feed'?"

"Capone is berserk because Caleb does not feed him. We feed off human life energy. There is no cutting corners. We have to. But we control the amount we take. Caleb holds back, denies Capone what he needs. He uses fake stimulation and it won't work anymore."

I nodded. "The sweets."

Nadine's head popped up. "You notice he eats more and more lately? It doesn't fool Capone anymore, and he is not satisfied. The spirit starves for real energy so he gives off heavier signals, like distress call, which is why women attack Caleb now."

"How can Caleb stop it?"

"Capone needs strict eating habits and discipline. And Caleb needs new stimulation, true pleasure, true connection. I believe he knows this, but he's too scared to try it." Green eyes looked pointedly at me.

I recoiled. "What? Me?"

"You make him happy. Why not?"

Slack-jawed, I stared at her for a minute, appalled at her lack of concern. "Do I look like a Happy Meal to you? He's *not* feeding off me."

"If he disciplines himself, there should be no problem. Besides, the spirit feeds off Caleb's joy."

"What if I'm not around? I don't want him depending on me to have joy, and I don't want our . . . whatever this is to be based off his need," I disputed, getting more annoyed with the argument, and the Hacky Sack boys who kept whistling at Nadine.

"You cannot fake or force happiness. It comes from within. This is Caleb's mistake. Anyway, this can be managed. My mom is carrier in my family, and she's been married to my dad for thirty-two years. My parents are happy and healthy. This malady can be contained and not be a burden."

For some reason, I thought of that Valtrex commercial where the couple skips along the beach, despite the fact that one of them has a highly contagious, incurable disease. I imagined Caleb and me in that situation.

We're holding hands and he looks at the camera and says, "I have a demonic parasite."

"And I don't," I say with a smile.

I got so lost in the daydream, Nadine had to repeat her question. "I said what will you do about Caleb? I know this is great pressure on you, but if you help him through this, just until he handles his demon, the transition will run smooth. He trusts you, and so do I. I know you won't compromise our situation."

I shook my head. "No, I wouldn't rat you out. I mean, who would believe me anyway?"

"So will you help? He needs you."

Oh hell, how could I refuse those sad eyes? Things would be much easier if Caleb was a vicious killer with no soul. But he was as much of a victim as those women, signifying him as the worst sociopath in the world. I'd seen bees attack with more organization. For the sake of the remaining female population, I had to help.

"I guess," I said after a long breath. "I've got nothing else to do this summer."

"Thank you," Nadine said before cutting her eyes at the frat boys, who motioned her to join them. I'd known it was a lost cause the moment they spotted her. Cambion or not, men came to Nadine, not the other way around. She would never be dubbed as vain or high maintenance, but she possessed an air of majesty that made her unapproachable, unattainable. I could only pray that the guys owned enough sense to keep their distance. It was a moral debate over what was scarier, her hostile rejection, or what would happen if she accepted.

"Does your spirit have a name?" I asked.

"Lilith."

I stared her down. "For real? Please tell me you're joking."

"She likes the name. It suits her." Nadine showed me the gold chain on her wrist. For as long as I'd known her, she'd never taken it off, not even to wash her hands at work.

I fingered the gold plate with the name engraved in the center. "Well, aren't you sentimental."

"Everyone in my family has one with the spirit's name. Trust me, it has deeper purpose."

Fiddling with her straw, Nadine's eyes met everything in the field but my questioning gaze.

I moved on to a safer subject. "What makes you happy? How do you appease it between feedings?"

Immediately, Nadine's body relaxed and stretched out like a lazy lioness, giving every male in the lawn something to think about late at night. "I meditate, do yoga, think of family, write poetry, and my job."

"Which one?"

She looked at me as if the answer was obvious. "At day care center."

"You like working around children?"

"Have you ever watch children at play? They are so full of life. They're saturated in it. Their laugh, their vitality; it is in the air. You don't need to touch them; just being near is feast."

My stomach lurched as an image of a witch in a gingerbread house flashed in my mind.

"You feed off *children*?"

"Not in way you think. I just watch them play. Like I said, their energy is concentrated; it coats the skin like heat. They bring me joy, and my spirit is pleased."

"That's gross, Nadine."

She sat up straight, her face hard with indignation. "I have never harmed a child, Sam. Never! Unlike Caleb, I can control my being."

"So what can Caleb do to control his?"

"Spend more time with you, and find something that makes him happy. He needs to know himself; find what excites him."

"He likes roller coasters," I offered.

"Adrenaline is good stimulate, but who wants to almost die all the time?"

I nodded in agreement. "We'll work on something. But in the meantime, I have to help keep the hungry women at bay. Caleb's afraid to fight them off."

Nadine scoffed. "Oh, he has to get over that."

"That's what I said. He needs to defend himself."

"He gets that from his brothers. They *love* women, but they are all gentlemen. They fear their strength, their power, and would face harm than hurt a woman. This aggression is new to Caleb."

Rubbing her chin, Nadine examined the clouds. "I'll take him under my wing for a while. Let me deal with spiritual stuff; you help with emotional stuff. Deal?"

"What about the women? He needs some protection."

"He will need to learn to fight. You and I can achieve this, yes?" She gave me a mischievous wink.

I flashed her an impish grin, for great minds think alike. "Operation Demon House Training will begin." We shook hands, and I thought about something that could play to my advantage. "When you feed from kids, are there any side effects?"

"No. They just get sleepy. Like I said, I do not take enough to harm. And children are pure and immune to my draw."

"In that case, next time I have to babysit my sister and brother, I'm taking you with me. Trust me, Lilith will be full in five minutes."

17

After our powwow, I spent the day searching self-defense classes online, but all the lessons were for women.

What was a man to do for protection in this town? I researched martial arts instructors and printed out a few classes located around the peninsula. At work, I looked up some self-defense books, but ended up finding the next book to share at our monthly meeting. I knew Caleb was too proud to ask for help. Avoidance and denial were his coping devices, so getting his cooperation would require an iron fist in a velvet glove.

The next day, I decided to go boot camp on Caleb. Scoring his address from Nadine, I took it upon myself to hunt him down. He lived in a simple town house in a middle-class neighborhood, one of those subdivisions where every yard looked the same. While casing the joint, I learned a lot about Mr. Baker. For starters, he recycled, he brought his sugar addiction home with him, and he had the nosiest neighbors on the planet. But then again, I did look a bit suspect peeking through his windows.

He was off on Tuesdays and the Jeep was parked in front, so I knew he was home. After the fifth knock, I added a kick to his door. If the pounding didn't wake him up, the whistle blow in his face as he opened the door got the job done.

He stumbled back, stunned and disoriented, and I took that moment to invite myself in.

Shaking out of his daze, he closed the door. "What are you doing here?"

"I'm gonna help you fight."

"At ten-thirty in the morning?"

"The sooner, the better. Now get dressed. We gotta meet Dougie in thirty minutes." I took a moment to observe his attire, something that he would've liked to have kept secret. With his tousled hair, rumpled white T-shirt, and plaid boxers, he didn't look a day over twelve.

Uncomfortable with his state of dress, he tugged at his shirt. "I still feel funky after what happened Sunday night. I just wanna relax, eat Fruity Pebbles, and watch *The Price Is Right*."

"Too damn bad." I blew the whistle again. "You want me to help you defend yourself, or what?"

He eyed me with distrust. "No."

"Well, you're getting it anyway. Nadine and I are gonna school you on how to handle your roommate."

"Nadine? What—"

"Yep, so get dressed and prepare for battle."

He rubbed his face, shaking the cobwebs from his brain. "Look, I appreciate your help and all, but you don't know anything about this. I can do this on my own."

"If you could handle this on your own, women wouldn't be dropping like flies." Having gained his full attention, I continued. "I want to believe you. And a part of me keeps trying to separate you from Capone, but that doesn't work.

You know that better than I do. I want to help you. If you don't do it for yourself, then do it for me. Because if you don't, this is the last time you'll see me."

One could hear a pin drop in the room.

I learned quickly that Caleb didn't cater to threats, nor did he fall out in a temper tantrum. Instead, he shut down, which was a whole lot worse. Of all the terrifying moments while in his presence, the glacial stare aimed at me ranked number one.

Lethal detachment darkened his eyes and made the temperature in the room drop twenty degrees. Time stood still while he deliberated the pros and cons of having me in his life. This debate took a lot longer than I would've liked. Only when he came to a decision did I realize I had been holding my breath.

"Can I at least eat some cereal?" he asked, thoroughly annoyed.

"No. Now get dressed."

"When did you get so bossy?"

"When I found out you loved it. Now go. There's much to cover."

Cursing under his breath, he disappeared up the stairs.

To kill time, I gave his place a good look. It was like a rave threw up in there: glow sticks, light machines, beanbags, and a wall shelf loaded with vinyl albums. The only recognizable pieces of furniture were the couch, a coffee table, and the biggest television I'd ever seen. The screen stretched the entire wall.

Caleb wasn't lying about the crossbow. It was mounted on the wall to my left in company with a longbow, a Celtic sword, and five international trophies. The sight of that just led to more confusion. Caleb had the ability to fight; he just didn't actually fight. He would rather get beat up than unleash the wrath of Capone, which wasn't going to fly anymore.

"This is a nice place, but a bit out of your price range, isn't it?" I called out.

"Yeah, well, I used my inheritance to pay for it!" he yelled from his room.

Caleb told me that his family had money, but I thought he was trying to impress me. I should have known better. Mom taught me that the wealthier someone was, the less they talked about it.

"Oh God, you're a trust-fund baby like Mia," I groaned.

"Not really. It's what my mom left in her will. Since I have five other siblings, my share isn't that big, plus I didn't get all of it at once. I'll get a small portion every three years until I'm thirty, which means, I still have to work like normal people." His sarcasm filtered through the walls.

I sucked in a sharp breath. "Wow. That's cold."

"My folks didn't believe in giving their kids a free ride. They made us earn everything we got. You tend to appreciate what you have and you fight hard to keep it."

I laughed to myself. Cake Boy was preaching to the choir. "Builds character."

Drifting toward the sound of footsteps, I found Caleb leaning against the wall banister, watching me. His eyes traveled to my legs, which were fully on display. I wore green athletic shorts with striped knee-high socks and cleats. Twirling the whistle in my hand, I said, "Put your eyes back in your head, Mr. Baker. We've got work to do."

He pushed off the wall and stalked toward me. "It's dangerous for us to be alone like this, don't you think?"

"It sure is, but I promise I won't hurt you."

"Come here," he commanded softly, his direct gaze never wavering.

I strolled forward until I stood in front of him. He reached to place his arms around my waist, but I thrust my hand out to stop him. Dropping his hand, he lowered his head, yielding to my unspoken decree: *Access denied.* We had a long road ahead of us, and trust was our number-one issue, a privilege he had taken for granted, an honor he had to reclaim. Dejection shadowed his eyes as he battled with some unmet necessity that raged within, a call that he fought to ignore. The shuffling of feet and itchy, fidgeting hands made his impatience hard to watch. Unsure of my own restraint, this served as motivation to break through his wall, to ensure that this was only a temporary exile.

He circled around me, close enough to share breathing space, but far enough for our skin to never meet. He stood behind me, and I fought the urge to lean into him. My joints locked in place, keeping stone still, or else the slightest move might rouse the beast.

Warm breath fanned across my earlobe as he whispered, "You're still here with me, Samara, and that's enough. For now." Then he moved to the door, leaving me to endure the high-powered voltage charging my body.

My breath shivered between my teeth; my skin felt raw and vulnerable against the elements. Once the tremors subsided, I followed him out with unsteady limbs.

As he locked the door, he asked, "Where are we going?"

"To Dougie's. He's gonna help you with some combat moves."

He stopped and looked at me. "Doug? Are you kidding?"

"Dougie's been dating Mia since freshman year. If anyone knows how to dodge crazy women, it's him."

"Okay, here's the thing: you gotta avoid the claws, especially the acrylic kind. Now a lot of girls like to get all in your face. That's when you back up. The key is to keep the distance." Dougie pivoted and jumped in circles around Caleb, throwing jabs in the air.

"When they get violent, most girls go into this weird windmill thing, like this." He flung his arms around his head. "It looks nuts, but you gotta duck to the side or jump around. If the girl's a shorty, you can do the face-mush, like this here." Dougie reached over and trapped his hand over my face before I could prepare.

"Okay, you see how Sam's swinging around? She might even bite; that's fine, as long as you keep her at arm's length. Now if the chick is tall, you can always trip her legs, or if she's wearing pumps, you can snap the heel. How fast can you run, man?"

Caleb looked puzzled. "Pretty fast."

Dougie nodded, still palming my face. "Good, you'll need it, especially if a chick is determined."

Pushing Dougie off, I joined the discussion. "Another thing, you might want to tighten your security around your house. Get a few more locks around the windows, and develop a relationship with the neighbors so they can keep a watch out on your place. You also need to find at least three different ways to get to work, in case someone follows you home. Oh, and—"

"Hold on," Caleb interrupted me. "Do I really need to go through all that?"

"Yes," I said. "These are crazy times, son."

"Never underestimate irrational women," Dougie said. "You ever see *Fatal Attraction*? You don't have any pets, do you?"

"No," Caleb replied.

I nodded. "Good. Now, you may have to carry a can of pepper spray with you. I would let you borrow my mom's stun gun, but, well, it isn't exactly legal in this state."

Caleb and Dougie eyed me askance.

Propping my hands on my hips, I stared them down. "All right, look, these are precautions females have to take. It only seems weird to you because you're men, but women had to go through this for years—always looking over their shoulders, making sure no one is following them. You can't travel alone, or wander into the wrong end of town. Welcome to my world, guys."

I sat on the sidelines as the two sparred for a few hours. Dougie's backyard was the perfect spot for basic training, with an acre-wide strip of green on a hill that overlooked the neighborhood golf course and duck pond below. I stared as the moving clouds glided over the clay-tiled roof. The house had more windows than walls, very Zen with foliage and smooth rocks strategically placed around the lawn. Much to Dougie's embarrassment, his folks were closet hippies—very big on Eastern culture— and their home reminded me of a Hindu temple on a sacred mountaintop.

I drank in the scenery while screams of agony came from the yard.

Dougie went down a practice drill and used his little sister Colleen as a crash test dummy. Caleb's insistence not to harm an eight-year-old girl was inevitably his downfall. She had him on the ground in a pretzel wrestler move until he cried uncle. When Dougie's back turned, the biting began.

"Would someone help me, please?" Caleb choked out.

"Just walk it off, man." Dougie gave a flippant wave of his hand, then joined me at the picnic bench.

"So why isn't Mia at our training session?" I asked.

"Oh, you think I'm stupid, huh?" Dougie snorted. "I don't want her to know my guard tactics."

"You know, Mia goes off to college next year. What did you guys decide?"

"I'll visit her on weekends," he stated.

"Dougie, long-distance relationships are hard. What if you two meet new people?"

"We'll work it out. I'll go to summer school next year if I have to," he affirmed in complete confidence.

"Oh, *now* you decide to think about passing class?" I gasped. "My god, man, what will your parents say?"

"*It's about damn time*," he quipped. "But seriously, I'll work it out. I can't go a whole year without her."

I shook my head, knowing his sickness had no cure. "You're just as bad as Mia with that clingy possessive thing you've got going."

"I can't help it. She's in my blood."

The sound of giggling brought our attention back to the yard. Caleb found a chink in Colleen's armor and got her on the ground. She curled on her side, wiggling as Caleb tickled her sides. Grabbing her feet, he dangled the little girl upside down.

"All right, kid, I'm not gonna hurt you, but you need to behave before I have you declawed. You gonna play nice?" he asked.

"Yes!" Colleen cheered with a tingle in her laugh.

"Don't fall for it," Dougie warned in a singsong tone.

But it was too late. The second Caleb set the girl down, she had his kneecaps for lunch. Caleb limped away, dodging flailing arms reaching for him.

Leaning on his elbows along the picnic table, Dougie called, "There you go. Run fool! Don't let her catch you! Never let them catch you."

"Thanks for doing this, Dougie." I rested my head on his shoulder.

Dougie smiled and looked down at me. "I wouldn't think Caleb would have trouble with women. He don't look all that, and he's kinda goofy."

"Trust me, he has to beat them off with a stick, literally."

Dougie stared out to the field, watching Caleb duck behind a tree. "Well, I'll do my best to show him the way of the samurai."

"Thank you, sensei. Between you, me, and Nadine, we'll whip him into shape. Who knows, with our help, he could probably take down Chuck Norris."

We got back to Caleb's house around eight, both sweaty and exhausted. We didn't bother with idle road chatter, but simply enjoyed the companionable silence. All the while, tension taunted us from the backseat, buzzing naughty suggestions in our ears.

Parking nose to nose with my car, Caleb turned off the engine and looked at me. "I had a, um, interesting day today. Quite instructive."

"I try. You need to call Nadine so you can be led to your next course of action."

He rested his head against the steering wheel. "You women are trying to kill me."

"Better you than us." I kissed his cheek. "I'll see you later."

Escorting me to my car, he asked, "You wanna come in for a bit?"

"No."

"Any particular reason?"

Leaning against my car door, I regarded him carefully. "Can I ask you something?"

His posture straightened and braced himself for impact. "Shoot."

"That pull you have on women, do you think it could be slowly affecting me?"

His eyes dimmed in a shade of mischief. "Come here," he ordered.

I closed the distance between us in seconds.

His hands clasped behind his back when he bent down and whispered, "Kiss me."

I leaned back, startled. "Oh, hell no."

"Kiss me," he demanded.

"I said no, Caleb." I pulled away from him despite my impulse to stay. "Your little pet needs a muzzle."

An easy smile brightened his face. "Then the pull doesn't affect you."

I blinked. "Really?"

"Any other woman would've come to me *without* me asking, and would've kissed me without question."

My shoulders slumped, not sure whether I should be happy or sad about my immunity.

"There's nothing wrong with you. I love that you're not helpless around me. You're with me because you want to be. I love that."

"Love, huh?" I grinned.

The color drained from his face. "Um . . . I mean, I . . ."

"*Yes?*" I prompted with a lengthy drawl.

His eyes met the ground, his hands kept busy inside his pockets. "Look, I'm not good at expressing my feelings, and I'm not sappy. I feel strongly toward you, but the feeling's new to me. Maybe someday I can convey it in words. I—I don't know what I'm saying."

"You can't say the L word. I get it. I have issues with it too. It's like cuss words: you say it enough times, it loses its power."

"Yeah."

"Well, find another way to express yourself."

"Okay." He went back to his car then dug in the ashtray. Finding what he needed, he returned and handed me a quarter. "Here. You can start a pool. Every time I wanna tell you how I feel, I'll add another coin to your collection."

"What's with you and quarters?"

"It's substantial and you can watch it grow."

Giggling, I took the quarter and tucked it in my sports bra. "Fine, we'll make a little love bank for you."

"What about me?" he asked.

"What do you want?"

"Right now, all I wanna do is kiss you. I've never wanted anything so bad. It's that simple and just as difficult." He bit his bottom lip. I'd never seen him look like that at anything that didn't include frosting.

"I know. How long do you think it'll take for Capone to get to know me?"

Closing his eyes, he pushed out a breath. "I don't know. It's too soon to tell, and I'm not risking anything around you."

"Good to know." With another wink, I went to my car but stopped short at the man in front of me.

Haden stood tall and proud, wearing more rumpled clothes and Caleb's grin. Judging from Caleb's rigid stance, this visit didn't bode well for anyone involved.

Eyeing the two of us in humor, Haden rubbed his hands together, ready to dig into his meal. "Well, look at you, little bro! Don't you look well. Got some color in your cheeks. A change in your diet perhaps?"

Caleb pulled me behind him to safety. "I told you not to come here."

"Ah-ah! You said not to enter your place of business. This is your house. And I wouldn't bother to impose on your precious time if it wasn't important." Haden stopped and studied Caleb's face. "Good to see you have a social life, but I'm concerned about your eating habits. Have you learned nothing from Dad?"

"Back off, Haden!" Caleb warned.

"She needs to know what she's getting into. You're not exactly the poster child for exemplary living. Does she know about your special regimen, or did you want to wait until her heart stops before telling her?"

"I know what he is, and what *you* are. So stop picking on him," I cut in.

Haden smiled in a light and infuriating manner. "And you're still breathing. Impressive. Not many women can say the same."

"Caleb isn't a killer." Well, he sort of was by association, but that didn't count. Or did it?

Haden regarded me with hooded eyes, a look too reminiscent of a hungry wolf for my peace of mind. "Samara, I've got news for you—we're all killers. Evil lives in all of us, but ours scream louder than most. We consume everything in our paths until there is nothing left."

"You speaking from personal experience?" I asked. "How many people have you killed?"

Haden smiled. "I'm not the one you need to worry about, thigh-high." He cut his eyes to his brother.

Caleb mirrored the look with clenched teeth. "What do you want? And why are you still in town?"

"Don't get too happy. I'm leaving tonight, but I have information that you might be interested in before I go."

"What information?" I asked.

"Whatever it is, I'm not interested," Caleb added.

"You might think differently when you hear what I have to say. Honestly, you really think I would stay here longer than I needed to?"

Caleb froze. "Fifteen minutes, that's all I'm giving you."

"I'll take what I can get."

Returning to me, Caleb said, "I have to go."

"What's going on? You're scaring me."

"Smart girl," Haden quipped.

"Shut it, Haden!" Caleb barked. His brother threw his hands in the air and strolled up the walkway to Caleb's front door.

Once we were alone, Caleb turned to me. "He's family no matter how much I want to back over him with my car. He wouldn't be here if he didn't need my help with something. I gotta at least hear him out." Caleb didn't look too thrilled about the idea. Under that facade of apathy lay a glint of worry and uncertainty.

I tilted my head to his front door. "Haden mentioned something about your father. Is that why he's here?"

"I don't know. Maybe." He shrugged. "But I refuse to get pulled back into that chaos."

"Is your dad all right? Is he hurt?"

"Yes, very hurt. Beyond repair. It's not good for him to be around people."

"Well, he's still grieving."

"It's not that." Caleb looked over his shoulder before saying, "His spirit is restless. It misses the energy it used to get when Mom was near Dad. It feels the loss as well."

I nodded. "Um, this is gonna sound really bad, and please don't take this the wrong way, but did your dad do something to your mother?"

His body jerked. "What?"

"I was just wondering if he . . ."

Caleb backed away; his expression displayed a mixture of shock and betrayal.

"You think my dad killed my mom?"

"No. I mean, I don't know. Look, Caleb, I'm just trying to figure all this out."

"My dad loved my mom, all right? I can't believe you would say that!"

Eyeing him with caution, I shook my head. "I didn't mean it that way."

"My mom died of cancer. She was already dying; she didn't need any outside help." That freaky glow returned to his eyes and I knew I had to tread lightly.

"Okay, if that's what you say, then I believe you. I'm not trying to offend you, and I don't wanna have to walk on eggshells around you either." I turned and opened my door, but a strong hand slammed it shut.

"Wait. Sam, it's not that." His breath bounced against my ear, cascading a sweet draft of warmth down the column of my neck. "You just hit a soft spot for me, that's all. Mom's death hit my family hard, and, well, you just voiced a suspicion I've had myself."

"Really?" I leaned into him, enjoying the feel of his body against me; dead to any other sense but touch. "Is that why you avoid him?"

He brooded over the answer before saying, "We don't deal with loss well. It's complicated, Sam, and I really want to keep you away from it. Hell, *I* want to keep away from it."

"All right, just don't do anything crazy, okay?"

"Too late for that." He dragged a hand over my cheek, his eyes half-mast, rejoicing in the smallest of touches. "My brother has a point, you know."

"What? That all the women in your life die?"

"No. We consume everything in our paths, but what he didn't say is that we can just as easily become consumed." His stare settled on my lips and stayed longer than it should have. A purple nimbus blossomed before my eyes, a visible beam of aggression not brought on by anger, but by something far too primal, too vulgar to name.

"Caleb!" From the front stoop, Haden's voice cracked through the air like a gunshot. It cautioned us in that familiar parental tone, an interference with perfect timing.

Caleb pushed back and increased the distance between us while his hooded gaze targeted me as helpless prey.

"Good night, Sam." It wasn't a valediction, but a warning that needed no repeating.

Wordlessly, I climbed into my car and set out, fighting to regain my control as well.

That night, I stared at the ceiling, flipping that damn quarter in the air. I didn't care what Caleb said; Capone was working his mojo on me. That was the only reasonable excuse to be still awake at three in the morning.

He seemed to morph before my eyes like some great revelation finally coming to light, a beast of innate sensuality rousing from its sleep. Then there was the way he would look at me, how he could disrobe and deflower me with his eyes yet still look innocent.

I refused to believe that the pull was voluntary. Everyone, including my mother, diagnosed me as a victim of *l'amore*, but my pride and my very sanity demanded a second opinion.

I wasn't falling for Caleb. I just had to tell my heart that.

18

For the next two weeks, Caleb became my pet project. I made him sign up for Master Lu's judo class for beginners, which started in August. In the meantime, I loaned him every Jet Li movie in my library and showed him some Tae Bo moves. Nadine insisted that Caleb needed to develop an internal dialogue with Capone, and she introduced him to Eastern meditation to aid his journey toward enlightenment. We even resorted to kidnapping him and organizing field trips to find a stimulating activity.

Unfortunately, children were not Caleb's thing, a fact we learned the hard way. I underestimated the number of single mothers who hung around playgrounds. Caleb wasn't lying when he said he was a fast runner.

Mia, Dougie, and I took Caleb surfing. Caleb almost drowned, but recovered in time to watch the sunset with me. We huddled under a blanket and witnessed the day's demise in Technicolor. I curled beside him, inhaling the ocean breeze and the smell of Tootsie Rolls on his breath.

Dougie's failed turf war with a jellyfish allowed Mia to

play boo-boo nursemaid. Caleb and I endured two hours of baby talk and lip-smacking during the drive home. Caleb was kind enough to distract me with his fingers. I sat in the backseat with my legs on his lap. He massaged my calves, enthralled by the texture and earthly material from which they were made.

"You've got the softest skin," he said with visible awe. "That's gonna be a serious problem."

"It already is," I replied, in light of the shiver that attacked my remaining limbs.

He wanted more, as did I, but we still had a ways to go. I wasn't a tease, and my demands seemed pretty reasonable: always be honest and try not to eat me. Though he respected my need for space, just the slightest contact granted a small reward for us both, a goal to work toward.

All my free time was spent rehabilitating Capone. Work simply faded in the background with the exception of those all too brief moments in Caleb's company. The harassment went both ways. While returning discarded magazines to the rack, I received Caleb's sneaky back-of-the-neck kiss and disappearing act, which kept my toes curled for the remainder of the day.

When I returned to the counter, I smiled at the sight of two quarters sitting on the coffee bar. Within the week, I accumulated ten dollars' worth of love coins in an old Mason jar under the register. The way things were going, I could pay off my car on my own.

During my break, I saw Alicia sitting on a bench in front of the store. I hadn't had time to really talk to her since the Fourth of July massacre, and her shifts didn't align with mine. Reaching the bench, I decided to rub a little salt on her wound. "What's up, Alicia?"

"Hey, Sam," she called, swinging a Buncha Books bag between her legs.

"Whatcha doing out here?"

She looked around the parking lot. "I'm just waiting for my dad. He should be here in a minute."

"You still in solitary confinement?" I asked.

Alicia rolled her eyes and exhaled noisily. "Dad was furious. My butt's still sore. I can't go outside, talk on the phone, or anything. I have to come to work just to get fresh air."

"That's harsh, but it's an effective device to deter you from any repeat offenses."

Her eyes lowered to her feet. "I never thanked you for helping me that night."

"Don't worry about it."

"I mean it. Thanks. I don't even wanna think about what could've happened. I never drank before, and I just wanted to try it."

I nodded. "Personally, I don't like alcohol, especially beer. It tastes like rubber bands."

"Dad was pissed when he smelled it on me." Alicia shuddered at the memory.

"I'm a veteran when it comes to punishment. From what I've learned, the harsher the punishment, the more you scared them. When I was seven, I wandered away from Mom in the mall, and she wouldn't stop crying, even during the spanking."

Alicia shrugged. "I guess. You know what's so weird? All these people are talking to me now. Word got out that I was the last one to see Garrett alive, and they wanna hear my story."

"Notoriety favors the dead. Use your fame wisely, Alicia."

A smile teased her lips.

Looking down, I pointed to her bag. "So, what you got there?"

"It's the third *Specter* book. Since I'm on house arrest, I needed some decent reading material."

I groaned. "I don't get the popularity with these books. It's unhealthy to obsess over it."

"You won't even crack open the book, so you can't really criticize it."

"Alicia, I could've helped edit the book, and my opinion would go ignored by you fangirls. I mean, what's the appeal? Did the author sprinkle crack between the pages?"

"It's an awesome read. It sucks you in, and the romance is so sad and stuff. Can you imagine being in love with a supernatural creature that you can't touch or kiss? The tension is always there, but neither of you can do anything about it."

All humor died as the story line hit a little too close to home. I didn't dare entertain the possibility that a book could shed insight on how to date a Cambion. The curiosity was there, but not enough to drink the Kool-Aid. However, the look on Alicia's face was well worth the argument. That buoyant light returned to her eyes as she gushed over the male character. She opened her bag and handed me her book.

I skimmed down the page, singling out random passages. The girl in me giggled over the corny dialogue and profession of undying love. Caleb never said anything that sweet to me. For a minute, I actually thought the book wasn't that bad. If it could bring a smile to Alicia's face and get her to read voluntarily, then there had to be some merit to it.

That is, until John Adams's wife walked by with her bonnet and apron, and peeked over my shoulder. "Oh, I love that book. Nicolas Damien is so hot!"

"Isn't he?" Alicia's eyes swelled as if finding her missing soul mate.

"I saw online that they're turning *Specter* into a movie. Can you believe it? I'm so excited!" The woman bounced in her buckled shoes.

Alicia's mouth fell open. "No way!"

"Oh yeah! Here, I'll Google it." The woman dug inside her petticoat and whipped out her BlackBerry.

And with that, my momentary insanity ended. It was one thing for kids to bug out, but adults had no excuse for their mania. Handing Alicia the book, I went back to work, leaving the two ghost chasers to compare notes.

At the main doors, I caught the feeling of someone watching me. The vibe had me looking over my shoulder toward the adjacent building. A man stood in front of a women's clothing store, ogling me in candid fascination. He all but licked his chops as he stared, his lips pulled into a smile that I knew from anywhere.

"Caleb?" I moved closer, trying to see his face clearly while weaving through foot traffic. The need to just touch him took top priority in my brain. Standing mere feet away, I just couldn't get close enough. Before I could reach him, he was gone, leaving no trail to follow.

Maybe he entered the department store without me noticing. But why would he stare me down only to run from me? Though miffed by his sudden flakiness, I didn't give it much thought.

At least, not until I saw Caleb ten seconds later, ringing up customers in the music department. Judging from the items shoved into the store bag, it was a lengthy transaction. I looked to the main doors, then to the music section, and did a double take. There was no way he could have passed me to get to his side of the store that quickly. I was sure the man who had been watching me was real, as was the unyielding need to go to him. The more I thought about it, the more that feeling drained from my memory.

Rubbing my temples, I prayed for quitting time and some much-needed sleep. I must have been seeing things, but considering the man in question, not a whole lot surprised me anymore.

19

Nadine agreed to give Caleb some field practice, so the three of us went to a club in Norfolk.

Only giving a week's notice, I had to offer up my first-born to get Robbie Ford to make me a fake ID. When I saw the results, it was well worth it. That little plastic time machine blasted me five years into the future. Twenty-two was a good age—not too old, but old enough to pass inspection.

The club was an overpriced meat market with an uninspired emcee. The usual suspects were in attendance: the girls with the spray-on tans who did anything for attention and free drinks, the wannabe players who did nothing but hang in the corner with other guys, that chick who laughed way too loud, that old dude who swore he still had game, and that greasy guy at the bar with the open shirt, gold chain, and taco-meat chest hair.

Navigating through the ocean of catcalls and dirty dancing, Nadine grabbed a table and went right to business. "Okay, Caleb, we start off with simple allure. You can control how much you use."

I sat across from Nadine and Caleb. "I thought it came naturally."

"Some. Just enough to turn heads, but not enough to turn someone into mindless zombie. That comes later." Nadine scanned the bar area, searching for a willing donor.

The pickings were a-plenty. I couldn't grasp the full scope of desperation women had these days. These women just showered and came to the club. Never mind clothes—that would just slow them down. Wearing a tube dress and sandals, I looked like a nun.

"There! See the brunette? Call her to you," Nadine ordered. When Caleb rose from his seat, Nadine pushed him back down. "No, do it from here. Look at her and will her over."

"Can you really do that?" I asked.

"Yes. The cool thing is so can you." Nadine disclosed this tidbit with shifty eyes.

"Really?"

"Yeah, you look at someone long enough, you get response. Never discount the eye contact. It's vital to our power."

"Is it like mind control?"

"In a way, yes. We deceive our prey. We don't need beauty. With one look, we become who they desire most. He is everything she ever wanted and she must have him. And her body responds, becomes a slave."

That was the freakiest thing I'd ever heard in my life, and I'd never been more turned on. I could only imagine what it was like to become enslaved by one glance.

"Now Caleb, keep your eyes on her. When she looks this way, reel her in." Nadine coached, steering my attention back to our mission.

Caleb did as instructed. The stare was so intense; I got sucked in from his peripheral. I redirected my focus on the brunette.

In seconds, she clapped eyes with Caleb and slid off her stool in half the time. The woman was pretty, thin, and what most men were looking for, especially in a club. I felt a bit self-conscious, not to mention awkward about the situation. The feeling only grew stronger as she crossed the room. I wondered what she saw when she looked at him.

Nadine leaned in toward Caleb and murmured, "Remember what I taught you. You do not need to pull directly from mouth; the energy around her body is enough. Just a taste."

When Nadine told me that she wanted to help Caleb feed, I was gung ho about it, really. But now there was something very *Animal Planet* about it. A sense of helpless curiosity overshadowed the need to act, like when a baby gazelle drowns in a river and no one helps, not even the camera crew.

Notwithstanding the inexplicable sense of ownership I had toward Caleb. It was one thing to have women all over him. It stroked the ego to know that women want your man. It was another thing when he encouraged it. True, we hadn't had the "relationship talk," but neither of us felt it was necessary.

So why did it still feel like cheating?

The woman slid inside the booth next to Caleb, barely blinking for fear of losing sight of the deity that struck her dumb.

"Hi, I'm Kelly."

He nodded. "Caleb."

Slinging her hair over her shoulder, she closed in on him. "I saw you looking at me across the room. I just had to come over."

My muscles tightened as Caleb whispered in the woman's ear.

When his mouth moved toward hers, Caleb's eyes met mine and he froze.

"Caleb, what's wrong?" she asked.

He looked away. "Nothing."

Not wanting to see any more, I slid out of the booth and made my way toward the bar. My mouth felt like cotton, and I would've paid serious money for a breath of fresh air. There were too many bodies, too much heavy breathing, too much music, too much energy, too much life to consume. Once I got the attention of the bartender, I ordered water to cool my fried nerves.

I felt Caleb's presence before he spoke.

"Are you all right?"

With my back to him, I said, "I'm fine, just thirsty."

His breath brushed across my neck. "You left your water at the table."

"That's okay. I got another. Besides, it's not good to leave your drink unattended. Someone might put drugs in it." I nodded my thanks to the bartender when he set the glass in front of me. "So what happened to your little friend, Kelly?"

"I ate her."

If Caleb was trying to provoke me, it worked. I almost knocked over my water. That statement held so many meanings, each more disturbing than the first. I took two strong pulls on my drink before asking, "Is she all right?"

"Look to your left."

The words directed me to the end of the bar. The brunette rocked back and forth with her head cradled in her hand. Anyone else would have attributed her sudden discomfort to alcohol, but I knew better.

"Will you look at me?" Caleb asked.

Slowly, I turned around. "Isn't it dinnertime?"

He let out a heavy sigh. "Sam."

"What?"

"I shouldn't have brought you here. I can't put you through this."

"Put me through what? I'm okay."

"No, you're not," he argued. "You can't understand what's going on. This isn't what I want, but I have to feed. It's nothing personal. I don't like this any more than you do. In fact, I dislike it more, which is why I've been fighting it all these years, and this is why I'm paying the price now. I've denied my spirit for too long, and I need to supply him with what he needs."

His explanation didn't help at all. "Go ahead, Caleb. I'll stay here."

"I'm not leaving you alone, so you can get that out of your head." He reached out his hand. "Come back to the table."

I collected my water and took his hand. By the time we reached the table, a muscular man sat in the brunette's place. Nadine leaned in, barely touching his lips when a white coil of mist pulled from the man's mouth. When the man tried to deepen the kiss, she pushed him away. Staring off in a daze, the man scooted from the booth and disappeared into the crowd.

Nadine sat back in the seat, basking in the afterglow of her intake. She swallowed a lungful of air and held it until the vein in her throat rose to the surface. With her eyes closed, she exhaled.

"So, are you okay, Sam?" she asked, peering through parted lids. A bright sliver of green light shot from her eyes.

"I'm fine."

"Good. Caleb, follow me. We will do a lap," she said before Caleb could sit down.

He paused. "A what?"

"We will mingle and feed. The key is to take little from each person, like sample platter. When you nibble regularly, meals are not necessary and your spirit will not want. Since yours starves, you will do more laps tonight. I will join you this time, but the next, you go alone."

His head volleyed between me and the dance floor. "I don't want to leave Sam."

I shooed him away. "Go on. I'll be right here."

"You sure?"

"It's cool. I've got my mace." I patted my purse.

Planting a peck on my cheek, he faded into the mob of dancers. The separation gave me a moment to think. And I had some serious brain work to do.

Caleb liked me, a lot, and he really didn't want to do this. I had agreed to come along, knowing full well what would happen. But why was I jealous? Caleb and I weren't a couple, not officially. And I wasn't sure that I wanted to be if I'd have to deal with this on a regular basis. What kind of relationship was that? What if I walked in on him sucking face with some chick? I would lose my damn mind!

The underscore of my soliloquy was this: I would never be enough for him. I could never sate him. Those negative thoughts corroded my inner peace until Nadine and Caleb returned to the table. Their little exhibition had left them exhilarated and oddly refreshed.

"Well, that was fun." Nadine fanned herself with a napkin.

"I never felt so . . . full," he added.

"Well, one more lap should do. Wait a while, then go back in," Nadine advised.

Caleb's eyes beamed like a kid showing off his new toy. "It's wonderful. I don't kiss them to feed. All this time, I thought I had to pull the energy from the mouth."

"That's good. At least now you won't catch mono," I mumbled.

"How are you holding up?" He seemed on edge, perhaps waiting for me to go into hysterics and toss my drink in his face.

"Great!" My response came out more chipper than expected.

Caleb didn't buy it for a second. "We can go home if you want. I know this is awkward for you."

"Naw. I'm good. Besides, I promised I'd help you train Capone, and I meant it. So I'm staying. All that matters is that you get better and no one else gets hurt."

"Thanks, Sam. You don't know how much this means to me. I'm glad you're here to support me." He kissed my hand.

When Caleb left our table, Nadine looked over at me. "You know he's in love with you, right?"

I looked around the club.

Her eyes locked on mine. "You, Sam. *You.*"

"How do you know?"

"Well, let us see. He can have any woman he wants, yet he chooses to be with you and your crazy friends. He lets you boss him around. He cannot stop touching you. He told you his secret, an honor only given to potential spouses, and the whole time on dance floor, he wanted to come back to table. Now if this is not love, I do not know what is."

"Have you ever been in love?" I asked.

"Yes. It was wonderful, painful experience and I enjoyed every second."

"What happened?"

"We grew apart. Oh, and he was married."

I choked on my water. "Nadine!"

"I never said I was saint, Sam. In fact, having demon inside me precludes nomination into sainthood."

I dabbed my chin with a napkin. "How long did you . . . date?"

"Two years."

"*Two years?*"

"It's in the past. I moved on and so has he. But we're talking about you here. Caleb loves you. He may not say this, but he shows it. I'm still helping him with his feelings, but he needs you."

"I haven't even kissed him—well, I haven't *really* kissed him."

Nadine's eyebrows rose. "You kid, right?"

"It's safer that way."

"For who?" she scoffed. "Why have you not kissed him?"

"Because of Capone."

"What about him?"

"If I kiss Caleb, Capone will feed off me."

Nadine stared at me as if I were insane. "If the spirit is appeased and not threatened, it has no reason to attack. Caleb explained recognition, yes?"

I nodded.

"This spirit feels what Caleb feels; it corresponds to it. If Caleb loves you, then you bring him joy. Joy produces most natural strain of energy. So of course Capone wants you around. You are meal ticket."

"I don't want Capone feeding on me."

"That should be no problem if Capone is full."

"How can a spirit be full? Aren't they supposed to be infinite?"

"By itself, yes. This spirit is limited within the body it inhabits. That's the cost of possession: cramped living quarters. I understand your fear; I would be scared too, but you must trust Caleb. He would never hurt you."

"It's not Caleb I'm worried about."

"You'll never know." She wiggled her eyebrows.

"What if you're wrong?"

"I take you straight to hospital."

"Nadine!"

"Go on." She nudged her head in the direction of the dance floor. "Make his day."

I slipped from the booth and steered through the crowd of sweaty dancers. It only took a moment to find him. He stood in a corner, sandwiched between two women who didn't mind sharing. Applying Nadine's teachings, I steadied my focus, barely blinking, and in no way faltering until he looked at me. In moments, his head turned in my direction. He pulled away from his company, ignoring the pleas and insistent tugs on his shirt.

I didn't move, nor did I have any intention of going to him. I simply withstood the fire in his eyes and predaceous method of his stride—a creature of carnal intent. In that instant, I was the only woman alive, the only one who mattered. Heads turned, envious eyes sized me up, lips tightened and curled, and I loved it.

When he stopped in front of me, I placed a finger over his lips before he could say anything stupid to kill the mood. I threw caution to the wind. Mom's horror stories and my own common sense flew right out the window. Trapping his head in my hands, I pulled him down and kissed him.

The next thing I remembered was lying on Caleb's lap, while Nadine fanned my face with a napkin. It took a moment to absorb my surroundings. I was back at our booth with a pounding headache that kept in time with the music.

"Oh thank God, she's coming around. Oh good, very good." Nadine stammered while checking my pulse. "It's my fault. I talked her into it. If anything happened to you, I—"

"It's all right," I said, reaching up to rub my face. "I was stupid enough to go through with it. Peer pressure: it can happen to anyone."

Cradling me in his arms, Caleb observed me with a

pained expression, marking each of my movements as a grand event. "Sam, are you okay? How are you feeling?"

After a few blinks, I no longer saw three of Caleb. "I'm fine. What happened?"

"You passed out on the dance floor," he said. "You scared me to death."

"Really? How long was I out?"

"Five minutes," Nadine answered.

My body stiffened as the truth of the situation sunk in. "Am I going to have a heart attack?"

He ran his fingers through my hair. "No. I didn't take much."

I sat up straight. "What? You fed from me?"

He looked flustered trying to find the right words. "I lost control for a second and—"

I pushed away from him. "What, Caleb? How much did you take?"

Nadine scooted from the booth. "Uh, I leave you to talk. I come back with orange juice. That should help."

When she left the table, I asked again, "How much did you take?"

"Not much. Sam, I'm so sorry."

"You should be sorry. There I was, trying to open up to you, and your pet tries to eat me."

His warm hand stroked my cheek. "I appreciate the effort. I just need a bit more time, that's all."

"Take all the time you want because it ain't happening again."

"You say that now, but give it time. I'll have to pull you off me," he said, all smug and sure of himself.

"Dream big, Cake Boy. Reach for the stars."

Smiling, he drew me closer. "Come on, lie back down."

"I'm fine, really."

Pulling me down, he held me tight in his arms. "Well, I'm not. So please, humor me."

20

climbed the walls with that nail-biting, floor-pacing, methadone-clinic restlessness.

I hadn't heard one word from Caleb in two days. He didn't return my calls or answer his phone. He barely looked at me at work, and when he did, it was only to ask me for Robbie's phone number. Granted, Robbie was the one to call when organizing a coup or partaking in espionage; however, what Caleb wanted with him remained a mystery—a mystery that he had no intention of sharing.

Sneaking a kiss on the neck, he purred, "All will be revealed in due time. It'll take a few days to get everything straight. I'll tell you then."

Caleb's motives came into question yet again. Did he hang out with me out of gratitude? Did he see me as a challenge or something safe to be around? Maybe I had been too hard on him for feeding on me and he wanted to give me space. It's not like I didn't have a right to be upset.

I'd never had a hangover, but if it was anything like

what I felt the day after our club adventure, then I'd stick to a simple concussion. Caleb assured me that he didn't take enough energy to cause harm, but no one told me about the disorientation that occurred while recuperating. Not to mention the obscure sense of loss. Caleb may have taken a drop, but I felt its absence, like a fading dream, a name on the tip of the tongue.

In either case, Caleb couldn't get away without a proper scolding only heard from drunken sailors with Tourette's syndrome. Despite the lethargy and the morning-after regret, there was an element of intimacy about it. A part of my life resided in him, sustaining him, bringing him joy. But that wasn't enough to dismiss the gross factor.

To keep occupied, I spent the day cleaning and reading. I made it halfway through the book for the monthly meeting, when Katy Perry's "ET" killed all tranquility. Reaching for my bag, I fished out my cell, then yelled, "Oh, so you know how to use a phone now?"

"The buttons are tricky, but I think I'm getting the hang of it." Caleb laughed. "I told you I was working on something."

"Yeah, you just left out what that something was."

"I wanted it to be a surprise."

"I don't like surprises."

"You'll like this one. Can you come over?" he asked.

I stared at the phone as if it bit me. "Now?"

"If you're free."

His nerve knew no bounds. I put the phone back to my ear and unleashed the pent-up anger. "You expect me to drop everything I'm doing just to see you?"

"It would be nice," he crooned, sounding amused at my frustration.

"You must've forgotten who you're talking to. I don't jump through hoops for a guy. And I'm not at your beck and call."

"I know. I'll make it worth your while," he enticed, and I wondered why he sounded better on the phone than in person.

"I'm not sure that I wanna go. What if I have a date?"

"Is that where you're going now?" His tone dripped with accusation.

"What?"

"I heard your car start. Are you meeting up with someone?"

I looked around and took in the new setting. There I was in pajama shorts and flip-flops inside my car with keys in the ignition. The last thing I remembered was sitting on my bed. I had never encountered a mental blackout like that before, and I wondered if Capone's mojo could travel through phone waves.

"Hello? Sam?"

I put the phone back to my ear. "Yeah?"

"I'll see you in twenty minutes." He ended the call.

I banged my head against the steering wheel. As Mom would say, "Ignorance was to not know, and stupidity was to not know and not care."

Pulling out of the driveway while still in my pajamas, I came to the conclusion that I was grade-A certified stupid for Caleb. I knew it, Caleb knew it. The entire eastern seaboard knew it. This was so unfair.

I could now sympathize with drug addicts. They understood the illness, fully aware that what they crave would probably kill them, and yet they go back for more.

For most addictions, the need accumulated through an ongoing course of events. Deep-seated tragedies and childhood trauma were common factors. The behavior was inexcusable, but the addict eagerly supplied excuses nonetheless, either out of self-pity or a way to pass blame to someone else.

My defense was blatantly simple: It was all Caleb's fault.

When I got to Caleb's house, he met me at the curb, jumping up and down with no shoes on. It was good to know that I wasn't alone in my insanity. I barely shut off the car before he opened the door and pulled me out, then herded me inside the house.

"What was so important that you ha—" I stopped at the sight of his living room. CDs were scattered everywhere with state-of-the-art music equipment, wires, cables, crates of albums, and a turntable in the corner.

"What's all this?" I asked.

Sweeping a hand across the open space, he said, "This is my surprise."

"What? That you need a maid?"

"No. I think I found something stimulating. Music."

"Okay." I struggled to follow the logic.

"I talked to Robbie and he set me up with the deejay that played at his party. We've been talking for the past few days—he's been showing me the ropes."

"Wait, back it up. You want to be a deejay, like on the radio?"

"No, a club deejay. I've always loved music, and I have a wide collection that no one has. Mark, the deejay at the party, came by and lost his mind at all the albums I have. Half this stuff you can't find in the U.S. I let him borrow some in exchange for coaching. I even got a turntable to practice on. Right now I'm organizing a set."

"Do you even know how to mix?"

"I dabbled in it in high school, but I never thought it would come to anything. But I'm learning. Give it time. Right now I'm compiling a playlist for Mark. He knows a promoter in D.C. that's looking for some new talent."

"That's great."

"Nothing's set in stone. I still need to hear back from Mark, but I'm pretty excited. And Robbie wants me to mix at his next party."

"What party?"

"He's having a birthday bash in two weeks, and he wants me to deejay."

"Why didn't I hear about a party?" And when did he start calling him Robbie?

Caleb patted my shoulder in sympathy. "I guess you're out of the loop."

"That's it; I'm leaving." I went for the door, but he pulled me to him.

"Aren't you happy?" he whispered in my ear.

"I'm happy, you're happy, Capone's happy; all is right with the world."

"But," he pressed.

I didn't like being so needy, but I had to know the score before whatever this was went any further. By clearing the air now, I could walk away with half my sanity intact.

"What are we?" I asked.

Caleb seemed a little slow on the uptake, so I gave him hand gestures to help him along. "Us. You and me. Are we dating?"

"That was my impression."

"What does that make me?"

He looked at me like I was slow. "My girlfriend?"

"I never got that memo. You expect me to read minds now?"

"I thought you knew. I've known since the night at Europia Park."

The news took me aback. "Really?"

Caleb had the gall to laugh, a deep, throaty laugh. "Yeah. I told you I wasn't into the lovey-dovey stuff."

"Well, a girl needs to know these things. What if a guy approaches me? What am I supposed to say?" I asked.

All humor left his face and tone. "You're taken."

Lifting my chin, I turned away from him. "By who? You haven't staked any claim."

Caleb obviously saw that as a challenge. In a blink, I sat on top of his kitchen counter with my legs wrapped around his waist and my arms around his neck.

Vibrant eyes burned into mine, singling me out as marked prey, a position most intoxicating and equally disturbing. "I never saw you as one for formalities."

"Me either."

Placing my hand over his heart, he said, "In that case, I, Caleb Nolan Baker, hereby declare you, Samara Nicole Marshall, esquire, as my main squeeze. I proclaim exclusivity and promise devotion and loyalty. I am internally, externally, and eternally, yours."

One could knock me over with a feather. I could now understand why brides cried at weddings. Though the declaration was overkill, my heart couldn't stop racing, and his nearness made me pant.

"Sam?" he whispered. "You okay?"

Probably sporting a half-baked grin on my face, I nodded. "Yeah, I'm just a little buzzed. I thought you said you weren't sappy?"

"It's not sappy if it's true," he countered.

"Well then." I placed his hand over my heart. "I, Samara Nicole Marshall, esquire, declare you, Caleb Nolan Baker, as my main squeeze. I proclaim exclusivity and promise devotion and loyalty. I appoint you keeper of my heart and champion of my terrestrial and celestial domain."

Fighting hard not to laugh, his cheeks reddened. "That's not much acreage."

I pushed his chest. "Hey, you put me on the spot."

"Didn't you bring up the topic?"

"I know, but I wasn't expecting you to get all syrupy on me."

He trapped my face in his hands. "We've been officially dating for ten seconds and we're already fighting."

"As long as we don't end up like Dougie and Mia, I'm cool."

Nodding in agreement, he said, "Mia loves Doug a lot."

"How can you tell?"

"She doesn't react to me. She might give me a look or two, but she's not attracted. That means she's happy."

Threading my fingers through his hair, I wondered why guys were blessed with softer hair than girls, or was it due to all the products girls put in their hair? I was learning a lot about Caleb Baker. He was a closet romantic with a caged ardor that had me anticipating his next move. He was also very sensitive around the ears. My playing invoked a response that left him gripping my hips and struggling for breath.

Seeing the internal conflict in his eyes, I decided to provide a distraction. "I have a question. When you fed from me, what did you learn?"

He stared off for a moment, rounding up his mental resources. Grimacing, he said, "When you were three, you drank from the toilet. Your favorite color is light green. You hate any type of injustice, no matter how small. You over-analyze too much, and you love very deeply. That's why you don't do it often."

I gaped at him. "All that from a drop?"

"It's fragmented. I only get small flashes. Um, why were you drinking from the toilet?"

"I don't know, but my mom's got pictures," I replied before noticing the sudden change in his demeanor. His breathing grew shallow; stress lines appeared around his face as he withstood a private torment.

I cupped his jaw and searched his eyes. "What's wrong?"

"Hungry," he growled and turned his head away.

Unsettled by the cold response, I attempted to slide off the counter. "We can go grab something to eat."

His hands kept me still. "Not for food."

"Uh-huh. What exactly are you hungry for?"

Despite his evident pain, an insidious grin split his face. "Get your head out the gutter, Miss Marshall. I'm referring to my roommate."

"Speaking of the gutter; let me ask you something. Have you ever . . . you know?"

"Had sex?" When I nodded, he answered, "Of course. I'm a walking chick magnet, but it's been a while for me though."

"How long?"

"Five months."

That wasn't the answer I expected, but I tried to keep an open mind. "Oh. I figured you'd—"

"It's a little dangerous to be involved with women like that, don't you think?"

Seeing his point, I asked, "How did you do it before and not hurt them?"

A nice shade of pink rushed to his cheeks and neck. "This aggression from women is only a recent thing, so it wasn't that difficult. The enticement works with eye contact, and I was in a situation where we didn't have to look at each other." He didn't say any more, and he didn't need to.

"Don't you miss it?"

"I'm a guy, Sam. Of course I miss it, but not enough to put a woman in danger." He closed his eyes and took a deep breath. "It's a great stimulant. Scratch that—it's one of the best—but there's something even better."

"What?"

"Feeding. Words can't describe it. Sex is more a physical thing, where feeding is far more intimate. I'm taking in life, the physical, mental, emotional blueprint of existence. It's intense; so much is coming at you at once. It's like you're dying and living in that exact moment. The rush is better than anything that you will ever know, which is why my celibacy hasn't driven me crazy yet."

Seeing the elation in his eyes, I could only imagine the thrill that came with the act. This man literally got high on life, and I wanted to become his supplier. I wanted that look to remain on his face whenever he saw me.

"When was the last time you fed?" I asked.

"Last night."

"How is that going, anyway?"

"Pretty good. I try to feed twice a day, but I haven't gotten around to it today. Being near you doesn't help."

I shrugged, offering no pity. "You invited me over."

"I know you're worried about what would happen, but is there any way it's possible for us to kiss again?" Biting his lip, he stared at me with the eyes of a naughty child who promised to behave.

"I don't know. I'm still freaked out over the last time." I hesitated, not sure how to get the words out. "But, if you need me . . . you can have me."

His eyes fixed to mine, trying to find meaning in my statement and any sign of objection. I answered him with silence.

He reached for my hands and dragged his lips across my wrist. "The pull isn't nearly as strong this way, but you may feel a little light-headed."

His moist lips, his hot breath, the stubble on his chin wreaked havoc on my nervous system. The warmth traveled up my arm to my vertebrae. During his slow exploration up my arm, every movement illustrated the need for control, which only heightened the excitement.

Closing my eyes, I presented trust and vitality as an offering, a gift that he handled with care. My thoughts flew back to our first kiss in the bookstore as the pulling sensation returned—the numb weightlessness, the icy tickle of static on my skin. Textures and heat I never knew existed invaded my body, assailing all reasoning. Not just touch, but all the senses fostered pleasure. I relinquished all purchases of self for the sake of the moment, for the sake of the pull. The longer the contact, the more of me bled away.

Feathery strands tickled my cheek when he reached my shoulder. His breath shivered against my throat. "Sam?"

"Huh?"

He tipped my chin, forcing me to meet his eyes. "What do you see?"

I stared into the vast plane of lavender and saw the life behind the world, that uncharted territory never seen by the living, where the flesh could never endure. I alone could see his eyes that way, which secured our bond long after all things of this world ceased.

Touching his face, I whispered, "I see joy."

The next three hours took place in Caleb's arms on the sofa. I rested against his chest, counting the spaces between each heartbeat and inhalation of air. I gave in to the moment: a feeling so convoluted, so pure, it was blinding. The slow descent from the clouds made me drowsy, and the fall settled me into a warm embrace that greeted below. Light fingers dragged across my arm and neck, coaxing me into sleep.

"What did you learn about me this time?" I asked.

His fingers coiled around my hair. "People gray early

in your family. When you found a streak, you dyed it white and red in defiance."

"Wow, I never told anyone that."

"I know. I like it. I also learned that you trust me."

I lifted my head. "Oh yeah?"

"I'm glad. I promise to keep that trust intact." He held me tighter as if his security blanket would be taken away. Though I couldn't see his face, I knew something bothered him. Before I could mention it, he asked, "How are you feeling? You need some more orange juice?"

"You made me drink a whole carton."

"It helps you recuperate faster; you won't get that hungover feeling."

"You should have told me that the last time."

He rolled onto his side and pulled me to him. "Must've slipped my mind." His lips brushed my forehead; his hands drew me closer. It seemed that we couldn't get close enough. I wanted to merge with him, graft my skin to his. He smelled like the inside of a bakery, warm and sweet, just like him.

Before I dozed off, I heard him say, "It doesn't take much to make me happy, but the simplest things are sometimes the hardest to get. But when it finally arrives, heaven help those who try to take it away from me."

21

The first week of August was an entertaining one. Mia and Dougie broke up that Monday on account of a pregnancy scare. Maybe she found death a turn-on, because the day after Garrett's funeral, Mia and Dougie finally sealed the deal. After three years of dating, they figured it would cement their bond as destined soul mates. Folly it was, considering she broke up with him the second her period ran late.

Dougie called, begged, even camped outside of my house the day of the test, so Mia had to park a block away and enter from the back porch. As we waited for the verdict to read from five home pregnancy tests, I told Mia the latest on me and Caleb—minus the demonic possession, of course.

She seemed happy that I was stepping into the relationship field, a feat thought impossible from all sides. Mia gave me crap the entire time, which served as a good diversion from her own problems.

"So, let me get this straight. Caleb likes you, but instead of declaring his love verbally, he hands you bus fare?" Mia rolled on my bed in another fit of laughter.

"Well, if you put it like that, it sounds pretty lame. We're both weird about couple stuff, and we're allergic to corny. Can you really blame us?" I joked.

She must have taken it seriously. Her face set in a line of brooding introspection. "Every time I ask myself if being with Dougie is even worth it, the answer is always yes."

"Then why do you fight with him all the time? One of these days he's just gonna leave and not come back."

Her honey-brown eyes narrowed. "I know. He can do a whole lot better than me. And he can leave at any second. That's why I have to be the one that ends it, not him."

"Why end it at all? He's not going anywhere. You two are crazy about each other, so the only fighting going on should be to stay together. Stop being a little bitch."

"Gee, thanks, Sam."

"I'm not gonna hold your hand and coddle you when you're in the wrong. You sure as hell wouldn't do it to me. So what are you gonna do about Dougie?" I asked.

"Time will tell." Mia stood at the sight of the clock on the nightstand. "And my time is up. Let's see the results."

Thank God it was a false alarm. I couldn't see Mia bringing a life into the world. People say children change everything, bring one's priorities into focus; but none of my friends were equipped to test that theory.

That Friday, Mia's monthly visitor dropped by, and she and Dougie made up just in time for Robbie's party. Being surrounded by my friend's relationship, my siblings, and my crazy mother served as an efficient chastity belt; however, time spent with Caleb weakened my armor.

Caleb survived Master Lu's orientation class by a thread. He stretched across his couch like a limp rag doll for two days, begging for someone to shoot him. Muscles he never knew he owned made their objections known. Soon he would be one mean fighting machine, and I was tempted to sign up for a class myself, especially if it could give me abs like his.

It wasn't fair that he could pig out and not gain one ounce, but if I walked past a vending machine, the button of my jeans popped. I conquered the freshman fifteen in eighth grade and it was a constant struggle to keep from backsliding. Caleb didn't seem to mind, if his relentless petting provided any clue. He told me that I felt better than the softest pillow. Though it was complete BS, I gave him points for effort.

Aside from having his ass handed to him twice a week, Caleb spent most of his time mixing on his turntable and seducing me after work. He kept his music selection under wraps, wanting it to be a surprise for Robbie's party.

Meanwhile, Mom decided not to let the speed-date fiasco bring her down. Jumping back on the saddle, she continued her online search for her better half. She was working on date number three, and I barely even noticed.

This Caleb makeover occupied every ounce of free time I owned, but I had to pump the brakes when Mom came downstairs wearing something backless and not very age appropriate. Apparently Mom's hunger strike had paid off, and the result had me doing a double take.

Picking my jaw off the floor, I asked, "Where you going, Miss Thang?"

"I told you all this week that I had a date tonight." She strutted—yes strutted—through the kitchen and grabbed her cell phone off the charger.

I leaned against the kitchen island. "You did? With who?"

"He's a retired engineer for the military, and he's gorgeous!" Mom squealed.

"Uh-huh. What else? Where are you going? What's the address? And what's his Social Security number?"

"Samara, I've already checked him out, and he's fine."

Not wanting to be upstaged, I said, "Okay then, have fun. I've got plans, too."

"Oh yeah? You hanging out with Caleb?"

"As a matter of fact, I am. Am I really that predict-able?"

"Nowadays." As Mom drew closer, her expression turned serious. "Samara, you're almost eighteen and you're old enough to make your own decisions. But some decisions are important, and your choices can change the rest of your life. Now if you and Caleb feel the urge to become intimate—"

"Mom!" I covered my ears. *Omigod, not the sex talk. Not the sex talk.*

"Samara, sweetie, you need to be prepared for any sit-uation."

"There is no situation. We just hang out."

Her stare pinned me still. "I see how he looks at you. He's a bit older than you and has worldly experience."

"Two years, Mom. That's all. And he's not using any of his 'worldly experience' on me, that's for sure."

"All I'm saying is that you have a bright future ahead of you. I don't want you ruining any opportunities over a summer fling."

"It's not a fling. We just—"

Mom spied the microwave clock behind me and jumped. "Honey, can we talk about this later? I'm run-ning late. Just remember what I said. I'll see you later."

I followed her to the door, hoping her skirt didn't ride any higher. "Okay, Mom. Have fun."

Not having an invite to the party brought me to Rob-bie's doorstep, demanding retribution. He told me that I was always welcome and no invitation was necessary. Though the response made me blush, some type of notifi-cation of the event would've been splendid.

The party was the epic milestone and fond farewell to civilization as we knew it. Robbie wasn't the balloon and cake type of person, but he was into performers of the clothing-optional variety. The turnout was ridiculous, proving that there was no such thing as bad publicity. Finding a dead body at a party shot one's popularity into the stratosphere.

The house was a fire-code violation with nowhere to stand, let alone sit down. But no one wanted to sit once Caleb's magnum opus invaded the speakers. Bodies swayed and bent like wheat in the breeze, contorting to the will of the elements. Movement and sound occupied their own cosmic string.

Mark stood in awe at Caleb's orchestration in the deejay booth. Every track blended with the other with customized precision, without any pause, or interference. Each song set a new mood, from panic to euphoria, all falling into a rib-rattling accordance with each other.

Caleb closed his eyes, letting the beat absorb into his pores, drinking the energy surrounding him. I watched him draw in the crowd's adulation. He waved to everyone and they returned the acknowledgement with reverence. It was now clear why so many chicks got hot over the deejay. They brought energy to the scene, but Caleb took it right back.

Caleb's eyes held mine prisoner as the last song of the night violated my body. His look revealed that he, as well as the song, was dedicated to me. I had never heard the tune before, and it was a good thing we were in public. Though devoid of lyrics, the sensual rhythm bordered on indecency. The beat alone would surely make a woman out of me.

This was the song that held planets in orbit; it was where babies really came from, and it wouldn't surprise me if it was on God's playlist. Smiling in gratitude, I lifted my head and allowed the music to steal my soul.

*   *   *

After the party, I went to Caleb's house for a bit. Mom must have been having some fun of her own since she hadn't called me about the time, so I figured another half hour wouldn't hurt. He needed a sound opinion on a new set he had compiled for Mark. I sat on Caleb's couch watching him work his magic on the turntable. His eyes came alive with activity and absorption. He definitely found his element and it showed through every cell of his body. He looked better, too. His skin had a healthy glow and he carried a spring in his step. Though Capone had begun to behave himself, women still huddled around Caleb at work and whenever we went out. They kept their advances nonviolent, but they stood oblivious of my presence. It took saintly grace to withstand that amount of disrespect.

Then there was the sex issue. I wasn't a prude; I just never found a guy worthy enough to go that extra mile. Caleb was a good candidate, but the risks overshadowed the reward. Everyone was entitled to their past, but the thought of him sleeping with other girls made me ill. He never gave an exact body count, but even *one* partner was enough to tie my stomach into knots. They partook in a joy I couldn't have, a gift only I could appreciate.

Shaking those negative thoughts away, I got up and moved to the kitchen.

"So do you like it?" he called after me.

"Huh? Oh yeah, it's great, Caleb. The girls are gonna hunt you down over that last song." The comment came out sharper than intended. He must have caught on, because he removed his headphones and followed me to the kitchen. My path to the fridge was intercepted by Caleb's body trapping me against the counter.

Frowning, he read my face like a map, examining the hidden flaws in the typography. "Jealousy is never healthy."

"I'm not jealous." The reply came out quicker than necessary.

A smile pulled at the side of his mouth as his thumb stroked my bottom lip. "No, but I am. Every guy who's kissed you, I envy."

"You don't have to." I sucked the roaming digit into my mouth and nibbled lightly.

His eyes darkened at the invitation. Just as he leaned in to kiss me, *The People's Court* theme rang through the kitchen. Trust Dad to kill the mood.

Caleb searched around in annoyance. "You might wanna consider changing your ring tone."

"Or just turning off my phone." I went for my bag. Caleb tried to hide his disappointment as he followed me to the living room.

Once I flipped open the visor, Dad yelled through the phone. "Samara, where are you? I tried calling you at the house."

"Dad, what's wrong?"

"Your mom's at the hospital."

I wasn't sure if I heard him correctly, even as he repeated it twice. "What?"

"They just brought her in. She collapsed outside a restaurant parking lot. She had a heart attack."

The bottom dropped from under me, and all the blood drained from my body. Somehow, I managed to keep the phone to my ear. "Are you with her now?"

"No, she's in the ER now, but I'm on my way."

"Thanks." After Dad gave me the hospital information, I ended the call. Hurling my bag over my shoulder, I went to the door, but I couldn't quite reach the knob. I tried a second and a third time, but all I caught was air. Something prevented my left arm from extending forward, a light resistance that originated at the elbow. Examining the limb, I realized a large, white-knuckled hand held it in place. I followed the hand toward the man who stood next to me with fear in his eyes.

"Samara, what's wrong?" His low, muffled voice seemed to come from another room. He rotated my shoulders in his direction. His eyes focused on every movement, every intake of breath. "Sam, talk to me. What's wrong?"

Coarse thickness clung to the back of my throat. My stomach tightened, my lungs heaved to get it out, the words, the sob, the scream. Nothing came but hot air.

A violent jerk snapped my head back, my body shook. Someone was screaming at me. Irritated, I looked up at those crazy purple-blue eyes. It looked like something was moving inside them, swirling in a whirlpool around the cornea.

"SAMARA!"

I jumped. "What?"

"What is going on? What did your dad say?"

After a long blink and shake of the head, my hearing returned along with the dizziness. I leaned my head against his chest. "My mom just had a heart attack."

His hands slid across my back and pulled me closer. "I'm so sorry. How is she?"

"I don't know. She's in the ER now."

"You need me to drive you?"

"It's fine. This is a family thing. I need to go alone."

"You can't drive in your condition; you're shaking. I don't want you to be alone. I'll drive you." Opening the door, he asked, "Do you need me to carry you to the car?"

I shook my head and passed through the doorway. Words took up more energy than I had available, and something told me that every bit of it was crucial tonight.

22

Sitting in the waiting room, I anticipated the doctor or my father appearing around the corner.

I had never felt so helpless in my life, and the nurse at the front desk just made things worse. I practically had to pass a lie-detector test to prove I was family, and she kept going on about insurance cards. Thank goodness Caleb was there; otherwise, I would've ripped that woman bald.

On that rare occasion when a doctor crossed my path, he explained the extent of the damage. Though a rare malady, a similar case a few weeks back allowed the doctor to diagnose Mom quickly. Mom endured something called stress cardiomyopathy, or "broken-heart syndrome," a type of shock caused by psychological or emotional trauma. The overwhelming stress released a heavy amount of adrenaline and other chemicals into her bloodstream. The toxic overdose weakened her heart muscles, creating symptoms similar to a heart attack.

The doctor said that they were able to regulate her heartbeat and raise her blood pressure, along with a great deal of technical terms I had difficulty translating. But the word "observation" caught my attention. That meant she wasn't out of the woods.

Caleb was a gem, not leaving my side for a second, always touching in case I forgot he was there. I needed the constant reminder, if anything, to redirect my thoughts from every worst-case scenario.

Dad finally showed up, looking like a warm place to rest. I reluctantly left Caleb in the waiting area to talk to Dad in private. Away from prying nurses and comatose patients, Dad pulled me into his arms so tight I thought my limbs would break.

He kissed my head and whispered words of support. "Your mother's gonna be all right."

"I hope so."

He looked down at me. "Where's your faith, baby girl?"

"I think I left it in the car."

"You can borrow some of mine." We walked back toward the waiting room when Dad spied Caleb standing against the wall. "Why is that boy looking at you?"

I turned to where he pointed and smiled. "That's my boyfriend, Caleb."

"Boyfriend?" Dad looked at me as though I sprouted an extra head. "When did this happen?"

"We've been talking for a while. It's only been made official recently."

Dad let out a low groan. "Samara, you know how I feel about boys."

"I know, but Mom's cool with it."

Dad blinked. "She is?"

I nodded.

"No criminal background check, no blood test?"

"No. He just talked to her, and she likes him." I smiled weakly.

Dad shot Caleb the death glare before saying, "Well, now's not the time for interrogations, so I'll hold off. You want anything from the cafeteria?"

"No, go on. I'll call you if something happens."

After another bear hug, Dad retreated to the elevators.

Caleb met me halfway, and I allowed him to lead me back to my seat.

While I waited for the doctor to walk in with updates, several questions replayed in my head like a broken record. What was Mom doing to cause a heart attack? Where was the guy she was seeing? Why was everyone having heart issues, physical and emotional?

I lifted my head and looked to Caleb. "I need you to be honest with me."

He waited.

"Are there any more like you in Williamsburg? I mean besides Nadine?"

"Not that I know of."

Running down the Cambion roll call, I asked, "Is your brother around?"

"No. As far as I know he flew back to Dublin the night he came to see me."

Satisfied, if only marginally, I returned to my stupor.

"I thought the same thing too. Your mom is pretty young to have a heart attack. She doesn't have any weird medical history, does she?"

"No. There might be something on her parents' side, but nothing I'm aware of."

He rubbed my back. "I think she'll be fine. The doctor says she's stable."

"What do doctors know?"

His hands caressed the back of my neck. "A lot more than you do right now, so just relax until we hear more."

My head whipped up. "It's easy for you to say. That's

not your mother in there fighting for her life." The words left my mouth before I could catch myself.

If he was offended, he gave no evidence of it.

"I've been where you are," he began, his voice even and calm. "Every memory you have is flashing in your head—birthdays, holidays, little things about them—their laugh, the way they smelled. Every skinned knee, every case of the flu, every loose tooth you tucked under your bed. It all rushes in front of your eyes.

"What makes it worse is when it collides with the self-deprecating sense of regret. You replay the last conversation in your head. Everything you wish you could've said, or done; a few more 'I love yous' here and there might've made the loss easier. 'If I were a better kid, I would have saved them grief.'

"Every thought causes a new ache, a pain that is so distinct, it's physical and inclusive. Then it reaches a point where you feel nothing else. You lose sight on whether you're really alive, and whether you even care. I think that narrows it down. If anyone knows what you're going through, it's me."

Scum of the earth was not an adequate description of how I felt. My body shrank into the chair as I covered my eyes with a trembling hand. I couldn't look at him; I didn't have the right. "I'm so sorry, Caleb. I didn't mean—"

He gently pulled my hand from my face, kissed my wrist, then climbed to his feet. "I'm going to the vending machine. Do you need anything?"

"No."

"You sure? You need something in your stomach. I can swing by the cafeteria."

"No thanks. I'll probably throw it up anyway."

"All right, I'll be back in a minute." He squeezed my shoulder, then made his way down the hall.

I let Caleb's words sink in. He had nailed it right on the

head. Memories, good and bad, drifted in a sea of "what ifs" with no sight of land.

The voice of a man talking to the nurse at the desk came in and out of my audible range. When he said my mom's name, I leapt up from my seat. Nearing the desk, I looked him up and down, trying to figure out how he knew Mom.

His age played up mature sophistication, and his casual, expensive suit was as cosmopolitan as he was. His large hands raked through his short, salt-and-pepper hair. When I reached the desk, he looked in my direction. The second he locked eyes on me, his expression changed. Deep blue eyes peered behind tinted specs and assessed the lines and bends of my features. Donning a confident smile, he approached me. "You must be Samara."

The sound of my name on his lips made my insides tingle. The feeling only got worse when he took my hand. "My name is Nathan Ross. Julie told me so much about you."

I hesitated a moment, willing the fluttering in my stomach to stop. "How do you know my mother?"

"Your mother and I have been corresponding for about a week now. We went out for drinks tonight when she collapsed. I was the one who brought her here. I left a while ago to get some air, but I had to come back and check on her."

"You're my mom's date?" I gave him another once-over. Mom had good taste. The guy looked as though he had stepped out of *Gentleman's Quarterly*. And that voice. It was an R & B slow jam waiting to happen.

"This kind lady informed me that your mother had an issue with her heart, and she's currently stabilized." He gave the blushing nurse a smile.

I glared at the woman behind the desk. I'd had to go through a retina scan and full cavity search to get my mother's room number, and this dude had details on the medical procedure. But then again, he could steal Pentagon secrets with that smile alone.

His warm hand rested on my shoulder. "I can't tell you how sorry I am."

"Thanks. I appreciate you sticking around."

"No problem—" was all he could say before Caleb's voice rang behind me.

I heard his footsteps approach as he called my name, but it took me a moment to understand why he'd asked Mr. Ross why he was there.

And why on earth Caleb called him "Dad."

23

"I asked you a question. What are you doing here?" Caleb stepped between us and pushed me behind him. "Did you have something to do with this?"

Mr. Ross shoved his hands in his pockets. "Good to see you too, son."

"Did you hurt Ms. Marshall?"

Mr. Ross blinked in surprise. "Why would you think that?"

"I don't know, you tell me." His tone, brusque and uneven, ground out each syllable as though speaking with proper inflection would invoke an unholy curse. Every muscle in Caleb's body tightened against me.

"I'm simply checking on a friend," Mr. Ross explained in complete innocence.

"A friend, huh? How exactly do you know Samara's mom? Did you draw her to you?"

"You know how women are around me. I couldn't help it even if I tried, and Julie and I happened to be at the right place at the right time. I'm sure you know how these things work. Speaking of which . . ." Mr. Ross looked around Caleb's blockade to face me. "Samara, how do you know my son? Has he bewitched you with his charm?"

When I tried to step around Caleb, he trapped me behind the solid wall of his back. The tense undertone of the exchange revealed that Mr. Ross's looks had deceived more than just me. There was some serious evil afoot, which proved reason enough to keep my distance.

"You stay away from her," Caleb ordered. "And stay away from her mother."

"Am I bothering you, Samara?" Mr. Ross asked, ignoring his son's warning.

Finding my voice, I managed to choke out, "No, but your demon is."

My words, driven by hate, hit their mark, leaving Mr. Ross stunned. He removed his tinted glasses and revealed that familiar shade of purple that I knew too well. His stare moved from my face to Caleb's in an attitude of defiance. "You two are closer than I thought. No wonder you've been preoccupied."

"Why are you really in Virginia? How did you find me?" Caleb demanded.

"You make it seem like a crime to keep tabs on my youngest child. It wasn't easy to track you, I'll give you that. You really know how to shut yourself down. Not very healthy, son. You can't deny who you are. You are a part of a whole, and you must return to the source at some point. I told you if you didn't come to me, I would come to you. I'm sure Haden told you that when he came here."

Caleb stiffened. "What did you do to him?"

"Well, what do you know? You still care about your family. Haden's someplace safe, taking a nice long nap." When Caleb prepared to lunge, he added, "Oh, don't worry, he's fine, but I couldn't let him tell you I was here. I wanted it to be a surprise."

Caleb closed in on his father, their faces barely an inch apart. "I'm only gonna say this one more time. Leave, and keep away from Sam and her mother."

"If you insist, I won't go near them, but I can't guarantee *they* will stay away from *me*."

Backing away, Mr. Ross gave me a wink, doling out that same devilish grin that was Caleb's trademark. He owned the same expressions, the same penetrating stare. It was like a peek into Caleb's future.

The stiffness in his right leg gave him a slight limp, but had little effect on his determined stride. In fact, it made it more dangerous. I turned to Caleb, who leaned against the wall, taking long, therapeutic breaths. "What the hell just happened?"

"The shit hit the fan," he replied with eyes closed.

"What is your dad doing here?"

"I didn't expect him either. I wasn't ready for this." He lifted his head to the ceiling. "I need to find Haden. If he's still in town, I need to see if he's all right."

"Would your father really kill his own son?" I asked.

"Kill, no. Hurt, yes. We're all connected, an extension of dad's spirit, and it won't destroy itself. We can sense each other's presence."

"Then why didn't you know he was in town? Couldn't you feel him nearby?"

"No. I've severed the ties and kept my distance for too long."

I took a step back, quickly losing my balance and what was left of my patience. The traffic in my head stood in gridlock and my nerve endings crackled with the need to inflict harm. Pushing out a long-suffering breath, I said, "I think you should go."

Blazing light shot from his eyes as they met mine. "You know I can't leave you alone now."

"I'm fine. I have my family here."

He didn't seem convinced. "Is that what you want?"

"No. What I *want* is the truth from you—all of it. No riddles, no subtle innuendos, no ominous pauses. I've respected your privacy and given you time to open up, but this shit is leaking into my world, and I'll be damned if my mom gets killed over what you're *not* telling me." Lowering my voice, I continued. "I know you weren't directly involved, but I'll only take it out on you. So please, just go."

He sucked in air through his teeth. It made a hissing sound in reaction to some invisible sting. Whether it was my words, the sight of his estranged father, or the totality of the evening, I wasn't sure, but he seemed to age before my eyes. When the worst of it was over, he pushed off the wall. "All right, I need to call my brothers and Nadine."

I tilted my head. "Nadine?"

"Yeah. I'm gonna need all the help I can get now." Holding my shoulders, he stared into my eyes. "Do me a huge favor. Stay with your dad. Go home with him, keep him nearby, and don't go to your house alone, okay? Tell one of the nurses what's going on and that they're not to allow any unauthorized visitors near your mother's room."

Was he serious? "They won't even let *me* in."

His brows furrowed in thought. "If they put security on the floor, it should scare him off. I'll call the police, not that they can do anything."

My chest throbbed from my heart trying to punch its way free. "You're scaring me."

"Good. Then you'll do what I say. Please?" His face was a mask of determination, refusing to take no for an answer.

"Will you call me if anything happens?"

He nodded and tucked his hand under my chin. "Be careful." He walked away and whipped out his cell phone, rushing by Dad before he could stop him.

When Dad reached my side, he asked, "Where's the fire?"

"Family emergency. He couldn't help it."

He harrumphed. "You sure he wasn't ducking out on me?"

"No. Something came up." Moving back to the sitting area, I sat next to Dad and tucked my head in his chest. My whole body trembled as the tears stained my cheeks, each drop bleeding the life from me. Strong arms wrapped around me and rocked me back and forth.

"It's all right, baby girl. Everything will be all right," he assured, rubbing my back in slow circles.

Dad was a great lawyer. He had a way with people and could talk his way out of anything. Such conviction and gentle persuasion almost made me believe his words.

Almost.

24

Work proved to be a useful distraction. The rapid activity kept me going for several hours. Through the drink orders and café chatter, I stayed in tune with my cell phone, anticipating the slightest vibration from my pocket. Dad checked into a hotel until Monday and promised to alert me on any updates.

Nadine watched me from the corner of her eye, waiting for that nervous breakdown right around the bend. Caleb must have told her the news, because she kept asking me if I was all right.

When Mia and Dougie showed up during my break, I lost it. Mia was the only one to ever see me do the Nasty Cry, so I didn't mind using her shirt as a handkerchief. I sat in the backseat of her car with my head on her lap.

"I like Ms. M., I really do." Mia brushed my hair with her hand. "She's way cooler than my mom."

"Your mom lets you do whatever you want." I sniffed.

"Because she doesn't care. She gives me things so I can get out of her hair. 'Go to the mall, Mia,' or, 'Take my credit card and go get something nice, on me.' You know, my first 'woman talk' was with your mom."

I lifted my head. "The ones with the sock puppets?"

"Yeah. That's why I always came over to your house. Your mom actually worried about me."

Dougie squeezed my shoulder. "I liked your mom too. She was weird, but she was pretty."

Mia's hands flew over my ears. "Stop using past tense, Dougie! She ain't dead. She's just hospitalized."

Dougie lowered his head. "Sorry."

"It's cool." I sat up and eyed the clock on the dashboard. "My break's almost up. I'll see you guys later."

After serving hugs all around, I climbed out and put my suit of armor back on. Nadine's eyes tracked me as soon as I entered the building.

"You going to talk to Caleb?"

Brushing past her, I reached for my apron. "I'm not in the mood."

"He worries about you. And you need to know what's going on as soon as possible."

I turned to her. "What's going on with his dad? I've never seen Caleb get so defensive. If anything, I should be the one freaking out. It's my mom he hurt, not his."

"Maybe you should talk to Caleb."

"You may need to wait in line, my dear." A voice called from the counter. Nadine and I jumped at the same time. Mr. Ross propped his hip against the counter, wearing a smile that personified conquest. "Good afternoon, Samara. How is your mother?"

"Like you care," I sneered.

Nadine pushed me behind her. "State your business and leave, Mr. Ross."

"Petrovsky, I remember when you were this tall." He

measured to his mid-thigh and smiled. "What a beautiful woman you've become. Just like your mother."

"What do you want?" Nadine asked again, her tone dripping with venom.

A hint of fear flashed in his eyes, breaking down his reserved disposition for a second. "Now Nadine, we don't want to cause a scene. I'm just remarking on how beautiful you are, especially when angry." Casting a sly glance to the customers, Mr. Ross said, "You're positively . . . *glowing.*" His eyes grew wide to underline his meaning.

Taking the hint, Nadine gasped and snapped her eyes shut.

Smiling in triumph, he continued. "Now that the pleasantries are over, have either of you ladies seen my son? I have a few issues to address with him."

"I'm sure you can contact him by phone," Nadine said, her voice trembling from anger.

"He's not exactly returning my calls, so I decided to see him in person." He looked around Nadine to lock eyes on me. "Samara, come here, sweetheart."

I approached the object of my scorn without question, without resistance, and without a bit of back talk. Though fully aware of my actions, and of the string of what I was sure was Polish cursing behind me, it didn't even occur to me to refuse. When I reached the counter, he brushed a curl away from my face and caressed my cheek. He looked so much like Caleb; it scared me.

"No wonder my son is possessive of you," he said with a secretive smile, as if amused at some joke that only he knew about. "We have a lot to discuss, you and I, but right now, would you be so kind as to tell me where I can locate my son?"

My stomach clenched in tight spasms, as if trying to regurgitate the words.

"Get away from her," a voice growled behind him,

shattering my enchantment. Mr. Ross turned to see Caleb in full attack mode.

Backing away from the counter, Mr. Ross lifted his hands in surrender. "There's no need for that. I simply want to talk to you."

Caleb nudged his head toward the exit. "Outside."

As Mr. Ross limped ahead, Caleb looked at Nadine with narrowed eyes and mouthed the words, *Watch her.*

Nadine nodded and pulled me inside the back kitchen before I could object. Her hands gripped my shoulders and she hunched down, making direct eye contact. Her limbs trembled as sweat broke from her forehead and upper lip. The intensity of her gaze startled me.

"Look at me!" Nadine commanded, shaking my arms. "Look at me, Sam. What do you see?"

"I see your face—more than what I would like to right now."

"Close your eyes." When I hesitated, she shook me again. I shut my eyes, and she asked, "What do you see?"

"Darkness. Nadine, what's going—"

"You don't see Mr. Ross's face, his eyes, any image at all?"

"No."

Pushing out a breath, she released me. "Good."

I opened my eyes and saw her slumped against the dishwasher. Her muscles locked as she gripped the metal surface. I'd never seen her so spooked out before, which only shot my panic level to an all-new high. "What was that about?"

"Mr. Ross is very strong Cambion, and he knows how to use his power."

"You think he used it on me?" I asked.

She sucked in a breath of air in an attempt to regain composure. "I know he did. I needed to know how much."

That didn't make any sense. "Caleb said I was immune to the draw."

She wiped the sweat from her forehead and readjusted her bun. "Caleb's draw, yes, because he is still young. His father is older and stronger. He can turn the enticement on and off in a flash. No woman can oppose him when he lays on the charm. Even I am affected to extent. He is too strong, in fact. This means only one thing." She trailed off as some great insight struck her.

"What?"

"I told you, it is not good to consume entire life. You become more demon than human, but you also gain power. Mr. Ross is on the brink and he wants more. Could you not sense his hunger?"

"Not really." It wasn't a lie; I was just too preoccupied by my own hunger to notice.

She nodded. "Your willfulness and purity counteract the draw, making your resistance high. Your reaction is not severe as most; you're still able to complete a thought on your own."

I shrunk back. Did everyone know about my lack of a sex life? Was it on a billboard somewhere? I guess if it served as a blockade against the forces of darkness, I'd have it tattooed on my forehead.

"I had a bit of a pull toward him, Nadine," I confessed.

She snorted. "That is expected. He gave heavy signals just now. Any other woman would have leaped over counter and taken him right there."

I couldn't wrap my mind around that. There was no way I would jump stupid or degrade myself for the sake of gratification. But then again, I still owned my free will . . . for now.

"Why would he want to mess with me or my mom?" I asked. "We haven't done anything to him."

Nadine inched to the swinging doors and peeked outside. "Doesn't matter. It will affect you anyway. And now you know what he is, he might come after you."

"Why?"

She remained on edge, her eyes shifting to every moving creature in the café. "If he sees you as threat, he will hurt you."

I joined her side by the door. "What about Caleb? I'm his son's girlfriend."

"That will not stop him if you're an obstacle. And as you can tell, he's not above hurting those close to him."

The finality in her tone made my ire skyrocket. Mr. Ross may have had everyone else scared, but he had messed with the wrong chick. I didn't do powerless and wasn't about to sit by and let tragedy happen to me. Regardless of blood ties, if things had to come to blows, then Caleb's dad was going to end up missing.

Nadine held the door for me. "We got more customers. Caleb will explain everything later, all right?"

Speechless, I returned to the workstation with a fresh batch of anger and paranoia. Nadine's consoling hand on my shoulder only solidified that everything was far from all right.

25

An hour later, Caleb returned to the café and conducted his own examination.

He checked my pulse; made me follow his finger, along with light and reflex tests. He all but whipped out a Breathalyzer to prove I wasn't under the influence of Big Daddy's mojo.

Once satisfied, he pushed out a long breath. "I'm following you to the hospital tonight, just in case."

"Just in case of what?"

"Just in case," he repeated with a determination that seemed foreign.

Nadine paced behind us. "Have you called your brothers?"

"Yeah, Brodie's catching a red-eye from London, so he should arrive tomorrow. Michael said he's getting the first flight out, and he should be here no later than Monday."

My head swung between them. "Guys, if you're trying to freak me out, you're doing a bang-up job."

Caleb rubbed my arms. "I'm sorry, but we need to make sure your mother's safe. That's our top priority."

"What did your dad talk to you about?" I asked.

"I'll explain it tonight when we have more privacy." He tilted his head, indicating the two dozen ears and eyes swarming the café. "Nadine and I will follow you to the hospital."

"I gotta stop by the house and change first."

"That's fine. We go where you go." His stern features told me that the decision was not merely a suggestion, but an undisputed fact.

After the store closed, I called Dad en route to the house and updated him about Mr. Ross. Omitting the otherworldly element of my suspicion, I provided enough reason for Dad to keep his eyes peeled. To my absolute horror, he told me that a man fitting Mr. Ross's description tried to visit earlier today, but was denied because visiting hours were over. I almost crashed my car. He assured me that there was an abnormal number of police officers circling the hospital, probably courtesy of Caleb's phone call, which brought my heart rate back to a reasonable pace.

As promised, Caleb and Nadine escorted me to the house. It was a good thing, too. Turning off the car engine, it then occurred to me how forsaken and sideshow-spooky my house looked with no inside lights. Holding a can of mace in hand, I crept toward the porch until the security lights brightened the lawn. Mom had spared no expense when it came to security. She had the interactive security service that called when stuff went down. The porch light afforded enough voltage to light Vegas for two days and blind any possible assailant.

Nadine entered the house and did a quick sweep of the

second floor while Caleb searched downstairs. I stood against the front door, clutching my bag, and feeling the terror rise in the back of my throat. When Caleb returned, he motioned me to the living room and took a seat.

Sitting across from him, I cracked my knuckles. "Is this the part where you tell me what the hell is going on?"

"Where do I start?" he asked, more to himself than to his audience.

"Your dad."

His weary eyes looked up at me. "How much time do you have?"

"As long as it takes."

Pinching the bridge of his nose, he laid it all on the table. "Okay. My father is not in his right mind and very dangerous."

"I figured that much, but what level of crazy are we working with here?" I asked.

He raked a hand through his hair. "Let me go back. It started around seven years ago when my mom was first diagnosed with cancer. There were a few signs then, but we were too focused on Mom to pay attention. When Mom died, he snapped, and a part of him died too. His spirit wasn't going to let him get away with that, so it took over for a while. And that's when the incidents began."

I shifted in my seat. "Go on. You can't be this foreboding without good reason."

His gaze lowered to the floor when he continued. "Shortly after mom's death, women in London were starting to disappear, as well as in Dublin. Their bodies were found days later, all dead from shock or heart failure. The coincidence was too uncanny, especially in those places. It was better than any fingerprint."

"Why those cities?" Nadine asked, strolling around the living room and eyeing photos on the walls.

"My mom was from London, and they met in Dublin," he replied. "He was reenacting the beginning of their relationship. Every one of his victims had curly brown hair and blue eyes, like my mom."

Nadine stopped in front of the fireplace and picked up my baby picture. "Like fantasy role-playing?"

Caleb shrugged. "I'm just explaining the motive here. He's going through a type of spiritual withdrawal. The emotions, the energy he had with mom were unique and potent, and it isn't there anymore. His spirit recognized it as a good source of energy. Now dad feeds irregularly, and he doesn't care if women die or not. He just knows he needs to soothe the loss. The spirit's energy deficit on top of my dad's own grief made him delusional. He thinks by finding women similar to Mom, it might pacify the need."

"Can't he use an alternative source of energy?" I asked. "You've been using sugar for years."

Narrowed eyes shot in my direction. "And look how far that got me. We sustain by consuming human life energy. Just like me, he's letting the spirit take over and binge, just to sate the ache. By the time we all figured out what was going on, he had already killed five women."

I jumped. "Five!"

Nadine spun around, wearing a similar look of horror. "What do you mean *already*? As in that was just the beginning."

"I only know about five," Caleb admitted. "I have no idea what he's done between the time I left and now."

"Wait a minute. You're telling me your dad is a psychotic serial killer who's after my mom." When Caleb nodded, I yelled, "And his ass isn't in jail?"

"There's no evidence that he was involved. All the autopsy reports prove is that the women suffered cardiac arrest. No charge would stick. Trust me, I've called the police several times."

"So your dad just runs around free and clear?" I asked.

"He's under suspicion. Detectives follow him, but they don't have any solid evidence to convict him."

I couldn't believe this. How could he just let his dad continue to murder innocent women? Women like Mom.

"Why haven't you done anything?" I yelled.

Caleb sat up straight, his face hard with indignation. "You think I haven't? I've done *everything* in my power to put him away. I've taken him to mental wards, but they release him a week later."

"Why?"

"From outside appearances, he's quite sane; and as *you* realize, very persuasive with females. Have you noticed how many nurses, psychiatrists, and medical directors are women?"

My jaw dropped. "Omigod."

"We've tried everything, we've drugged him, and we've put him on house arrest. My brothers take shifts staying with dad, making sure he's cared for. Haden is more connected, more sympathetic to dad than the rest of us and spends the summer at his cottage in Brussels. Lately, Dad's been asking for me specifically, needing to reacquaint our spirits, as required. But I couldn't be anywhere near him. I haven't returned his calls, and I usually delete his messages. He even sent Haden to come and find me, and we all know how well that turned out. Since they share a strong connection, dad tracked Haden to Virginia in order to find me, and he's been here ever since. Three weeks, exactly." Caleb stared at the opposite side of the room.

"He's been biding his time, moving slow so not to rouse suspicion. He's been following me, watching me at work. . . ." Caleb's eyes, wide and haunted, latched to

mine. "Watching me with you. He was there at the poetry meeting, and yet he couldn't work up the courage to
show himself."

Using my fingers, I did a head count of the casualties.
"So, including the lady at the poetry reading, that's six
women total—that we know about. You're dad has
killed six women, and no one is doing shit about it. He's
really hell-bent on becoming a demon, isn't he?"

Caleb blanched, then cut his eyes to Nadine.

Nadine returned the look, but with more hostility.
"She shouldn't be in the dark about us. Not now."

In silent acquiescence, Caleb continued. "The transformation requires several lives to be consumed at once. The
murders were spread too far apart for the energy to build
up. The power that comes with it is addictive. As he gets
stronger, so will his hunger. He'll certainly reach his
quota if not stopped.

"My father is beyond redemption. Before, he was consumed with grief, but at least he felt something remotely
human. Now, he's becoming what Cambions fear most, a
creature of vice. But there's a calculated method to his
madness. He told me today how he met your mother
with every intention of feeding, but he couldn't do it right
then. He wanted to take his time with her, play with his
food. He's made his pursuits a sport, singling out those
who resemble mom."

My stomach lurched. "You think he's going to go after
my mom again?"

The light and warmth behind his eyes was snuffed out.
"I know he will."

I pushed back the bile creeping up my throat. "Why?"

"She triggered a response in my dad that he hasn't had
since mom. He's curious and hungry."

"Curious?"

"The fact that your mother is still alive makes him curious. She must have had a hell of a resistance. She might be lonely, but she acts like you: guarded, sarcastic, no-nonsense. That's kinda what drew me to you."

My upper lip curled. "That's gross."

"It's the thrill of the chase. And your mother sparked his interest. That's all he would talk about today, but he slipped once and called her by my mom's name. And then there's you."

I jumped. "What about me?"

He held me with a look that stopped my blood circulation. "He might go through you to get to his prize."

Having heard enough, Nadine stood up, ready to take action. "How do we stop him?"

Caleb dropped his head into his hands. Curling his fingers into his hair, he said, "Keep Sam and her mother away from him until we can figure out what to do. He's not full demon yet, so he can still be killed. That's one advantage we have. And I plan to use it."

I took a shower, hoping to wash away the past twenty-four hours. I'd never delved into such spirituality before, but this tiled cubicle became my temple, a place of peace with healing waters of absolution.

I should've left while I had the chance. As soon as Caleb told me what he was, I could've kicked his scrawny butt to the curb. No measure of stupidity could equal mine right now, and Mom would pay the price for my error.

It was easy to identify the irony in this situation. People hailed Samara Marshall as the last person to get into a relationship, and now, here I was, smack dab in the middle of the weirdest kind imaginable. If this summer's events weren't a reason to steer clear of guys, nothing was.

And my poor mother's warnings and cautionary tales

did nothing but make her another victim. There was a belief that one perpetuates one's fears. The amount of energy and concentration invested in something will force it to manifest. The trick was to use that brainpower for good, yet it had clearly backfired on my mother.

I tried not to notice Mom's shampoo and loofah on the shower rack. I couldn't look at her monogrammed towel hanging on the door, or her toothbrush and contact solution on the sink. Caleb told me I would go through a stage of guilt, but no amount of forewarning could soften the blow.

Stepping out of the shower, I cataloged the little things that used to annoy me, how my perfume and conditioner would wind up missing, or how Mom used my bathroom instead of her own, or the eighties rock ballads that blared through the walls while she got dressed. This house was a three-dimensional postcard of my mother. Everywhere I turned was a relic of her existence, a shell with no life inside it. All good things must end, but this one just might take me with it.

Once dressed, I packed a bag while plotting an exit strategy. I was in over my head. School began in three weeks and a law degree waited in my future. My dream car sat in a dealership parking lot, calling my name. I had a family to protect, but all thoughts shot back to Caleb. I cared deeply for him; a part of me ached and feared for him, but not enough to throw my life away.

The knock on the door made me jump. "Who is it?"

"It's me," Caleb called through the door. "Are you decent?"

"No, but I'm dressed. Come in."

Poking his head inside, he surveyed the war zone of my bedroom. "Wow, are there any bodies in here?"

"Not yet," I grumbled. "What's up?"

"My brother called while you were in the shower. He

should be here some time tomorrow night, but he told us to start looking for hotels now. Brodie says dad likes the smaller inns, like bed-and-breakfasts or boarding houses. If we find him, we can find Haden. So after I take you to the hospital, Nadine and I are going to check around and ask if anyone's seen him."

"That's fine, do what you gotta do." Knowing it was a long shot, I still had to add, "In fact, I can go to the hospital by myself."

He stepped closer and tipped his head to the side. "I really don't want to argue about this. I promised to protect you and that's exactly what I'll do."

"No offense, but that's not gonna help me sleep at night, Mr. I-don't-fight. And your judo classes just started."

"I won't need them if I have this." Caleb lifted his shirt, exposing the butt of a handgun poking out of his pants.

Why wasn't I surprised? This was the South; everyone and their mother owned a weapon. Since Mom practically raised me at the shooting range, my only concern was whether Cake Boy knew how to use the damn thing. Those who couldn't fight were the first to whip out a gun.

Although, I had to admit, nothing said "back the hell up" like a loaded firearm, which was exactly what I did.

"Good luck getting that through the airport," I quipped. "Where did you get that anyway?"

"Brodie gave it to me the last time he was stateside." Watching my slow retreat, he dropped his shirt and hid the gun from view. "Don't worry. I know how to use it."

I wiped the imaginary sweat from my brow. "Phew, that's a load off my mind. Too bad you didn't use it today when your dad came into work."

"It was locked in my car; I couldn't get to it. My dad isn't stupid. He wanted us to meet out in the open for a reason. I know you're scared, but please trust me."

I tumbled back, utterly blown away by his audacity. Squaring my shoulders, I let him have it. "Trust you? Are you serious? Since day one, you've been hiding the truth from me, and your communication skills suck! I know this isn't something you want to alert the media about, and I appreciate you trying to save me from the 'Big Bad,' but giving your *girlfriend* a heads-up that your dad is a demonic psycho would've been ideal! I've seen enough weird shit this summer to dull me to whatever shock you might throw my way. And I'm *still* here with you, yet I barely know who you are, Mr. Baker—if that is your real name." I jabbed a finger into his chest for good measure.

He caught my hand in his and held it to his heart. That firm yet gentle touch stopped the flow of venom from escaping my mouth.

His eyes shimmered on the brink of tears, but never shed a drop. Crying and heavy bursts of emotion seemed alien to him, like the many languages he couldn't understand.

"Baker was my mother's maiden name. I changed it once I turned eighteen in rebellion, and it made it harder for them to find me. And you know three main things about me that matter: I'm not like most people, I promised to protect you, even from myself, and that I'm in love with you. Everything else is gravy."

The sound of the L word from his lips made my knees buckle, but I kept my resolve. I simply logged the sentiment away to review at a later date, a free time when people I cared about weren't in mortal peril.

Taking my hand back, I grabbed my bag and threw it over my shoulder. "I don't wanna talk about this now. I gotta go see my mom."

He lowered his gaze to the floor and nodded. "But we will talk about it," he vowed as I brushed past him to leave the room.

26

The sleepless night began once I entered the waiting room and caught the angry look on Dad's face.

With language that would get him banned from his church, he revealed how Mr. Peter Marshall, otherwise known as Mr. Absentee-Grandpa, had graced the hospital with his presence. Ignoring Dad, Grandpa had thrown his weight and money around, as if he had a right after seventeen years of abandonment. When he insisted that Mom stay at his house to recuperate, Dad just about hit the ceiling.

The two went into a long-awaited scrap, bringing up two decades of animosity and making their personal business available to staff members and patients. Security intervened before the two men came to blows. Grandpa shot a parting threat to enforce legal action and some crap about power of attorney.

I was thankful for missing the fallout. I haven't cussed anyone out in a good minute, and Grandpa was a perfect target to unleash my manner of hell. Once the nurse's back turned, I snuck inside Mom's room for five minutes, just to touch her and find physical evidence of her vitality.

She looked so fragile lying there, wrapped in tubes with monitors twittering away. The nurse had reported that Mom was coming in and out of consciousness, so I wasn't too surprised when her eyes fluttered open. Attempting a smile that looked painful, she asked if I was okay. Even now, she worried about her baby, which brought another bout of tears.

The medicine made her a bit loopy, but that didn't prepare me for the next question from her mouth. "Where's Nathan? Is he all right?"

I had to shake myself out of the daze and reel in all composure. There was no proper response to that question, none that would prevent my admission into the loony bin. Recalling her reaction when Caleb first came to my house, I knew it was a lost cause to pitch a fit about Mr. Ross. I assured her that he was fine, and insisted that she get her rest.

After leaving her room, I ate stale Cheetos and juggled phone calls from Mia, Nadine, and Caleb. The game of phone tag lasted for hours, resulting in several trips outside to use my cell, because my service provider doesn't like hospitals. Nadine and Caleb had searched over twenty hotels on the main strip and found not a whisper of Mr. Ross or Haden's whereabouts. The frustration and fatigue channeling through the phone were becoming contagious.

"Yes," I said, assuring Caleb for the millionth time. "I promise I'm—"

A tall figure stood between the cars, watching me. The night masked his face, but not the chill of his presence. The man embodied a persistence that put Mia's stalker technique to shame, practically daring me to make a move.

"Sam?" Caleb called.

I tried to respond, but nothing came out.

"Sam?" Caleb said, his voice pitching a little. "Are you okay? What's happening?"

Two words managed to escape. "He's here."

I ended the call and raced back inside. That probably scared Caleb into the next life, but I needed to find refuge and stand guard around Mom.

Peering out of the window, I did surveillance of the parking lot when a commotion by the entrance caught my eye. A team of doctors pulled a man under a sheet out of a car and loaded him on a gurney. Caleb and Nadine raced onto the scene, shoving their way toward the doors. Seeing the man under the sheet, Caleb grabbed at the sheet, almost pulling the man off the stretcher. Telling by how Caleb fought and reached for the victim, it couldn't have been Mr. Ross, but someone of more significance. A doctor pushed Caleb back, urging him to stay behind and let them work. After a few attempts at reason, Caleb complied and remained behind the procession.

I searched the parking lot and saw no sign of Mr. Ross, not that I expected him to remain at the scene. He may have disappeared from sight, but this wasn't over. The question was, could I fight him off? If what Nadine had said was true, if that draw could persuade me, how could I repel it? It was one thing to fight an outside force, but it was another thing to fight one's own mind.

Staring out to the waiting area, I took in the illusion of normal: the plastic chairs, florescent lights, and the dozing loved ones of the sick. All these things met the naked eye, so people had no reason to look any further. Even Dad, the strongest man I knew, was blind to what lurked in the dark.

A part of me envied it, wanting more than anything to go back to the first week of summer, a time where I could say in all confidence that the bogeyman wasn't real. But that dream had ended and there was no going back to sleep. There was nothing left to do now but find another insomniac to help me.

All arrows pointed to Caleb, which ticked me off even more. I didn't want to need him, but he was the only operative in my brigade, forcing me to break down and dry swallow that pill of pride.

As if thought alone conjured him there, Caleb rushed from the elevators, panic-stricken and out of breath. His sweaty brown hair was plastered to his forehead as he whipped around the hall. After spotting me, he stopped short and pulled me into his arms.

"You scared the hell out of me," he whispered.

I knew he wasn't lying. His body shook as his heart pounded against my chest. Peering over his shoulder, I saw Nadine standing next to us.

A somber cloud darkened her features. "We found Haden unconscious in a car in the parking lot. His father must have brought him here. He's got a nasty knot on his head. The doctors are looking at him now downstairs."

It wasn't what I expected, but at least one puzzle got solved. "Is he all right?"

"He's alive. That's all that matters."

His response gave me a chill. "What happened to him? Was your dad holding him hostage the whole time?"

"Looks that way. He's wearing the same clothes he had on when he came to my house. I can only imagine what he's gone through."

"You said you saw Mr. Ross?" Nadine broke in.

"Yeah, he was standing in the parking lot, just watching me."

Nadine frowned with concern. "Did he make eye contact? Did you feel an urge to go to him?"

"No, I didn't stay long enough for his roommate to pull me in."

She looked puzzled. "His roommate?"

"That's what she calls it," Caleb joined in. "But anyway, we need to wait until Brodie and Michael get here to work up a plan. How's your mother?"

"She's doing pretty well, except for the fact that she asked for your dad."

Nadine shook her head. "That's not good."

"I'll say," I said.

"No, that means she might still be under his draw." Nadine looked around the waiting room. "We should be fine for now, but once she is strong enough, she might try to seek him out."

My smile dropped. "Tell me you're kidding."

"Trust me; we need to grab him before he does any more harm," Caleb said grimly.

A deep voice behind me made me jump. "Excuse me."

"Dad!" I cried, whipping around to see him.

"Aren't you going to introduce me to your friends?" Dad asked, sizing up the man next to me.

"Um, yeah. Daddy, this is Nadine Petrovsky. She works with me at the café. And this is my boyfriend, Caleb Baker." Stepping aside, I motioned for Caleb to walk toward his imminent demise.

When they shook hands, Caleb didn't even flinch at Dad's kung fu grip.

"Nice to meet you, young man. I hear you've taken an interest in my daughter?"

Caleb held his own, looking the big man square in the eye. "I have, sir. I care a lot about her."

"I was wondering if I could take a moment of your time to talk." Dad stretched his arm to point toward the chairs in the back, indicating that his statement wasn't a question.

Lifting his head high, Caleb began his death march toward the mother of all inquisitions.

"Want a Jolly Rancher?" Nadine held a bag of hard candy in front of me, a welcoming distraction. "I have feeling this will be a while. Let's sit and you can tell me how you'll make honest man out of Caleb."

I fished out a cherry-flavored one, then took a seat. "It's a little too soon for that."

"It is never too soon to plan, and the best ones require time." Nadine sat next to me and sucked down her sour-apple treat.

"Since the beginning, you've been pushing me on Caleb. Why do you think I'm such a good match for him?" I popped the candy in my mouth.

"Because you're both stubborn and guarded, yet secretly crave passion. You both battle duality and war with your identity. You know what it's like to exist in two worlds, and you love sweets as much as he does." She looked at me, her eyes twinkling with humor. "He speaks of you often. It is usually complaint, yet his eyes glow with desire. He loves the fight in you."

Wow! It's hard being called out on so many issues at once. I wasn't ready to look into that mirror, so I steered the conversation elsewhere. "So, his spirit likes willful women?"

"No, is not that. Women constantly throw themselves at Caleb. To have one out of hundreds not give a damn if he lives or dies is refreshing. The human side of him gravitates to it; it is intriguing. In time, the spirit will recognize your presence and accept it," she encouraged, but I wasn't getting my hopes up.

"I can't think about that right now. This is all new to me, and I need to get my mom squared away."

"I understand, but those who know about us stay close to us. We have difficulty letting them go, hence the issue with Mr. Ross." Nadine took a deep breath. "The torment of losing his wife drove him insane. We love very, very deeply, Sam, because we don't do it often. We cannot afford to, as you can see."

"Caleb said that about me."

"Maybe you two are meant for each other."

I gave her a hard look. "Can we focus on Mr. Ross instead of playing matchmaker?"

"I call it like I see it. Caleb never acts this way around any woman. In fact, he has been distant these few years."

"I should say so. His dad is a killer. When an animal is lame or ill, the humane thing to do is put it down," I intoned.

"You sound like Caleb. You know real reason he's in the States? To flee his father and avoid temptation to kill him. He was determined to do what his brothers could not. Caleb tells me that he tried to kill Mr. Ross twice: once with poison, then tried to shoot him in his sleep."

The reply was like a punch in the face. That didn't sound like the Caleb I knew. "Really? What happened?"

"Obviously, it didn't work. Caleb says he came close, but he couldn't do it."

"Why?"

"Our spirits are connected to their source. Their instinct is self-preservation. The spirit will not harm itself, and it will not allow us to either."

"So Caleb didn't kill him because Capone is still tight with Big Daddy's spirit."

Nadine's lip twitched, fighting the urge to laugh.

"You have strange way of summing things up," she said. "But yes, that is the problem. The deeper the bond to spirit, the less we can harm its source. Caleb is not close with his spirit. He ignored it for years, ignored our advice and teachings. His detachment is blessing and curse. I heard he shot Mr. Ross in the leg. Caleb has excellent shot, by the way. Have you seen his crossbow?"

Nadine boasted as though having a trigger-happy friend was run-of-the-mill. But at least it explained why Mr. Ross had a limp.

"So what do we do now?" I asked, steering the topic back to our present dilemma.

"You can tell me whether or not you love Caleb."

I scowled. "Oh, so you gonna grill me now?"

"Better me than Caleb's brothers. They don't play nice." She looked at me for a moment and repeated her question. "Do you love him?"

"If I do, I can't identify it. I have no source to draw from. I feel deeply, but that could mean anything. Plus, he's got enough baggage to sink a cruise liner. How could I possibly get past this?"

Nadine nodded. "Now you see why we can't love freely like others do? It takes a strong person to love who we are, and when we find that one person, it's impossible to let them go. I know the grief of lost love, a pain I wish on no one. So if you are not sure, you need to end it now before it's too late, before his spirit is used to having you around."

"That sounds sinister."

"It doesn't have to be if you feel the same. You must be sure. For your sake as well as Caleb's."

"No pressure, Sam, really," I sighed.

"No pressure at all," Nadine returned with a wink.

When the Man Meeting adjourned, Dad dismissed Caleb with a handshake laced with fatal caveats. Seated in the corner, Dad flipped open his laptop as if pleased to know that my virtue was intact. Caleb reached our side of the room, looking exhausted and confused.

"How did it go?" I asked.

He shook his head slowly. "I'm not sure."

I patted his arm in consolation. "Well, you're still alive, so I guess it went stellar."

"What did he say to you?" Nadine asked.

Caleb kissed the top of my head, then pulled up a chair to sit across from me. "He asked me what my intentions were. I told him that we were just dating, and it was too early to make any major decisions."

"See." I bumped Nadine in the arm.

"He was pretty concerned about our age difference. He called me a cradle robber and a few other names that I didn't understand. Then he said something about you, and then I was completely lost. What exactly is a tenderoni?"

"The San Francisco treat?" Nadine offered.

I rolled my eyes. "No, that's my dad showing his true age. He and Mom need to let the eighties rest in peace."

"He wanted to know why I haven't gone to school, and I think he understood my reason."

"Did you tell him what's going on?" Nadine asked.

"I told him that your mother's date frightened her and probably caused her attack. And that he was creeping around the hospital, and we shouldn't risk anything until she's recovered. He was pretty shocked that your mother didn't take extra precautions. Your mom has a reputation for being a bit paranoid."

"Understatement of the decade, dude," I scoffed. "Did you tell him who the mystery date really was?"

Caleb stared at me. "Are you kidding me? The less he knows about this whole thing, the better. I just need him to keep guard around your mother until we handle this."

I concurred. The last thing anyone needed was my dad to get involved. "So what have you decided?"

"We gotta trap Dad somehow. Maybe drug him again?" Caleb suggested.

"We will see what your brothers say." Nadine rose from her seat. "I'm going to check on Haden. You two love-birds talk. You have sorting out to do." With a knowing smirk, she moved toward the elevators.

Once we were alone, Caleb turned his focus on me. "What's she talking about?"

"She's a-fixin' to get us hitched," I drawled in my best country accent.

"And what did you say?"

"I said, 'No thank you, I'll just have the salad.'"

Looking down, a wide, face-splitting smile crept forth. "You know, if someone asked me that two months ago, I would have laughed in their face, but now . . ."

"But now what?"

His eyes met mine again. "It's still funny."

I winked. "Right back at ya."

He held both my hands in his own, his fingers tracing over each knuckle. "Sam, we have plenty of time to sort it all out. I just need to know that you're willing to try."

"Do I have to answer you now? I can't make decisions like that at the moment. Wait until my mom recovers and your dad is dealt with before I give you my answer."

"Fair enough. Am I still the champion of your celestial domain?" He tucked in his lips to fend off the laughter.

This guy would never let that go. "For now. You've survived my father's gauntlet. Wear your badge with honor."

"I will." Wetting his lips, he pinched his eyes shut. "Sam, I wanna kiss you so bad. My lips are burning."

Boy, did I know the feeling. I also knew that neither of us was going to do jack about it. Taking his hand, I stood up. "Come on, they've got ice cream in the cafeteria. That should cool you off."

The prospect of dessert brightened his face. "Really? What kind? You know I have a thing for chocolate."

"Obviously," I muttered, leading him to the elevators.

27

The next day at work, I was a walking zombie, immune to the electroshock treatment of caffeine and energy drinks.

My head remained plastered against the counter, not caring if Linda walked by, or if the Four Horsemen of the Apocalypse needed an iced latté. Nadine was a saint to pick up the slack.

I was glad it was Sunday. The store closed at six, and I could make it to the hospital in time for visiting hours. Nadine must have read my mind, because she zipped through the workstation, wrapping food and cleaning like crazy. I didn't even bother to change. I went straight to the hospital with Nadine following me in her car.

When I got to the waiting room, I saw Dad in varying hues of pissed off. Turns out Grandpa made another attack, demanding that his daughter be released and placed in his custody as soon as possible. As the king of tobacco and a lofty contributor to the city's funding, the Marshall name carried some serious weight in this town. Having the state senator and local officials as golf partners made it unwise for anyone to get on Grandpa's bad side.

The doctor insisted that Mom wasn't ready to be released for another few days, which gave us time to stall. In the meantime, Mom was transferred to a private suite on the ninth floor.

The ninth floor, which I soon nicknamed "The Penthouse," was a private retreat set away from those filthy HMO peasants. With hotel motif, soft lighting, and a cushy sofa, all that was missing were the cabana boy and the complimentary hot towel. Grandpa's guilt sure rode him hard, because he spared no expense in seeing that Mom was well-treated and heavily guarded. I had to show ID and sign in at the front desk before I was escorted to my mom's suite.

Opening Mom's room door, I found her sitting up in the middle of the bed, looking out of the window. She was in no condition to move, let alone attempt to stand. Every motion looked painful, especially with the IV shackling her down.

"Mom, are you all right? You need to lie down."

She didn't seem to hear me, so I stepped closer. She didn't look at me when I reached her side. Her gaze stayed glued to the window. Orange sunlight leaked through the blinds, making the room look and feel like the inside of an oven.

"I know you hate being cooped up in here, but you need to keep still until you get better." I brushed her curly hair from her face. She was unresponsive, at best. She barely blinked and the only sounds in the room were the monitors and her heavy breathing. Soon, she was panting like a dog in heat.

"Mom, are you warm? I could open the window," I offered.

Lifting the blinds, I searched the pane and found no opening. Just as I was about to turn away, I saw it: the reason for Mom's zombie state, the cause of her erratic breathing, and the source of my ever-increasing panic.

Mr. Ross stood in the middle of the parking lot, staring up at the window. How Mom knew he was there was a mystery, but she seemed in tune with his presence from a mental antenna. His stare reached through twenty yards and half an inch of glass to assault my sanity. Everything in my body screamed for me to turn away, to not look at his eyes, but my feet couldn't move. Slowly, my hand reached for the string of the blinds and pulled. The band of shade sliced across my vision, shattering the trance. After closing the blinds, I rushed to Mom's side and laid her back on the bed.

"No, no!" she moaned. "I need to go. He needs me. He said he needs me."

"Mom, calm down. I need you to lie back."

"No! I have to be with him. I need him!" Her arms flailed around her head.

Ducking fists and nails, I pinned her shoulders still, all the while my heart was breaking. Mom was the bravest woman I knew, and to have things come to this brought me to tears. Summoning strength I never knew she had, she shoved me to the corner of the room. Screaming, she pulled at her hospital gown, clawing at her neck and chest as if she caught a rash and in the process ripped her IV from her arm. A shrill beeping noise filled the room. In seconds, orderlies rushed to our aid.

Mom made a valiant effort to fend them off, but she was outnumbered.

"No, please, I have to be with him! He needs me!" she screamed, her torso lifting off the bed, as her head tossed from side to side. The veins of her neck rose in bas-relief as her face reddened with blood.

"It's all right, Ms. Marshall, just relax," the nurse crooned, sliding the IV back into her arm.

Fighting every step of the way, Mom spat curses at everyone within reach, including me. Realizing that didn't work, she tried a guilt trip. Her head whipped in my direction; her mop of curls fell over her face.

"Samara, baby, why are you doing this to me? Why are you keeping us apart? I thought you would be happy for me. Please, let me go," she begged as the nurse injected a sedative into her arm.

The weight of my sorrow pulled me to the floor, where I curled up and cried. I didn't realize Dad was there until he lifted me into his arms and ushered me outside.

"It's okay, baby, I got you," he whispered and kissed my hair. "Your mother's on heavy medication. She's just having a reaction, that's all."

Man, if only that were true. She was having a reaction all right, and it had nothing to do with drugs. There was too much activity in my head, different themes playing in a series of fear. Having only a blink of sleep and a swig of courage, I needed a target, an outlet.

When we reached the waiting room I found Nadine and Caleb standing by the sign-in desk, watching me in horror.

Dad looked at the familiar pair, then back down at me. "Samara, you wanna tell me what's going on? Why are all these people here?"

"They're here for me, Dad. I told them to come."

"Why? This is a family matter."

"I needed to talk to them. If it's a problem, I'll leave."

"No. It's just . . ." He shot a heated look at Caleb before closing in on me. "You've been acting strange lately, and if it has something to do with that boy—"

"Dad, it's not him. If anything, he keeps me sane. That's why he's here. He's my counselor of sorts."

"You sure? I've got a weird feeling about it."

"That's just because he's a boy. It'll pass. Besides, do you really think I would have him as a boyfriend if I hadn't put him through the wringer?"

That made him smile. "You *are* your mother's daughter." He glanced up at them once more and sighed. "All right, but all these people can't stay here."

"I know. Are you gonna stay with Mom?"

"Yeah, but I gotta head back home before nine. I got work in the morning."

"Not to mention a family at home. I'm surprised Rhonda hasn't dragged you out of here yet."

"Rhonda and I have an understanding that you don't need to worry about. But I do have to get back home." He pulled me in for another hug. "Go on, get some rest and something to eat, and tell that boy to keep his hands to himself."

"Love you, Daddy." I pulled back and made my way to Caleb.

He stood with wide eyes and a huge question mark on his face. Before he could open his mouth, I said, "Let's go. We're having a little meeting. You're gonna tell me what you plan to do about your dad, because if you're not going to handle it, I sure as hell will. Cambion or not, your dad's going down. And if you stand in my way, you're going with him."

It didn't surprise anyone that Mr. Ross had vacated the parking lot. The hospital was placed on high alert, and the increased security on the ninth floor was the only reason Dad left in good conscience. No one but staff and family would pass the sign-in desk.

Police compiled a detailed description of Mr. Ross, though that would do little good if the female staff members had unhappy love lives. This was the only time when equal opportunity was a bad thing, and Mr. Ross exploited women's liberation as his personal playground. Women were everywhere: airport ticket holders, flight attendants, hotel receptionists, police officers, doctors, lawyers, and nuns were all at his service...and his mercy.

We went to visit Haden in recovery. He didn't say much between apologies and swearing, but offered his hand in marriage if Caleb didn't have the "bollocks" to do so. His words, not mine. He confessed that he had been drugged and held against his will for two weeks. Beyond the point of civil compromise, he was more than willing to aid in his father's capture. Seeing that the sedatives and major concussion might slow our progress, Caleb advised that he sit this one out and recover.

For the next three hours Haden's room became our headquarters, where Caleb conducted a conference call with his other brothers. Brodie explained—with a very posh English accent—that he was in the air and would land in a few hours.

In light of all this, both brothers sounded delighted to meet me, more than anyone should given the situation. As the oldest, Brodie gave me a crash course in Cambion 101, via speakerphone. Most of it was pretty simple, stuff I already knew. It intrigued me to learn that Cambions could sense the presence of their chosen mate. Also, the death of a host will result in the spirit's release from the body, a departure that could be seen with the naked eye. All that was well and good, but we were still no closer to finding out how to deal with Big Daddy.

With a phone book splayed on her lap, Nadine called every hotel in the city, which was substantial considering Williamsburg was one big inn. No one knew where Mr. Ross boarded, or how he even entered the country seeing as the brothers confiscated his ID and passport ages ago.

The man had to be stopped. The question was if we wanted him dead or alive. At the moment, all we could do was wait until Michael and Brodie arrived. After the party line ended, Caleb and I worked on alternate means to lure Mr. Ross out of hiding. The method of his father's demise steered the debate, and I could almost see the ten-ton weight settle on Caleb's shoulders.

The loud boom of a phone book hitting the table shot us upright. Finally, after hours of silence, Nadine spoke up. "You may not be able to do it, but when the time comes, I can. I will make it quick and painless."

Caleb left Haden's bedside and touched Nadine's shoulder. "I can't let you do it."

"This man has killed innocent women and will continue to do so if not stopped," she argued. "We have no choice and we are on our own. Lilith is well-disciplined and strong enough to overpower his spirit. When the occasion arises, I am down."

Nadine's enthusiasm melted away some of my stress. At least Caleb and his brothers wouldn't have to take down their own flesh and blood.

"We seem to be the only women who aren't badly affected by the draw," I added, rubbing my throbbing temples. "It only makes sense for one of us to do it."

Caleb rounded on me in fury. "Sam, I don't want you involved in this."

"It's a bit late for that. I'm neck deep in it, and my mom nearly lost her mind over this mess. So whatever you plan to do, I want in."

"I'm not putting you in danger."

"I already am in danger!" His overprotectiveness grated my nerves. "No one is safe around this man, and he has to be stopped. Now quit bossing me around and tell me what you plan to do."

I stood up and moved away from the table—perhaps

too quickly because I developed a head rush. Fatigue finally caught up with me at the most inopportune time. My body and all its components joined together in revolt and abandoned their post. Stumbling in the hall, I leaned against the wall for support. The world grew fuzzy as little lightning tadpoles swam across my vision. Blood pounded my skull as the distance between my head and the floor decreased. But for some reason, I never hit the floor. My feet kicked from under me when an unseen force lifted my body upward.

"I got you." A low, familiar voice whispered in my ear.

Though I enjoyed not having to walk on my own, I made some attempt at protest. "Put me down. I weigh a ton."

"Stop that. You're just fine. Now keep still," Caleb answered tartly as we began to move.

Nadine's head peeked over Caleb's shoulder. "Sam, you need rest. When have you eaten?"

It was difficult to recall. The days congealed into one collective moment. "Last night?" I guessed.

Caleb let out a loud and irritated sigh. "Sam, you need to take care of yourself. You're no good to anyone like this. I'm taking you home before you end up sharing a room with your mother."

Worry crept through his stern demand, and I didn't own the strength to rebel. I buried my head in his chest. The soft thud of his heartbeat and the gentle rocking lulled me in to a dreamless sleep.

After what could have been days or five minutes, a hand shook me awake and a car engine cut off. Voices murmured around me, filled with concern and sympathy. Keys jingled and a car door slammed, making me jump. I was airborne again and cradled in the safety of a man's arms, a man who smelled a lot like cake. A humid blast of air trapped my face and snatched the breath from me, then soon fell away to blessed air-conditioning and a strange beeping noise.

"Sam, you need to turn off the security alarm," Nadine said nervously.

It then occurred to me that I was home, so Nadine's anxiety came with a good reason. With one eye open, I reached over and disabled the security system before the entire Williamsburg Police Department caravanned to my front lawn. With that accomplished, more murmurs occupied the room on my behalf. Nadine remained downstairs while Caleb transported me upstairs in the direction of my bedroom.

"No, I wanna sleep in my mom's room," I whined, pointing across the hall.

"Okay."

We crossed the threshold like a newlywed couple, and Caleb played the role of happy groom to the hilt, laying me ceremoniously on Mom's bed. Keeping with the matrimonial theme, Caleb knelt in front of me as if ready to propose. Instead, he gathered my left foot and unlaced my sneaker.

His nimble fingers pulled at the laces, removing the offending footwear. The footie socks soon followed along with a slow exploration up my ankle before moving on to the next foot. Caleb could make any action look X-rated, or maybe it was just me.

He worked with silent efficiency, engrossed in the solemnity of the task.

I stared, almost hypnotized, as his hair hung in a feathery veil over his face. He looked distant, almost complacent, like a servant who had accepted his fate. There was no task too belittling, to base for him, for he had seen and probably done it all. I also saw the love in his eyes, the wordless devotion, and the longing for true physical contact. Though it was clear what would happen if we went too far, it didn't stop him from dipping his toe in the water.

I couldn't quite put a finger on my feelings about this crazy boy, but somehow he had managed to slip under my radar and steal a piece of my heart.

My shirt fell away, with very little effort on my part. I didn't respond; I grew too distracted by clothing flying in the air in a colorful blur. I must have been out of it, because there was no way in hell I would let a guy undress me. But I was too tired to care if Cake Boy got an eyeful of my goodies.

Caleb was far from a saint, and his wandering eyes validated that point. They drifted down my body, stopping at my small chest and not-so-small abdomen. He'd seen naked women before, but he approached the situation with the fascination of untried youth. Cupping the back of my head, he eased me to lie back, his eyes expanding under a haze of indigo light.

"Well, since we're here, I might as well go all the way." He gave a playful smile and reached for the button in front of my slacks.

"Caleb, if you try anything, I swear . . ." I warned, with little conviction, especially while lifting my hips to aid the disrobing.

"Oh please," he scoffed as the fabric crawled farther away from my body. "You would like that, wouldn't you? Now shut up and keep still."

Ever the gentleman, I thought.

His hands traveled over my inner thigh, making me burn with fever, but Caleb remained diligent in his task.

"Relax, Sam. I've got you," he promised, tossing my pants to the opposite side of the room.

"That's what I'm afraid of."

He stopped. "You're afraid of me?"

"I'm afraid of what you do to me," I confessed.

"Lethargy: the ultimate truth serum." He chuckled and set me up straight. "For what it's worth, you have the same effect on me, if not worse."

"This is abuse, you know," I mumbled under a cloud of cotton that suddenly cast me into darkness. Once light returned, a T-shirt draped my body in a baggy tent.

"Oh, I can tell you're really suffering, you poor baby." He pulled the covers back and tucked me inside.

A moment later, soft pillows and blankets swallowed me whole. The environment embodied safety and familiarity, an oasis for the weary traveler. Enfolded in a cocoon of Mom's floral perfume, I drifted deeper into peaceful oblivion. A warm body spooned behind me, its fingers tracing my arm and rounding the ball of my shoulder. "Sam?"

"Hmm?"

"I have to pick up Brodie in a few hours. Nadine will stay here with you while I run to the airport. You promise to behave while I'm gone?" he teased.

"Uh-huh," I mumbled into the pillow.

Soft lips pressed against my temple, and the weight of his head settled next to mine. His arm snaked across my stomach and dragged me closer to his warmth. With an assuring squeeze, he whispered, "I won't let anything happen to you. I finally found the one thing that's mine. He's not taking that too."

"Okay," was all I could get out before the world disappeared.

28

Somewhere between comatose and coherent, I heard movement stirring in the house.

My eyes fluttered open and focused on the darkness soaking the bedroom. The high beams from a passing car filtered through the blinds, dragging bands of light across the ceiling. Turning onto my back, I traced the left side of the bed, which was now empty. Events of the day slowly returned to memory, and I immediately wanted to go back to sleep. But Nadine had played babysitter long enough, so I forced myself to get up.

More noises came from the bottom floor, low murmurs and thumps; then a light footfall treaded up the stairs. It drew closer, those foreign feet unfamiliar with the creaking wood on the eighth step. That sound could break the deepest sleep, and I gained just enough clarity to recognize the figure in the doorway.

I smiled up at him and admired the familiar bends and slopes of his face. "What are you still doing here? I thought you were going to the airport."

Purple eyes twinkled in the dark in response. Moonlight cut across his features, which took the smooth consistency of marble. "I'll leave in a bit," he said. "Sleep well?"

I sat up and stretched. "Yeah. Where's Nadine?"

"She's asleep, so we have to be real quiet, okay?"

I leaned over to turn on the lamp and noticed that the digital alarm clock was off. No bright red numbers glowed in the dark. In fact, no lights were on in the house save for two purple spheres following my every move.

"Caleb, what's going on?"

Instead of answering, he drew deeper into the room, his eyes locked on mine. His gentle hands slid around my waist, luring me to him with the slightest persuasion. His warmth was inviting, and I couldn't find one good reason to argue. My lids grew heavy as I drifted within that purple mist, surrendering to the weightlessness of dreaming.

"Don't be afraid, Sam. I'm here," he whispered.

Soft fingers touched my cheek, and I welcomed the affection, needing the closeness to ease my fear. The comfort only lasted a second as I began to note something off center. Caleb lacked that sweet, sugary scent that seemed to ooze from his pores. His touches were heavy handed, greedy, and pinched my skin as his grip tightened around my waist.

"Caleb, stop. You're hurting me."

"Not yet."

He wasn't acting like himself. Questions rose to the surface and spread like a violent rash. Had he fed today? Was Capone lashing out again? Maybe seeing his father again had triggered a reaction. Whatever the case may be, I had to get away from him, but I could barely look away, let alone manage a good shove. All my energy had been tapped by one glance, and the luminous glow in his eyes told me he wasn't satisfied. Only when his mouth lowered to kiss me did I find the strength to look away.

"Caleb," I choked out, evading his lips. "Snap out of it. It's Sam."

"I know," he rasped and dove in for another kiss.

"Where's Nadine?" And where was Caleb for that matter?

The more I struggled, the more I realized that this dream had taken an unpleasant turn. My head tossed from side to side, dodging his hungry mouth and fighting to shake out of this nightmare. So imagine my shock when I discovered I was already awake.

Fingers pinched my cheeks and firm lips found mine. A pulling sensation soon followed, and trickles of energy passed my lips, pure, unencumbered potency. I kicked and punched, but he wouldn't move.

"You're a strong one, just like your mother. You've made it difficult for me to get to her now, so you'll make a good substitute. I can wait until she's released to finish what I started."

That was all the clarification I needed. Though he shared a visual and vocal likeness, this was not Caleb. This only meant one thing. I was under the draw, and a powerful one at that. I'd pondered the idea for a while, but now I understood what the draw entailed; that strange gravitational pull that lured women to their death.

No matter how many times I blinked, Caleb's face stared back at me, mocking me for giving away my heart and lowering my guard.

We deceive our prey. With one look, we become who they desire most.

The phrase played over and over in my head like a bad nursery rhyme. Every word of it dug into my brain, its truth striving to take root. It was my mantra, a reminder of who he *really* was. An imposter.

Applying strength born from sheer panic and adrenaline, I served him an upper cut to the jaw. Seizing a window of escape, I raced to the door.

"Get back here!" His hand trapped my waist and tugged me backward.

I clung to the doorjamb for dear life, my nails biting into the wood. "Caleb's your son! How could you hurt him like this? I hope you rot in hell!"

"And what do you know about hell?" he yelled. One tug sent me flying back into the room. My head struck the wall, the impact breaking the picture over Mom's bed. My weight collapsed to the bed, and I shielded my face from falling glass.

The back of my skull felt like a cracked egg, while the shots of pain trickling down my face were its yoke. My ears rang; red lightning bolts flickered across my vision. A hand latched on to my ankle brought me back to the present.

"You've never given your soul to someone you love as I have." His grip moved up my leg, reeling me to him like a rope. "I'm sure you're fun for Caleb and all, but he'll find a replacement."

Screaming and kicking, I reached out for a weapon, a miracle, something. My fingers found the squared edge of Mom's nightstand. I remembered the blade Mom kept hidden inside. I pulled open the drawer, fished out the knife, and allowed Mr. Ross to pull me to him.

As he rolled me over, he yelled at the blade slicing across his face, neck, and arms. I carved and diced blindly; hoping disfigurement would erase the image of Caleb from his face. I knew I struck bone and a couple of good arteries. My shirt clung to my chest, damp and sticky with what I knew was blood. This was a good sign. If he could bleed, he was still human.

A human who could die.

While he wailed and cupped his face, I leapt off the bed and rushed to the door. The knife tucked firmly in my hand, I ran downstairs.

I tried to click on the light, but nothing worked. Judging by the lampposts and the tiny lights glowing through the neighbors' houses, my home was the only one affected. The power might have been out, but that wouldn't prevent the security system from operating. Then it hit me. I had disabled the alarm before I went to sleep, which explained how that monster entered undetected. I stumbled to the door and pushed the panic button on the security box when something caught my eye.

Outdoor light leaked through the living room, casting a glow over a pair of feet poking behind the couch. The pale skin told who it was immediately. Normally, I would have been halfway across town by now, but I couldn't just leave Nadine if she was hurt. With the knife stretched to the air, I slinked closer, all the while listening for movement upstairs. I peered behind the couch, then caught the scream before it escaped my mouth. The sight froze the blood in my veins and my heart plummeted to the center of the earth.

Nadine lay in the middle of the floor in a boneless sprawl. Her hair fanned across the carpet, her limbs bent in skewed angles like a discarded doll. I knelt down and touched her pulse. Everything was quiet, which was reason enough to stay vigilant. The night left shadows around the room that made the imagination run wild. The ticking clock over the fireplace pronounced the departure of time. Five after one—not that time really mattered. There's no such thing. It's a device that keeps everything from happening at once.

In that moment, the front door swung open and a familiar form stepped into the foyer. "Sam!"

I yelped in surprise and pointed the blade at him, the blood-stained edge flashed in the moonlight. "Stay back. Stay away from me!"

He froze. "Sam. It's me. What happened?"

"Don't come any closer! You killed Nadine!" My clammy fingers began to slip from the knife's handle, but I wouldn't let go.

"What? I just got here. I was halfway to the airport when Nadine called me. We got disconnected. What happened?"

How could I believe him? Mojo or not, I had to defend myself. The man bleeding upstairs looked a hell of a lot like Caleb and almost killed me. Scrutinizing the man in front of me, I noticed his clothes and face—spotless, with no trace of blood or injury. But I had to be sure. "How do I know it's really you?" I asked.

He reached out his hand in appeal. "It's really me, Sam."

"Prove it!" I yelled, the knife wobbling in my hand.

He looked around the room, searching for a solution in the dark. As if one had appeared, he dove into his pocket and flipped a coin over to me. When it landed, I caught the shiny plate of a quarter lying face-up on the carpet. In light of my dilemma, I realized this was the second time I was scared out of my mind, holding a sharp object in my living room. Slowly, I lowered the knife and collapsed under the weight of grief.

Caleb joined our side and lightly touched Nadine's throat. "Her neck is broken. She's still alive." He leaned closer tilting his ear toward her mouth. "Nadine, can you hear me?"

No response.

I just waited, each breath holding a prayer that Nadine didn't become victim number seven.

"She's still breathing; that's a good sign. Keep an eye on her," Caleb instructed as he placed the cell phone to his ear.

I listened to Caleb's calm voice relay our crisis to the operator, glad that at least one of us maintained use of speech. After a series of nods and affirmatives, he snapped the phone shut. "The ambulance should be here in a few minutes."

"How can she still be alive with a broken neck?" I asked.

"Not everyone dies from a broken neck like in the movies. It depends on where the spine is severed; she could be paralyzed. They said not to move her and make sure she's breathing or else she'll asphyxiate. You know CPR?"

I nodded, then jumped when the floorboard upstairs creaked.

Caleb looked to the ceiling and then back at me. "He's here?"

I nodded again as footsteps rumbled over our heads, slow and sluggish, but very much alive.

Caleb reached behind him and pulled the nine-millimeter pistol from the back of his pants. He slid the clip in the butt of the gun and unlatched the safety like a pro. Gone was the arrogant flirt with an eating disorder. In its place stood a livid demon hunter ready for action, and he had never looked hotter.

Pointing the gun ahead, he scanned the perimeter. "Does he have a weapon?"

I shook my head, brushing the strands from Nadine's cheek and forehead. "I triggered the alarm. Help is coming." I pressed down on her chest, knowing that the force of time was against us.

My body shared her tremor when she tried to fight for one more breath. A hissing sound leaked from her lips as the breathing stopped altogether. The color leached from her face, her knuckles whitened, but managed a steady clasp to the phone in her hand.

I pumped her chest harder and began counting. "No. No! No, Nadine, hold on for a few more minutes! Just hold on."

"Sam, come on, we should go. There's nothing else we can do for her. She's turning blue," Caleb said behind me.

"No!" I yelled.

Caleb extended his hand. "Sam, let's go. We'll come back with help."

"No!" I slapped the hand away, then buried my face in her chest. No man on earth could take me from her now. If this was how it was going to go, I was staying with her. She would not be alone.

"Fine. Stay here. Keep giving her CPR, but don't move her neck, just the jaw." Caleb inched to the foyer, his head volleying between the door and staircase. "Where is he?"

"Mom's room."

Caleb vanished from sight with a thunder of footsteps climbing the stairs.

I absorbed myself in my chore, pumping her chest and counting the seconds as they slithered along like tree sap. My eyes blurred with tears, my hands trembled, my throat scraped with every swallow.

I placed my mouth on hers to give her air. When her eyes flew open, my body halted and remained stationary throughout the most frightening part of the evening. Something cold and thick entered my mouth. It attained the material of vapor, but clumped and burrowed down my throat like a worm.

My eyes locked on hers, and I saw that peculiar swirl

of light in her eyes, the same one I saw with Caleb. I needed air, but the force of what entered my body pushed back the oxygen. Whatever this thing was had me in a chokehold, and I couldn't move. Slowly, the light in Nadine's eyes vanished, taking her and the last thread of my reasoning with it.

Finally pulling away, a searing jab had me doubling over in pain. Grief, rage, confusion, and helplessness advanced to that of substance and could now punish within the laws of the flesh. A gut-wrenching scream echoed the walls, and it took a moment of me to realize it was mine. Every molecule ached as claws stretched and ripped at my insides. Hot and cold tangled knots around my spine, sending me into a full-blown spasm. Something invaded my body, angry, alive, and grappling for an exit.

The last thing I remembered was a piercing white light before everything went black.

And even after the curtain fell, I still saw Nadine's face, inert and forsaken as she stared off to some other plane never perceived by sight.

Neither fear nor remorse played a role on this stage. But every truth, every inch and ounce of life assembled in that final glint in her eyes.

Those glowing green eyes.

29

A gunshot wrenched me out of my dreamless state. My eyes met the ceiling, and I could almost see the struggle taking place upstairs. Sirens wailed in the distance, increasing in volume and urgency. But none of that seemed to matter now. I no longer owned the responsibility to care. I stretched out my hand, my fingers spread wide, but it didn't feel like they belonged to me anymore.

I knew my body stood upright, but I couldn't feel the floor beneath me. Something obviously took place when I moved my eyes, but I couldn't quite associate it with sight. The clock on the mantel indicated one-fifteen, but it felt like years had passed.

I looked to my left and saw Nadine's lifeless body sprawled across the floor. I touched her face, which was not yet cold, but rigid and hollow, lacking that gentle hum of animation. All brilliance and strength expelled, evicted from its home to find refuge elsewhere. This violent exit had come too quickly for me to prepare, leaving me raw and chafed from the friction. Realization hit me hard and stole the air out of my lungs. The hows and whys remained hazy, but the finer points of my predicament became crystal clear. From that moment on, I became truly and mercifully numb.

I had always wondered about out-of-body experiences, but had never known how to put it into practice, until now. My inner being, my soul, or whatever fell under the jurisdiction of conscious thought, relinquished all authority and watched the events play out without my participation. No longer able to function by my own strength, I let go of the leash and allowed the beast within to take the reins.

I made it to the foyer, where sirens blared like an air raid attacking the house. Shattering glass, cracking wood, and pounding fists against flesh led me to the second floor.

Leaping three steps at a time, my body moved at a natural pace, but the world slowed to a crawl. Time didn't seem to be a factor in this crucial moment of consciousness, neither did the act of mercy. The frenzy supplied me with adrenaline and one tunnel-vision objective.

My mom was weak, Nadine was dead, and Caleb was in the clutches of a psycho. Mr. Ross had gone too far. And it was high time he learned that messing with me and mine was detrimental to his health.

I entered Mom's bedroom and landed in the throes of chaos. The bed and dresser had been knocked over, the mattress leaned against the wall, and clothing was scattered around the room. Mr. Ross, in his true form, knelt on the floor, clutching his bleeding arm.

I simply watched with amazement, not truly feeling anything within my physical confinement; only simmering rage.

All movement ceased when Mr. Ross caught sight of the gun barrel pointed to his head.

"I can't kill you. That doesn't mean I can't hurt you,"

Caleb warned with his finger firm on the trigger, his eyes runny and glowing with fury.

Mr. Ross stared up at his youngest son in defiance. "You know this won't end. Not until I have my wife. Adriane is mine. She's always mine."

"Adriane is dead, Dad," Caleb said, his voice wavering slightly. "She's not coming back."

With eyes swimming in tears, Mr. Ross charged at his son.

His shoulder slammed into Caleb's chest, sending them both careening against the wall, and knocking the gun out of Caleb's hand. Once the pistol hit the floor, several things occurred in a rapid string of calamity.

Caleb stepped from the wall, leaving a crater of crumbling plaster. He pushed back, hurling Mr. Ross to the opposite side of the room. Purple eyes clashed in the darkness, father against son, demon versus demon.

Before Mr. Ross could recover, another onslaught came his way in the form of a body slam to the floor. The impact cracked the wood, carving zigzags over the surface. Mr. Ross reached behind him and grabbed Caleb's collar. With one swift tug, Caleb flew over his father's shoulder and lay facedown on the floor. Mr. Ross loomed over his son with a hand on his throat.

The sirens and flashing lights told me the cavalry had arrived. The police weren't equipped to handle this sort of domestic dispute, so I stepped in.

"Stop!" I yelled.

Both men looked up at me.

"Sam, run—" Caleb's words were cut off, as he lacked the air to push them out. Not from nearly choking to death, but from sheer terror. His eyes widened, his lips parted as if to warn me of danger only he could see, a truth that he didn't know how to tell.

Mr. Ross smiled and climbed off his son. He stumbled closer, his movements jerky and week from massive blood loss.

I drew deeper into the room, meeting him halfway. My eyes locked on his, not blinking, and applying the teaching that now felt second nature.

"Adriane?" he asked, his teary eyes fevered and unfocused.

"Yes." I smiled.

"Sam, run!" Caleb struggled to his feet and slipped.

Men entered the house, radios and commands bounced off the walls. Revolving lights turned the bedroom into a kaleidoscope. But everything faded away, and in its place stood me, Mr. Ross, and the draw. I reached for him and encircled his neck. He looked down at me, his eyes glowing with surrender and need. I could only imagine what he saw in my eyes.

We deceive our prey. We don't need beauty, Nadine had said. *With one look, we become who they desire most. The body responds, becomes a slave.*

Footsteps climbed the stairs, and time was running out. If there was a chance for second thoughts, I didn't take it. Swallowing a deep breath, I leaned in and opened my mouth wide.

Yells and flashlights faded into the background. Violence, rage, and despair compiled into a mind-blowing exhibit of pure chaos. Caleb had told me that the pull made sex pale in comparison. Though ignorant of that truth, nothing shot my soul to orbit like the taste of life.

Hands tried to pull me away, voices screamed my name, but nothing on earth could steal my glory. The hunger consumed us both, and I wouldn't be satisfied until I had claimed it all. The loss of blood made Mr. Ross weak and uncoordinated, and I took the opportunity for what it was. Somehow, he knew how this would end, and that thread of humanity, that tortured man who missed his wife, wanted the madness to stop.

His cheeks sunk inward, tiny veins rose in bas-relief under his skin. His eyes rolled to the back of his head as the violet light retreated into the cornea. Too much of everything came at me at once, drowning me in an ocean of lifetimes, folding and overlapping in waves of electricity and power. My knees buckled, the foundation of my legs collapsed. Sound, movement, my breathing, and even my heart had stopped. Forever intertwined, gravity plunged us into a free fall into the abyss. If this was how I was going to go, I would take my hostage with me.

I owed that much to Caleb, to my mother, and to Nadine.

30

There once lived a girl with hair the color of sunlight. She was meek, but determined to see the world outside of books and television. Though her parents worried, they nurtured her need to explore. Despite its cruel indifference, the world held her captivated. Every answer created another question, granting an infinite source of wonder for her young mind. Her imagination knew no limits, propelling her journey to distant shores. The sights and sounds of this new land left her spellbound with the promise of hope.

I became her companion in the voyage, sharing her curiosity as the dawn unveiled its intent. To her, the world transformed every day, and one rediscovered its terrain to solve its mystery. We braved this frontier together, adhering to each other's strength to press forward, to seek the reward behind the horizon. Me and my guide. Me and my friend.

When consciousness returned, soft linen and warm sunshine engulfed me. The room looked familiar, the home furnishings and beige wallpaper, like a hotel suite with medical equipment.

Turning my head to the door, I saw Mom sitting in a chair by the bed, watching me. Her milk-white skin showed not a whisper of makeup. The dark shadows under her eyes marked her frailty and fatigue. The rosy fullness of her face melted into hollow cavities of stress. Her silk blouse hung on her body in a formless heap, proving that hospitalization was the best diet in the world. Her body curled inward, shielding itself from any further violation.

"Mom?" I called, not sure if it was the same woman.

Her smile was the only thing familiar. "How are you, baby?"

"Thirsty."

Mom reached to the end table for a bottle and poured water into a glass.

Sitting up, I asked, "Where am I?"

She handed me the glass. "You're at the hospital, in one of the private rooms."

"Why?"

She nodded. "We agreed that this was the best place for you now." The look in her eyes was an odd one to define. Several emotions dueled with shattered logic. "How are you feeling?"

That was a damn good question. I couldn't understand what I felt. Pieces cluttered in my head and mixed with others that weren't there before.

"I'm not in pain," I offered, hoping that was enough for her. "How did I get here? What happened?"

Mom lowered her head. Worry lines appeared around her forehead in strain to find an explanation. "What do you remember?"

"I remember being at home and Nadine . . ." My breath caught, my hand covered my mouth. I stared out to the far end of the room, numb to everything but the brutal arrest of knowledge. "Nadine," I whispered.

"Baby, I'm so sorry." Ignoring her own pain, Mom rushed to the bed and pulled me into her arms. She felt brittle against me, thinly spun glass that would leave a million paper cuts if shattered. She hadn't held me like this in years and the gesture felt like home. Her nearness restored one of my first memories: the vanilla of her hair and the spearmint of her breath. Warm fingers threaded through my hair, massaging the scalp and untangling the ends.

The crying continued when Mom whipped out the big guns, and the song of songs caressed my ears. She would always sing it to me when I was a little girl, the only thing that would end my tantrums and dry my tears, that "Baby of Mine" song from *Dumbo*.

I lay still against Mom's chest, clinging to her warmth and comfort, needing more than anything to have something alive next to me. I demanded proof that such a thing existed.

I didn't know how long I cried, but Mom's blouse was a sopping rag of tears and spittle by the time we pulled apart. Wiping my eyes, I said, "Tell me what happened."

She kept silent for so long, I didn't think she heard me. When I was about to repeat it, she spoke. "A great deal. I don't know where to begin."

Despite her shaky state, Mom got it all out. I listened with a sedate disbelief, not interrupting until she finished.

I remained unconscious for four days, and in that span of time, all hell broke loose. I had encountered severe psychogenic shock. Though my blood pressure had plummeted, I'd had a fever of a hundred and six degrees and climbing, which made no sense. The doctors had been able to revive me before enough oxygen left the brain. Mom had little memory of what happened between then and the night she met Mr. Ross, but the threat of losing her child had shattered her trance instantly.

Dad had gone ballistic when he returned, threatening to sue the entire city of Williamsburg. It had taken three security guards to hold Dad back from killing Caleb. By that time, Caleb was ushered away in handcuffs for shooting his father in the shoulder. He was released hours later due to his claims of self-defense.

Grandpa got wind of the fallout and unleashed his wrath on everyone, from the hospital to the police. Grandpa got into another scuffle with Dad, blaming him for interference. After all was said and done, and the entire city of Williamsburg had the fear of God put in them, Mom and I were placed in the penthouse.

"I didn't know that Caleb was Nathan's son," Mom said.

"It caught me off guard too."

"There are so many holes in the past week."

I nodded. "What happened to Nadine's body?"

"Her parents arrived yesterday. They're taking her body back to Poland for the funeral. Oh, Samara, I'm so sorry. The look on her mother's face. I pray I never wear that look." She held me tighter. "Caleb's brothers are talking with them. Apparently their families know each other."

"Yeah." I buried my face in her arm.

"Samara, I know you're still weak, but there are a few things I need to know. Is there any way you can explain it to me?"

My body stiffened. "I don't wanna lie to you."

"Then don't. I just wanna know the truth. Something happened that night, something that neither I, your father, nor the police can explain." She swallowed thickly. "But I have a feeling you can piece it together for me."

"I don't know if I can."

"Try. I'll believe anything you tell me. Do you trust me?"

"Yes, but you're gonna think I'm crazy."

"If you are, you've got plenty of people bunking next to you in the nuthouse, namely the police officers who found you."

Mom had a right to know. I knew she needed the closure. Taking a deep breath, I unloaded my burden on Mom, from the woman in the BB parking lot, to Garrett, to Nadine, to Mr. Ross, to Caleb and his brothers. Mom stayed quiet for several moments after I finished. I waited for the scream of horror or the insistence on medication, but none came.

She simply held me and sighed. "Interesting story, Samara."

I blinked. "It's not a story. It's true, all of it."

"I never said you were lying. I just said it was interesting. Honestly, I don't know what to say." She climbed off the bed and moved to the dresser. "As outrageous as it all is, I can't see any other explanation for your . . . condition."

"What condition?"

Mom returned to the bed with a small mirror in her hand. "I think you should see for yourself."

That statement alone brought a chill to my spine. Taking the mirror from her hands, I looked at my reflection, then screamed. Mom seemed to have expected this. She continued to rub my back and shush me quiet, when Grandpa rushed into the room, ready to swing.

Ever since I was little, he had looked like that oatmeal guy on television. Though plump with white hair and beard, there was nothing jolly about Mr. Marshall. The man had a frigid disposition that numbed the fingers. His gruff appearance was better suited for a life of solace in a log cabin than a boardroom.

He stood by the door, searching around for the ax murderer in the room. "What happened?"

Mom looked up at him with weary eyes. "She saw her reflection."

Grandpa's shoulders relaxed and he stroked his beard. "The doctors still have no idea how it happened. They want to analyze her, put her as a special case study."

"They are not making a lab rat out of my baby! She's fine." Mom's voice cracked with anger.

"That girl is far from fine, Julie. Look at her. She wasn't like that before." He stared at me in accusation.

"And how would you know? You haven't been around to make that assessment."

"I've been around more than you realize, and I know what my grandchild looked like. And that"—he pointed to me—"is not normal."

Too caught up in my shock to join the argument, I scurried to the edge of the bed and curled into a ball.

"Daddy, I appreciate your help, but I need you to leave. I need a moment alone with my daughter." Before he could reply, Mom crossed the room and shut the door in his face.

Shuffling to the bed, she cupped my face in her hands. "Samara, honey, look at me."

Slowly, our eyes locked.

"This doesn't change anything. You are still you, no matter what this means. I love you no matter what. Remember that."

I nodded. What *did* this mean? I knew there was something off, but I didn't know to what degree. Only one person could shed some light on this.

"I need to see Caleb. Where is he?" I asked.

"He came by a few times, but Grandpa sent him away and placed a restraining order on him. We couldn't risk him going after you."

I shot upright. "What!"

"I didn't know what to think, Samara. All I knew was that his father tried to hurt me, and I didn't know what the rest of his family was capable of."

"Caleb was trying to help."

"Samara, calm down. When you're feeling better, I'll invite him over." She eased me back down. "This is a lot to take in and you need to sleep on it. We don't need to solve this now. Get your strength back." Mom tucked me in and kissed my forehead.

When she left the room, I climbed out of the covers and went to the adjoining bathroom. I stood in front of the mirror for a half hour, examining the subtle nuances of the change, the odd flecks of color that rebounded light. No wonder Mom had freaked out. This was a hard thing to dismiss and an even harder thing to explain to people I knew. If anyone looked long enough they could tell it was natural.

My thoughts shot straight to Nadine. The girl sure knew how to leave an impression. I would like to think that she had given me this as something to remember her by. This little souvenir wasn't an easy thing to forget. I had constantly joked that I would kill to have her eyes. She must have taken the statement seriously. It was my favorite color after all. Jade green and tiny flecks of gold shimmered inside swollen, bloodshot eyes.

Caleb told me that his spirit used the eyes to show itself. Well, mine had no problems making its presence known.

31

The rest of the night took place in bed, though little sleep occurred.

I tossed and turned, toiling with an inner battle that had no victor. The efforts left me too exhausted even to use the bathroom. Memories from past lives tangled and spread like weeds, stunting the growth of healthy dreams.

Seeing Mr. Ross's life story play out before me didn't help my sleepless night. I envied the undying devotion for his wife, I rejoiced with him when Caleb was born, and I commiserated the events that sent him down this dark road of perversion. I became the hostile witness to the sick thrill, the conflicted guilt, and the demented reasoning to continue. I knew and felt it all, and I wanted it gone.

None of the food the nurse brought me filled me up that night. I scarfed down two sandwiches and half a cheesecake, but that only pacified the hunger for a few hours at a time. Nadine had warned me of how substantial human energy was when taken in its entirety; that it would take weeks to digest. One would think consuming two lives would fill me up for the next month, but the trauma from the body swap must have burned through most of the reserve.

Whatever the case might be, this thing inside me was unhappy with the new arrangement and demanded compensation, like a child who kept crying for her mother. I didn't have the heart or the wherewithal to explain that she wasn't coming back. That would only produce another meltdown and the diagnosis of schizophrenia.

I had teased Caleb about his spirit being a pet, but it was more like an infant that needed food and attention at regular intervals. There was no self-help book or instruction manual to handle this affliction, and evasion was not an option, no matter how hard I tried.

The tapping at my door the next morning was a welcome diversion. Mom popped her head in the room and smiled. "Hey, sweetie, are you in the mood for company?"

"Who is it?"

"Nadine's mother. She wants to talk to you."

I sat up straight. This visit was unexpected, but a part of me anticipated it. I wondered what she would say. Would she blame me for her daughter's death? Would she detect the being in my body? Curiosity and the need for acceptance outranked my fear. Though walls separated us, I could feel her presence and I couldn't pass the opportunity to meet its source.

"Yeah, sure, let her in."

Moments later, a tall woman entered the room. I almost jumped out of the bed.

She lifted her hand for me to stop. "It's all right, child. Calm yourself."

Seeing her up close, I could detect the years and wisdom in her features. At first sight, a surge of information rushed before my eyes—images, sounds, smells, and events in which I had not participated. I knew everything about this woman, her favorite song, her favorite food, her political views; I even knew what she looked like naked, which was kinda gross.

Mrs. Petrovsky was the mirror image of Nadine, give or take twenty years. She had the same golden hair, green eyes, and pouty mouth. From head to toe, she carried that tasteful European poise, a fashion plate in casual wear. I'm sure she had to beat men off with a stick in her youth, and probably still did.

"Forgive me, child, but your grandfather is an irritating man. I had to use great deal of charm to get on this floor." Her thick accent rolled off her tongue like a purr. Her voice soothed my bones, drifting me to warm nights by a roaring fire and stories before bed. The familiarity was intimate, giving me ease and safety that only a mother's presence could provide.

She took a seat in the chair by the bed and placed her hands on her lap, just watching me. She seemed quite comfortable with the silence, but I wasn't.

"Mrs. Petrovsky, I'm so sorry about—"

"Don't. Do not apologize for something you couldn't control. Nadine made her choice, and we all must live with it."

"I'm still sorry. It's not easy to lose a child."

"No, it's not. But, you must understand, I cannot dwell on her absence, but only her presence. The years she spent with me were precious, and I'm thankful for each one. We do not celebrate death, but life. Mr. Ross and others like us forget that key principle of what we are. Life is what sustains us. The sooner you realize that, the better. Besides, my child isn't really gone. I'm looking right at her."

"Mrs. Petrovsky, I—"

"You need to be aware of what is going on with you.

You will need teaching and support. I'm here to help you, Samara."

"I don't understand."

She leaned forward. "I think you do. This is quite an unusual situation, something that has never occurred in our lineage, but there it is. You will not face this alone. I promise you that. You are family now, and I embrace you as my child." Sitting up, she handed me a small envelope. "I want you to have this."

I opened the envelope and a thin bracelet fell into my palm. Recollection made my heart jolt in pain. "I can't take this."

Mrs. Petrovsky closed my hand over the chain. "You can and you will. Every one of my children have them, for their protection."

"But this was Nadine's."

"She no longer needs protection, but you do. You know it is not simply a bracelet, yes?"

I nodded with a hard swallow. This wasn't just a sentimental gesture, but an initiation, a rite of passage given to all the Petrovsky heirs. A privilege that I hadn't earned.

"I will take no refusal on this matter, little one. Nadine would want you to have it," she asserted before I could protest. "For my love and peace of mind, never take it off."

My shoulders sagged in defeat; then I fastened the clasp around my wrist. My fingers traced over the inscription.

I knew Mrs. P. was grieving and any coping device would do, but I wasn't trying to have another Nathan Ross on my hands. "I'm not Nadine."

"I know that, but Nadine is in you and so is her spirit. You feel it, do you not?"

"I—I don't know."

She cocked a blond eyebrow. "You don't? Have you not noticed your eyes, or the strong hunger that has nothing to do with food, or the fact that we have been speaking in Polish since I walked in the room?"

I flinched. How on earth did I know Polish? How did I know this woman's voice as well as my own?

"When I first heard what happened I had my suspicions, but now seeing you has removed all doubt." Seeing my baffled look, she continued. "Let me explain something to you. When a host dies, the spirit will try to fight it, grabbing at life, consuming as much energy as it can. When all traces of life are gone, it will leave the body and it takes the life of its host with it. Something happened to interrupt the ascent, and now the spirit is with you, and with it, Nadine's energy."

"Then what happened to Mr. Ross's spirit? Is it in my body too?"

"I highly doubt it. Our beings are gender specific. The human body is small compared to the vastness of a spirit. There is barely room for one. Nadine's spirit staked her claim on you and will not let go."

I knew what she was saying was true. I just couldn't accept it. How does one cope with a possession? Nadine, Caleb, and his brothers were born with this malady; they knew no other way, no other life. But I was now tossed in a whole other world with no map or compass to guide me.

"I am sure this is difficult for you to accept. And the alteration may be awkward, but we will help you through it. Caleb and his brothers understand the situation and are willing to aid you through this transition."

"Transition," I repeated dully.

"Being what we are has its advantages and consequences. I am sure you are aware what some of those are." Her firm stare dared me to contest.

"You say that I ingested her life energy. How long will the energy last?"

"A week or so. However, the memories are another story. I still have memories from my very first donor, and that was but a taste. So I can only assume the knowledge that came from Nadine and Mr. Ross is now yours. Once seen, it cannot be unseen. I can tell that you are burdened by his past. Do not dwell on the evil that comes to you. Preoccupy your thoughts and let them pass away. Only learn what you wish to learn and block the rest, for it will stay with you for life. What you do with such knowledge is up to you."

She reached in her purse and pulled out a white business card. "I would love to stay longer, but I must catch my flight. I will contact you after the service. These are all my contact numbers, my fax and e-mail address. Call me day or night, all right?"

When I took the card, she said, "This will not be our last meeting, Samara. We will have time together soon."

The promise of her return made my chest swell. I reached for her hand as she got up to leave. Smiling down at me, she bent and kissed my forehead.

The meeting was brief, but nothing she could say would enlighten me any further. It was like I'd known her for years. I knew because Nadine knew. I loved this woman as much as I did my own mother, and the likelihood of reciprocation brought more tears.

"Thank you, Mrs. Petrovsky."

"You're welcome, Samara. And please call me Angie." At the door, she looked over her shoulder and smiled. Stopping in mid-turn, Angie pulled a clear sandwich bag from her purse and unraveled the top.

"Oh yes, Caleb told me to give you this. He said you would know what it means." She placed the money in my hand and with a small grin, left me to my sentimental and starry-eyed daze. God help me, I had the love bug in the worst way. Smiling down at the four quarters inside my palm, it was nice to know I was in good company.

32

I was released from the hospital two days later. Grandpa had everyone sweating bullets, so the staff almost threw a parade when all members of the Marshall family left the property. Grandpa insisted that we stay at his house until we fully recovered, and Mom didn't have the strength to argue with him. I could tell the extra security and having a man around made her feel safe, even if it was her father. I slept in Mom's old room and she took the guest room up the hall. My new roommate drained every ounce of energy I owned, leaving me too exhausted to do anything but sleep.

Mom must have sent out a press release announcing my recovery, because the Marshall residence turned into Grand Central Station the next morning. Police, doctors, and relatives I hadn't seen in years dropped by to check on me. I didn't feel like getting dressed for visitors, so I stayed in the frilly white nightgown Mom had loaned me.

The police grilled me on the incident with Mr. Ross. I kept my answers vague and straight to the point, not giving an inch of rope. Even after I had disclosed my life story, the officers didn't seem to be in a hurry to leave. They just kept staring at me like I was lunch. That's when it occurred to me that they were under the mojo, so I had to sic Grandpa on them.

My man problems didn't end there. As soon as John Law left the premises, Mia and Dougie rushed into the room and hopped on the bed. I got the same reaction as the rest of the visitors: that look of unease and confusion, followed by the unanimous question, "When did you get contacts?" There was no good explanation for that question. No doubt it would come up often, so now was as good as any to rehearse that lie.

The more we talked, the more uncomfortable things became, especially with Dougie finding any reason to touch me. I enjoyed the attention; however, the look in his eyes was not one would give a friend. When he tried to kiss me, I pushed him off the bed.

Knowing what his deal was, I felt nauseous. Dougie was like a brother to me, and just the sight of him in swim trunks triggered my gag reflex. Mia and I were tight, but not tight enough for her to have Dougie all over me. Even now, she took the offensive and served me the glare of homicide. At that point, I decided to cut the meeting short.

Dougie seemed reluctant to leave, but Mia's hard yank on his arm got him moving. At the door, she shot me a parting scowl of confusion and female rivalry.

I hated keeping Mia and Dougie in the dark, but things like these were kept quiet for a reason. Nadine told me that this secret was only revealed to those closest to us. There was no one closer to me than Mia, but she would have to wait a while to learn the truth.

Plopping back on the bed, I covered my head in my hands. I didn't know how much more I could take. I needed to get a handle on this thing before I lost every friend I had.

That afternoon, Dad and the kids paid me a visit. Not wanting to disrupt the peace, Grandpa stayed in his study and polished his guns until Dad left.

Dad was unusually quiet and just held me, which I appreciated. Recounting the event to the police and family had taken its toll on me, and it was refreshing that Dad didn't press the issue. He was just glad his baby girl was safe. Though his presence gave me peace, I felt that awkward vibe from him that I had gotten from the other male visitors, and I wondered if I'd ever be normal around guys again. He apologized for threatening Caleb, but I could tell the entreaty was just for my benefit.

I was surprised to learn that the twins weren't dragged to the house by gunpoint. They showed genuine concern, and dare I say, fear that their big sis had been so close to death. I knew the affection wouldn't last, but I counted my blessings and welcomed their hugs and wet kisses.

The spirit in me enjoyed their company as well, proving Nadine's view on children to be true. Their boundless energy was potent and cased their skin like an aura. Aside from the usual marathon of questions, Kyle and Kenya were well behaved. They only managed to break two of Grandpa's antique vases and tracked dirt on the marble foyer.

Once everyone had left and the house was quiet, I wandered around the estate, mainly avoiding the in-house nurse who kept hounding me. Mom was still on the mend, so she took a nap in the guest room, and God only knew where Grandpa had disappeared to.

I only visited this house once when I was ten and not much seemed to have changed. It was a miniature castle that spoke of champagne wishes and caviar dreams. It had a traditional design with a spiral staircase and oil portraits of ancestors lining the main hallway. I almost fainted on sight of the last portrait at the end of the corridor.

I recognized the gown and pose, but not the reason for its existence. I had to commend Mom; she kept her correspondence with Grandpa under wraps. My junior-prom picture had been used to render the masterpiece of me in flowing green gossamer. Appraising the brush-strokes and clarity, I realized that he would now have to alter the eye color.

Mr. Marshall had hinted that he kept tabs on me, but I didn't realize to what extent. Grandpa's compassion was showing, a sight that I wasn't quite ready for. Maybe there was a silver lining in all this. Maybe one day Grandpa and I could share the same breathing space without gagging. Only time would tell on that score.

Around sunset, I wandered to the backyard and breathed in the crisp tang of cut grass. The one thing I hated about ailments was the confinement. My inner chi demanded sunshine, clean air, and quiet. The yard was a two-acre stretch of Eden, adorned with dogwood and lilies. Surrounded by God's crayon box, I lay across the marble bench and watched the night make its debut.

The quiet solitude of the day called up memories of Nadine. I learned so much about her, more than she could've ever shared, more than what I could've discerned in years of conversation. She wasn't as pessimistic as she let on and she had a flair for romance. She loved this time of day.

Much like her, I slowly became more in tune with the things around me, examining life through a poet's eye. I could hear her voice, and identify with her philosophy on the world. This revelry brought a sentiment that I would've never entertained, so I knew at once belonged to her.

What happened to all the fireflies? I haven't seen one since I was a little girl, and until this point, they never entered my mind. What else went overlooked along this troubled path of maturity? What other long-forgotten memories lie in wait to be revisited? Have they all died out? Or has the endless procession of time and circumstance allowed them to abandon me? Are fireflies magical creatures that can only capture the eyes of children, the most observant of mankind? Or is it some chimerical entity whose existence depends on one's belief in it?

How I wish for the days of the firefly; for that childlike wonder and to follow without question, to lie in a field of warm twilight in the company of a drifting galaxy at my fingertips.

Those days are gone, I'm afraid. Like a second language, if not put into practice, it fades away. Perhaps, unexpectedly, I will see that fickle light again. And with it, all that is pure and once good in humanity will resurface. That brilliant but ever so delicate light will ward me from the uncertainty of shadows, and I will be once again ignorant of the evil that lives there.

"Well, at least it doesn't rhyme," I told myself, then swallowed the sob in my throat.

"I hope you're thinking about me," a familiar voice called from behind.

My head turned and found Caleb leaning against a tree, wearing a week's worth of stubble and a huge grin on his face. Judging by the ripped T-shirt and leaves in his hair, he had resorted to breaking and entering to see me. My chest hummed with activity at the thought of my knight scaling the walls in search of his maiden fair. I don't know what thrilled me more, the sight of him, or the slushy in his hand.

Reaching out like a needy toddler, I bounced in my seat. "Please tell me that's for me."

He pulled the cup behind his back. "Maybe."

"Don't play with me. I'm a girl possessed."

"I'll say." He handed me the cup and watched me guzzle the frozen goodness. "Easy now—you'll get brain freeze."

"I can't help it."

His smile dropped as he lifted my chin to face him. He stared into my eyes, regarding the new life behind them. "Extraordinary," he whispered. "Absolutely extraordinary."

I snatched away from him. "Don't you start. The last thing I want is everyone treating me like a sideshow freak."

"I'm sorry, but you gotta admit, it's freaky as hell. I mean, I've never known anyone to acquire a sentient being. We're just born with it. How do you feel?"

I gave him room to sit. "Hungry."

"I figured as much, but the slushy's not gonna cut it. I guess I'll have to train you on feeding."

"You don't have to. I know how to do it."

"You do?"

I tapped my forehead proudly. "I know what Nadine knows."

He nodded and kissed the top of my head. "Have you named your spirit yet?"

I winced. "Um, no. I haven't even acknowledged it yet, and you're talking about naming it?"

"The sooner you identify with it, the easier it will be to tame it."

I stared sideways at him. Caleb had a ton of nerve trying to school me, when he dealt with the same issue less than a month ago. Not having the strength to fuss him out, I kept my mouth busy with strawberry-flavored ice.

After a moment, he asked, "Did your mom tell you what happened?"

"Yeah, I heard about the arrest. That must've been fun."

"Time of my life," he said. "Haden is out of the hospital, cussing mad for missing out on the action. But I can tell he's grieving. Brodie and Michael are taking care of Dad's funeral arrangements."

The mention of his father lanced a blade through my heart. How could he even look at me after what I did? I had succeeded in not thinking about Mr. Ross and his past for a full three hours, praying that those memories would pass away with his energy.

Hesitantly, I touched Caleb's arm. "I'm sorry, Caleb. This must be hard for you. I don't know how I could handle it if my dad died."

Caleb's lips pulled into a tight line. The sudden drain of color in his face became as clear as the restrained anger fueling his next words. "My father died five years ago in a hospital room in Paris. I've already grieved for that loss, and I don't feel anything now but disgust. That . . . thing killed my friend and it would've done the same to you, and I wasn't strong enough to do anything about it. I don't blame you, so stop feeling guilty. You and your mom are safe, and my brothers and I can move on with our lives. I should be thanking you. But I won't." He attempted a smile that didn't quite reach his eyes. "I'm here for you. Whatever you're going through, I've been there."

I stared out to the dimming garden as that night replayed in my head. "The whole thing was insane. I didn't have control over my body, like I stepped outside of myself."

He caressed my hand. "Now do you see why I don't like to fight? The spirit takes over and your control is gone. You can never lose it, Sam. You have to be aware of yourself at all times."

Whether it was the brain freeze or the onslaught of information, I developed a headache. "I know, and I appreciate that. Right now, I just need time." Standing up, I moved to a more secluded area of the garden. The moon spied through the blossoms overhead; nocturnal life chirped and buzzed around us.

Caleb followed me, his movements careful and unhurried. It was hard to explain how one sense can mimic another. It took an exceptional mind to understand how animals can smell fear, how the deaf can see sound, or how I was now able to relate to the skill. But Caleb's anxiety wafted off his body like a dense cloud of funk.

The extrasensory was unnecessary; his disheveled clothes and the bags under his eyes told it all. Cake Boy was worried sick. I sat in a soft patch of grass and waited for him to join me.

He remained standing. "You're tired. You need rest."

I felt the void of his retreat immediately. Before he could take another step, I pulled him back. "I don't want you to go. In fact, you're the only one I need with me now."

With feline grace, he crawled along the grass, stalking closer with eyes zeroing in on my every move. His nearness had me inching back until my head struck a tree. He hovered over me with his weight resting on his elbows.

His fingers brushed against my lips. "Have I ever told you how pretty you are?"

"No. That would involve, you know, romance."

"Wouldn't want that, now would we?" he whispered against my neck. Lips and tongue dragged along my throat. His stubble scraped against my skin. He was goading me on purpose. I was in a delicate state and vulnerable to his advances, or at least that was my excuse for pinning him to the ground. The new position got his attention.

He stared up at me with his hands on my waist as I straddled his hips. "You're hungry. I can feel it."

"Starving." I wagged my eyebrows.

The look in his eyes told me we weren't on the same page. He sat up until we were face-to-face. "You can use me for now. I'll talk you through it."

All humor fell away when I saw the determined look on his face. "I can't feed from you."

"Why not? I'm human. My energy is as good as anyone else's."

"I don't know. What if I go too far, or what if you pass out? I mean, what about that recognition thing, does that apply to us now? And what if—" A finger to my lips silenced me.

"This is a new experience. And the only way to learn is through trial and error. I'll make sure you don't take too much. But you need to feed. It's better you do it now than wait. It will only get worse, and I don't want you starving your spirit like I did." He extended his bare arm to me. "Start here and work your way up."

"Caleb," I objected.

"I'm right here." His other hand held my cheek.

Turning my head, my lips touched his hand, kissing the palm and each finger.

"What do you feel?" he asked.

"Nothing."

"Close your eyes and feel me around you. You'll sense it without touching me."

I closed my eyes and pulled my lips away, barely grazing the hair on his forearm. Then I felt it, the lightning bolts of energy, the palpable zing of living. Inhaling slowly, I felt the wave of warmth pass my lips, tickling my throat, the lining of my windpipe and lungs. The rush inflated and shattered in fragments of electricity, each with its own distinct sensation, all delicious, all inexplicably potent to the extent of agony.

Only then did I know what Caleb meant when he described feeding to me. Everything was invested in this force, condensed within its own galactic province; space without distance, direction without aim, rotation without an axis. The senses jumbled in a calculated disorder, the sequence of coincidence and fate rooting down to the tiniest particle. It tasted like music. It smelled like sunrise.

The knowledge only underlined the limitation of man's true potential. This insight was never meant for human consumption; therefore, it could never be vocalized. Key elements would get lost in translation and lose their meaning. Somewhere in the outskirts of my buzz, just beyond the haze, I heard Caleb's voice.

Firm arms held me close, warm breath lapped at my face; soft lips soothed my aching skin.

"I can't leave without doing this," he rasped as his mouth captured mine.

Instantly, I felt the spark, that gigawatt jolt of delirium. Our inner beings grappled together, giving, and taking like two mutts fighting over a bone. The tug-of-war continued without forfeit or triumph. As the two spirits went at each other, Caleb and I partook in a make-out session of that of legend. We came together with a violent urgency that had eluded us for too long.

Caleb may have an arrogant streak, but when it came to kisses, it was warranted. Mr. Baker had mad skills! No clinking teeth, no sloppy spit, no weird lizard tongue, but the gentle assertion that made it clear who was running the show. I welcomed each silent profession of love, drinking in his joy, and inhaling the scent of sugar cookies on his breath.

Slowly, his lips drifted to my cheeks and forehead. "Sam."

"Hmm?"

"How do you feel?"

Wallowing in the high, I allowed reality to return to my body, its weight forcing me to rely on Caleb for support. I collapsed against his chest and nestled my head against his shoulder. I never knew he had it in him, but he branded me, ultimately ruining all interest in anyone but him. It was just me and my other half in the garden under moonlight and a swell of lightning bugs. Before sleep took over, I whispered, "I feel joy."

I woke up the next morning having no idea how I had returned to bed. All I knew was the heady glow of fulfillment that claimed my body. Though my stomach rumbled for earthly sustenance, my spiritual hunger was sated, for the time being.

Stretched across the pillows, I thought of Caleb and our close encounter. I had fed from him, consumed his life, and attained knowledge that he could never reveal himself, a naked truth that exceeded all other intimacies. Though the amount was small, I caught a glimpse into his inner sanctum. That sneak preview banished all jealousy for the women in his past. They could never reach his soul, his heart.

This feeling was definitely the drug of choice, and the thoughts of feeding again excited my roommate. Its presence hummed and vibrated under my skin, scraping the posterior lobe, much like a puppy that couldn't wait to go outside. This was something I had to get used to, and there was no time like the present to get the ball rolling.

I crawled out of bed, went to the dresser, and conducted a face-off with my reflection. The flickers of light around my corneas told me I had its attention. I can't explain how awkward and absurd it was to converse with one's personal demon, so I won't try. I just knew it was necessary to get everything out in the open. Caleb explained the principle of recognition the best he could, but it was something one could only experience firsthand. I started off with a simple introduction.

"Lilith?" I called.

An icy chill trickled down my spine in response. I took a deep breath, knowing my suspicion was confirmed. This was Nadine's spirit, which meant it already had a name.

"If it's all right with you, can I still call you Lilith?" I asked. "I think Nadine would like that."

Another tingle zipped my spinal cord.

"Okay, Lilith, my name is Samara, but you can call me—" Before I could finish, an image flashed in front of my eyes.

I now stood by the barista machine at the café with the sound of perking coffeepots and steam hissing in the air. Wiping the sweat from my forehead, I noticed my creamy white arm and a blond ponytail that fell over my left shoulder. Looking up, I saw a young girl approaching the counter, with black eyes and fidgeting hands. Her hair was curly with a red and white racing stripe on one side of the head. Despite the apparent unease, she looked excited about her first day. Her high chin exemplified strength and courage toward any challenge that may come. On the spot, I knew I would like

this person, and I knew my spirit would benefit
from her presence.
The girl extended her hand and said, "You
must be Nadine. Linda said you'd be the one
who'll show me the ropes. I'm Samara, but you
can call me Sam."

It was hard seeing one's self from the outside—a direct externalization a mirror failed to accomplish. A torrent of information rushed to the forefront, flooding my brain with emotions and opinions that weren't mine.

This spirit knew me, long before I ever knew her. She had loved and grieved as I did, conveying humility that would never lose value. This was an intelligent life form inside me, cognizant of its origin and its past. I had to respect its power and embrace it as my own.

The vibration stopped for several moments as if waiting for a response or command. Her obvious discipline and eagerness to try gave me hope. In order to coincide, in order for me to live a normal life, we had to work together. And it was now up to me to open the lines of communication.

"All right, Lilith, it's just you and me now. I'll try my best to do right by you. But you're in my house now, and I have a few rules we need to get straight."

LIVING VIOLET

Jaime Reed

ABOUT THIS GUIDE

The following questions are intended to
enhance your group's reading of
LIVING VIOLET.

Discussion Questions

1. The story is told through Sam's point of view. How might the book differ if the story was told in Caleb's point of view or in third person?

2. The narration gives a slight satirical view of the paranormal world. How do you think the story would have been told through a more serious tone?

3. Do the stories mentioned in the book meetings have relevance in the story as a whole? If so, in what way?

4. Would the story have had a different impact if the main character was white? If so, how?

5. Is there a parallel between the demon-human inner struggle and the racial inner struggle in the story?

6. Sam admits to feeling like an outsider because she's biracial. Have you ever felt like an outsider? How did you overcome it?

7. Sam's view on love is greatly influenced by her family and friends. Do your family and friends influence your beliefs on love? Are they positive or negative? Is your view like Sam's? Why or why not?

8. Caleb battles with many issues: self-control, over-indulgence, acceptance, and the fear of opening

himself to another person. Have you ever battled with these issues? How?

9. Do the existence of souls and the consumption of life have deeper meaning? What's your take on it?

10. What do you think it would be like to consume the life and memories of someone you know? What would you do with that power?

11. Was Nadine's outcome at the end of the story necessary?

12. How do you think Sam will handle the transformation?

13. Does anyone else (besides me) wish for an invite to one of Robbie Ford's parties?

14. Who is your favorite character? Who is your least favorite character?

15. If you had a sentient being, what would you name it? What color would your eyes be? Why?

Turn the page for an excerpt from

Burning Emerald.

In stores in June 2012.

It surprised me how things stayed the same at Buncha Books, much like how cartoon characters never aged or changed clothes.

Fusion jazz pumped through the speakers. A group of girls giggled and read steamy paperbacks from the erotica section. Young entrepreneurs hovered over their laptops, abusing the free Wi-Fi the store provided. Old men who mistook the bookstore for a rest home hogged all the sofas while reading the newspaper. Yep, business as usual at Buncha Books, set under a thick aroma of fresh cookies and hot espresso.

Alicia Holloway was on duty with me at the café, perky and animated as ever, which put a damper on my afternoon. Her elfin face, hopeful brown eyes, and spiral curls always reminded me of a black woodland sprite who couldn't find her way home. She stood by the barista machine, watching a tin of hot milk bubble with foam.

"I'm not judging or anything, but it's just weird," she began, concerning the unlikely attraction between Caleb and me. "Isn't there, like, a rule somewhere about not dating your co-workers?"

"Isn't there, *like*, a rule about minding your own business?" I mocked while toweling off my wet hands, taking extra care to dry the gold bracelet on my wrist. I rotated the chain so the nameplate stood face-up, and Lilith, my internal roommate, hummed on recognizing her name engraved in elegant script.

Alicia let out a shrill meow and set a row of fixed drinks on the coffee bar. "Somebody forgot to bring their charm to work. I'm just saying, you should be more low-key. People talk, you know."

I watched her rush to the register to ring up the next customer. "Yeah, like people are talking in school about your tragic romance with Garrett Davenport."

"What!" she squeaked, dropping the customer's change. She quickly apologized, then turned to me with alarm. "What did you hear?"

Shifting my lips left and right, I crooned, "Oh, stuff. Like you and him secretly dating before he died and now all three Courtneys want your head on a platter, that's all. You're making enemies in high places. Be careful. Girls in our school are vicious."

Lifting her chin high, she poured coffee mix and ice in the blender. "I'm not scared of them."

My gaze wandered to the book floor and I smiled. "Oh, so if say, Courtney B. rolled up right now, you wouldn't be scared?"

"Not at all."

"Good to know, because she's heading to the counter right now."

By the time I turned around, Alicia was a ghost with the blender still running. Only the swinging door of the back kitchen told me where she disappeared. After finishing the drink order for her, I took my time going to the register and prayed for patience while in contact with the redheaded diva.

Decked out in designer labels from head to toe, Courtney B. approached the counter with a strut only suitable for the runway. All that was missing was the wind machine and the slow motion camera. The three Courtneys were renowned in my school for their reign of tyranny, and Courtney B. ruled as the bloodsucking queen of the dammed. Aside from her being painfully vapid, she owned the unmatched talent of squeezing insults into every conversation. Succeeding in working my last nerve could very well be considered an achievement, but for fear of getting fired, I decided to limit my responses to two words or less.

Her handbag thumped on the counter while she scanned around for the prey that vanished from sight. Disappointed, her icy gray eyes narrowed at me. "Hi. You're in my Spanish class. Sam, right?"

"Sí," I said, deadpan. I couldn't believe this chick. We've shared at least two classes since sixth grade and she still didn't know my name?

"Is that, like, short for Samantha?"

"No." I pointed to my nametag.

"Oh. My bad. Anyway, you know that hot guy that works here, Caleb something?" She looked around the store.

Tapping my finger to my lips, I contemplated. "Six-foot-two, brown hair, purple-blue eyes, always smells like cake? Yeah, that would be my *boyfriend*." I stressed the last word.

"Oh!" She looked surprised for a moment, appalled even, then swept a cursory glance up my frame. "Well, maybe you can help. I was wondering if you could talk him into deejaying my party on Halloween. He did such a great job at Robbie Ford's birthday party; I'd love to have him, um, spin for me." She twirled a lock of hair around her manicured finger.

I should be used to women drooling all over my man, but that required more patience than I could afford. "I'll be sure to run it by him, but it would be more business-like coming from you. You can find him in the music section. That way." I pointed to the other end of the store using my middle finger, a gesture too blatant to overlook.

Applying loud suction, Courtney slid her tongue over her teeth, perhaps to see if her fangs elongated. "Thanks. Doesn't seem to be your kind of thing, but I'll see if I can add you to the guest list too." With a neck-spraining flip of the hair, she flounced away.

Resting my weight against the counter, I exhaled slowly, absorbing the sting of her verbal attack. This was an interesting turn of events. Courtney's Halloween bashes were the talk of school, but unlike Robbie Ford, her parties were for A-list only. Mia would be so jealous if I got an invite before she did. The only downside was subjecting Caleb to that harpy's whims.

This was a good opportunity for him. Soon he would leave his position here to "scratch" with full force, but his budding deejay career already left us juggling sched-ules to see each other. Music was the mistress in our union, the only love I didn't mind sharing with him.

"Is she gone?" A timid voice called from the back kitchen.

When I confirmed, Alicia crept out, and a wash of re-lief ran across her face. I shook my head, knowing this doe-eyed sophomore needed more life experience and pessimism to survive high school. The mother hen in me wanted to keep her innocence intact, so my watchful eyes were never far from her.

Seeing her trepidation, I said, "If it gets too bad, you have my number, okay?"

"Thanks." She gave me a weak smile and went back to the register.

Though I only worked a few five-hour shifts during the weekdays, time seemed to run at a snail's pace. Alicia tried her best to entertain me with the latest gossip, but it didn't seem the same with Nadine gone. Nothing was the same with her gone.

I found myself comparing Alicia to Nadine, noting how she took forever to wrap the food when we closed, where it would only take Nadine ten minutes. Alicia chatted and laughed with the customers, where one was considered lucky if they got service, let alone a smile, from Nadine. Alicia was an old friend and I would flip out if something happened to her, but the injustice prevailed.

After shutdown, I clocked out at customer service then ambled to the break room in an almost dream-like state. Our monthly book meeting was tonight, which was reason enough to wallow in sorrow, but seeing where Nadine once sat deepened my depression another notch. A part of me expected to see her pass through the door, her blond hair bobbing behind her head in a haphazard bun.

The staff's seating arrangement was an unspoken rule, so I wasn't the only one who paused at the empty folding chair by the soda machine. Even Linda, the store manager, shifted her eyes to the chair, as if an unholy curse awaited anyone who sat there.

"It's just a chair, Sam. It's not haunted," Caleb said as he guided me to a seat and sat next to me. His smile produced broad dimples, two parentheses buried deep in his cheeks. His maple tresses fell past his jaw and slightly curled at the ends. Behind the curtain of locks, his eyes brightened to a blazing amethyst hue, a color that projected his mood and his spirit's needs.

"Not the chair, just us," I mumbled as my mind drifted again.

Even if I knew all that would happen that fateful night,

would it make a difference? If Nadine hadn't died in my arms, Lilith wouldn't have needed to abandon ship and move into my crib. Maybe Lilith was her farewell gift, a small consolation that numbed the ache of her loss.

Nadine's life energy—the ones that came with Lilith—eventually dissolved, but her memories were kept on file for safekeeping—every birthday party, every bedtime story, every wild adventure, save one. It was strange how every facet of Nadine's life opened at the ready to me, all but that tiny blank spot of her history, a scene spliced during post-production.

To say Nadine was a jaded woman would be a blatant understatement, but even she loved deeply at some point, a memory that was hard to penetrate. This feeling I detected was far more dangerous than the ones she had for her family, a love that those with good sense shouldn't have for a faceless man. So it shocked me that someone with a fairly decent, albeit morbid, head on her shoulders would entertain such mush. And not tell me about it! We used to tell each other everything.

Even in death, the pain of that relationship wouldn't release its hold. The dull throb was there, like a bruise I couldn't remember attaining, so it had to be hers. That single, minute detail prevented me from finding closure, and I kept picking that scab until it bled. Time might patch it up, but the open wounds remained untreated and at risk of infection.

The mystery entertained me through the meeting to the point where Caleb shook me to attention when it was over. I completely lost track of time, not to mention I didn't get to share my book. While the crew filed out of the door, Alicia tossed me a parting glance, grinning in triumph.

Caleb extended his hand, helping me to my feet.

"What did I miss?" I asked.

"Alicia got her wish. *Specter: Part III* got voted book of the month. She went through a ten-minute dissertation of the intricacies of having a 'totally hot' ghost boyfriend." Caleb mimicked Alicia's squeaky voice perfectly. "You know there's a movie coming out about it?"

"I heard." I collected my bag then followed him out.

Wishing everyone good night, I stepped into the cool night with Caleb practically stuck to my back. His arm wrapped around my waist and squeezed, lifting me off the ground. I squealed, which caused the crew to leer at us from the parking lot as he carried me to his jeep.

A honking horn came from a blue SUV driving by. "Get a room!" Alicia yelled from the passenger side window as her dad drove her away.

"That's not such a bad idea," Caleb whispered in my ear before kissing the back of my neck.

I wiggled against his hold. "That's it. You are unfit to be in my company, sir."

"Aw, come on! Don't be that way."

"Unhand me, contemptible cur! Else purge such lechery from thine purpose, you nave!"

Snorting a laugh, he set me down. "All right, Lady Macbeth, have it your way."

I pressed against his car door and frowned.

"What's wrong?"

I rubbed my eyes with the ball of my hand. "Nothing. I've got a lot on my mind. And I didn't get to share my book."

He leaned into me, getting good and comfortable, not in the slightest rush to leave. "Share it with me. What's it called?"

I put a finger to my lips. "*Shh.*"

He looked around the parking lot. "What?"

"No, that's the title, *Shh*," I explained. "It's about angels and the battle between Heaven and Hell. According

to Hebrew myth, an angel enters the womb of every un-
born child and places a finger over the lips. They silence
the baby from revealing the secrets of Heaven, including
God's true name. The proof of that secret is that small
dint in your top lip." My finger danced over the outline
of his mouth, making him shiver. I could tell he felt the
gravitation, a pull rooting from the chest, joining our
two magnets together.

Dropping my hand, I continued. "Anyway, this autistic
boy doesn't have that dimple. He's a mute, but he's been
leaking secrets all through his writing and artwork. A
group of angels come to Earth to kill the kid, because
once heard out loud, humanity will remember the secrets
told to them and all of Hell will break lose, literally. It's a
race against time because the kid starts mumbling in class
out of nowhere."

"Sounds good! Let me borrow that when you're done."
His lids grew heavy as he inched closer.

I tried to push off his jeep, but his nearness made it impossible. He was stalling, squeezing a few more minutes
alone with me, but our time was running out.

"Did you want to come over to my place for a bit? I
made a new playlist that you haven't heard—" He
stopped mid-sentence when I flashed my bracelet in his
face.

The gold chain shimmered under the parking lot lights,
creating a sufficient force field against his libido.

Caleb's shoulders slumped under the weight of defeat.
"I thought that was only activated for emergencies."

"So did I, but Mom's got it hot wired to her laptop to
track where I am. Cambion or not, my curfew still applies until I'm eighteen and out the house. It's just a
safety measure. Can't be too careful these days." I offered him a gentle smile.

"Fine. I'll see you tomorrow." He pulled back and allowed me to pass.

My new ride, a metallic green Nissan Juke parked in the next row—new being a relative term. It was new to me, and love allowed me to overlook the high mileage and stench of fried bologna that an entire bottle of Fabreeze couldn't remove. It was mine and I earned it, and that was enough for me.

I didn't make it two feet when Caleb's hand caught my wrist and pulled me back into his arms.

"Caleb," I whined, but felt just as needy. "I have to go."

"Well, am I at least allowed to kiss you? I've waited all day to do so. Indulge me." He lowered his head for a kiss that never came.

It's funny how situations can change. One minute I held my boyfriend, the next I was on the ground, curled into a ball. Caleb's body fell over mine, his weight crushed me as tiny shards rained on my head, over my shoulder, and tinkled against the concrete.